A Fatal
Chapter

Berkley Prime Crime titles by Lorna Barrett

MURDER IS BINDING

BOOKMARKED FOR DEATH

BOOKPLATE SPECIAL

CHAPTER & HEARSE

SENTENCED TO DEATH

MURDER ON THE HALF SHELF

NOT THE KILLING TYPE

BOOK CLUBBED

A FATAL CHAPTER

Anthologies

MURDER IN THREE VOLUMES

A FATAL CHAPTER

Lorna Barrett

BERKLEY PRIME CRIME, NEW YORK

BERKLEY
PRIME
CRIME

An imprint of Penguin Random House LLC
375 Hudson Street, New York, New York 10014

This book is an original publication of the Berkley Publishing Group.

Library of Congress Cataloging-in-Publication Data

Barrett, Lorna.
A fatal chapter / Lorna Barrett.—First edition.
pages ; cm
ISBN 978-0-425-25266-6
I. Title.
PS3602.A83955F38 2015
813'.6—dc23
2014049829

FIRST EDITION: June 2015

PRINTED IN THE UNITED STATES OF AMERICA

10   9   8   7   6   5   4   3   2   1

Cover illustration by Teresa Fasolino.
Cover design by Diana Kolsky.
Interior text design by Laura K. Corless.

Penguin
Random
House

ACKNOWLEDGMENTS

Writers live in isolation. That's how we work. But sometimes we need the companionship of others to help us write our books, and these days that most often comes via the Internet.

I'm so lucky to be a member of the Cozy Chicks blog. We're a group of eight cozy mystery authors who talk about our lives, our writing, and everything in between, and share it with you, our readers. We are: Ellery Adams, Duffy Brown, Kate Collins, Mary Kennedy, Mary Jane Maffini, Maggie Sefton, and Leann Sweeney. Check us out at cozychicksblog.com.

As always, I'm grateful to have a wonderful editor in Tom Colgan, and my agent, Jessica Faust, is always there with help on the business side of things. They, too, are just an e-mail away.

Did you know I have an author page on Facebook? You can find me there, as well as on Goodreads, Pinterest, and Twitter. Don't forget to sign up for my periodic e-mail newsletter on the contact page of my website: LornaBarrett.com.

Happy reading!

A Fatal Chapter

ONE

"Say cheese," Russ Smith called, and Tricia Miles watched as her sister, Angelica, and Pete Renquist dutifully smiled for the camera. They stood at the north end of the Baxter Building, a three-story brick edifice that housed By Hook or By Book, Stoneham's crafty book-and-craft shop. Its owner, Mary Fairchild, stood to one side, waiting her turn to grin for posterity.

Pete kept his gaze on Tricia and not the camera, waggling his eyebrows, smiling, and winking at her. After interacting with him for the past few months, she knew not to take him too seriously. Although he had a glib tongue, she knew he was all talk and no action. Still, his charm won out and she couldn't help but like him.

The camera clicked as Russ took another shot. Angelica posed à la Vanna White, showcasing a gilded plaque that proclaimed the year the building had been constructed, 1842, and that it had been presented by the Stoneham Historical Society, which Pete, its current president, represented. Eventually all the historic structures in the village would sport such plaques—but as the oldest structure along Main Street, the Baxter Building had the honor of being first.

What seemed odd about this gathering was that the building's owner, Bob Kelly, who had never missed an opportunity to toot his own horn, was not present. As far as Tricia knew, he'd been invited, but perhaps because his former lover Angelica, who now also possessed his former position as head of the Stoneham Chamber of Commerce, was present, he'd chosen not to attend. It was just as well. Lately Bob had become an even bigger pain in the butt than usual.

Since the fire at Tricia's mystery bookstore, Haven't Got a Clue, almost seven months before, Bob had been pressuring Tricia to buy the building, something she'd be quite happy to do—if the price was right. Bob was asking for much more than Tricia wanted to pay. Of course, for months she'd been paying rent on a building she could neither use nor live in while she waited for the insurance company to decide what they'd pay toward her losses. Angelica had rented out the top floor of the Chamber's new home to Tricia for a modest fee, since Tricia, who had nothing better to occupy her time, found herself working for the Chamber as an unpaid volunteer.

"Let's get Mary in the shot," Russ called, his eyes suddenly visible above the viewfinder and flash on his Nikon.

Tricia moved aside to let Mary slide into position.

"Say cheese," Russ called again.

"Enough with the cheese," Angelica chided, and then cheerfully called out, "Whiskey!"

Tricia smiled, but then her gaze shifted as she caught sight of Selectman Earl Winkler, a cranky older gentleman with his hair styled in a brush cut and a mouth that never seemed to sport a smile. His perpetually sour disposition gave one reason to suppose that perhaps his diet lacked the necessary fiber for a happy life. His profession was vermin extermination, which somehow seemed to suit his negative outlook on life. How he had ever gotten elected was a mystery to Tricia, since Earl was a bundle of negativity. Of course, there was a whole contingent of local residents who weren't happy with all the changes that had come to Stoneham since Bob had brought a shot of prosperity back to the once-dying village. They cursed the increased traffic, the tour busses, and the rise in property taxes that good fortune had brought. They were also peeved by the acts of serious crime that had increased within the village's boundaries and had cost Stoneham its former title of Safest Village in New Hampshire— and they blamed Tricia for that. It was her misfortune to have either been present at the time of the crimes or nearby. That bad luck had also earned her the despised title of Village Jinx.

The sun disappeared behind a big fluffy cloud just as Earl halted beside Russ and stood, hands on hips, scowling.

"Good morning, Earl. Come to have your photo splashed across the next issue of the *Stoneham Weekly News*?" Angelica asked, her voice sickeningly sweet. Tricia took a step back. She knew to watch her back when she heard that tone of voice, for Angelica only used it on people she could barely stand.

"Hardly," Earl answered. "I have more self-respect than the rest of you publicity hounds."

"Oh, come now, Earl. All of us who've attended town meetings know how much you love the sound of your own voice," Pete said. He was no fan of Earl, either.

"You're blocking the sidewalk, which is against the law," Earl asserted.

Angelica's eyes narrowed. Tricia took another step back. "There is no one around—except you, and we will happily stand aside while you pass."

"I'm not going in that direction," Earl declared.

"Then why are you here? Did you need to speak to one of us?" Pete asked rather sharply.

"No. I just wanted to encourage you to hurry up and clear the sidewalk for pedestrian traffic."

Russ replaced the lens cap on his camera. "I think I've got enough for the paper, although I may come back later in the day when the sun will make the gold leaf on that sign glow."

Earl turned his angry glare on Tricia. "And what are *you* doing here anyway?"

"I'm a resident of Stoneham. I don't have to have a reason to stand on the sidewalk at any time of the day or night," Tricia said politely.

"Don't get snippy with me, young woman," Earl warned.

Before Tricia could defend herself, Angelica, bristling with indignation, stepped forward. "Please don't speak to my sister in that tone of voice."

Tricia reached out to touch Angelica's arm. "Ange, don't bother—"

"You're a bully, Earl Winkler," Pete accused. "You may now be just a skinny runt, but from what I hear you haven't changed your ways since you were a schoolboy."

Earl glared at Pete. "That sounds like slander to me."

"I hear tell that in the past you operated with questionable business practices—what some might even say were highly unethical."

Earl's eyes blazed while the rest of them stood there in stunned silence. "Lies—all lies by my competition. In all the years I've been in business, I've never been taken to court," Earl grated.

"And that was a mistake made by far too many of Stoneham's honest businessmen," Pete asserted.

"Now, now," Russ said, spreading his arms and patting the air in a gesture of peace, for which Tricia was grateful.

"Ange, we need to move on," Tricia told her sister, hoping to further deflate the tension. "You've got a meeting in Manchester later today, and you have a lot to accomplish before you leave."

"And I need to check my messages," Russ said.

"Any sign that baby is on the way?" Mary asked. She'd knitted the most adorable outfits in shades of blue for Russ and his wife Nikki's first child. They'd decided they wanted to know their baby's gender and had selected boy-friendly colors for the baby's nursery.

"About a week or two," Russ said. "I'll be glad when it's all over."

"Ha! That's what you think," Pete said, and laughed. "Once the baby arrives, your life will never be the same. I speak from experience."

Oh? Tricia knew Pete lived alone, yet in all their conversations he'd never mentioned his living situation. Did he get cards on Father's Day from his offspring?

Earl's face twisted with anger. "If you people are finished with your business and gossip, you should just move along."

"Oh, you are a party pooper," Mary said, and turned to enter her store. "See you later," she called to the others.

Since the rest of the group was all heading in the same direction, they turned en masse and headed up the sidewalk with Earl following a few steps behind—and, truth be told, not *enough* steps behind, as he was obviously trying to eavesdrop on their conversation.

"Angelica, I'd like to formalize plans for the Chamber's sponsorship of the upcoming ghost walks. Will you be available to talk later this afternoon?"

"'Fraid not, Pete. I've got a networking session with other Chamber presidents in Manchester this afternoon. But I could pencil you in for tomorrow morning."

"Great. How about ten o'clock?"

"Make it eleven. I've got a grand opening to attend at ten, but after that I'm free. Come to the Chamber office, and I'll have coffee and warm muffins waiting."

"I'll be there," Pete said, and grinned.

"It's desecration," Earl said from behind them. Pete stopped dead, and Earl nearly ran into him.

"What is?" Pete demanded, sudden anger flushing his face.

"People traipsing across the cemetery looking to be entertained. It's hallowed ground. The dead deserve respect."

"The cemetery can't support itself. The money the ghost walks bring in will help with the property's maintenance. Of course, they wouldn't have to worry about fund-raisers if one of the village's select-men hadn't instigated a vote to kill their funding."

"The property needs to be self-sustaining," Earl very nearly shouted.

"That's hard to do when all its clients are *dead*—and some for hundreds of years," Pete pointed out.

"Please, gentlemen," Russ said, again playing peacemaker. "Why don't you take this up in an interview in the *Stoneham Weekly News*? It would be a great forum for you both to get your points across to the rest of the villagers."

"I'm game," Pete said, squaring his shoulders.

"I'm not so sure," Earl hedged. "I'd want to see a draft of the piece before you print it."

Russ shook his head. "There's such a thing as freedom of the press."

"If Earl won't talk to you, I'd be glad to do so anytime you want," Pete offered.

"How about later this afternoon?"

"Four o'clock?" Pete suggested.

"Great. Do you want to join us, Earl?" Russ asked, pointedly staring at the Selectman.

"No," Earl barked, then stormed off down the sidewalk.

Angelica sighed. "He's not the nicest man in the world."

"Come on, Ange. You've got a lot to accomplish before your meeting later this morning," Tricia said.

"You're right, Trish." Angelica turned to the others. "Pete, Russ, it's been a pleasure." Tricia nodded a good-bye to the others, and she and Angelica jaywalked across the quiet street, which they hoped would be full of cars and tour busses within the hour.

"That Earl," Angelica grated as they headed for the Chamber's office. "He's as likable as the Wicked Witch of the West. He ought to be careful, or someone might want to drop a house on him!"

"I think Pete might agree," Tricia said, trying to suppress a grin, "but don't let Earl bother you. Most of the Board of Selectmen are on the side of village development, and they're in our court."

Angelica stopped suddenly, her frown turning upside down. "You said *our* court."

Tricia smiled. "I did, didn't I? Well, Stoneham is my home, and I want to see it prosper."

Angelica positively grinned. "I'm going to miss you once you go back to running Haven't Got a Clue. You know, you could do the same as me; let Pixie and Mr. Everett manage it while you do other things, like—"

But Tricia shook her head. "No. Playing office at the Chamber these past few months has been fun, but I want to go *home*! I want my old life back—and the sooner the better."

7

"Well, I can dream, can't I?" Angelica said wistfully.

"Dream on," Tricia said, and laughed.

Tricia and Angelica returned to the neat little building that housed the Stoneham Chamber of Commerce and were joyfully greeted by Angelica's bichon frise, Sarge. "Was Mommy's little boy the best ever?" she asked as Sarge bounded up and down as though on springs.

Mariana Sommers, the Chamber's receptionist, laughed from her desk in the heart of the office—what had once been a living room. "As good as gold."

Back in February, the building had been just a shabby little house, but with some serious elbow grease in the way of paint, sanded floors, new shutters, and window boxes filled with petunias, it now looked like a darling little cottage. It was a shame that the building would probably be razed in another year when Nigela Ricita Associates, the development company that owned it, would replace it with a brick commercial building more in keeping with Stoneham's past. Still, despite it being only her temporary home, Tricia had come to enjoy living there.

Her quarters consisted of a bedroom, a tiny bathroom, and a sitting room on the upper level, and until she could go back to her own home, she was making the best of things. Since she had escaped the fire with only the clothes on her back and her cat, she'd had to start from scratch. A bed and a bookcase had been her first purchases. And she'd been steadily filling the bookcase with copies of her favorite mysteries.

Goodness only knew how much longer the insurance company was going to take to finish their investigation. What investigation? An angry man had dropped a lighted piece of paper on a vintage (and highly flammable) doll carriage and torched the first floor. Why was it taking so long to make the logical conclusion and pay up?

Once Sarge was rewarded with a rawhide stick, the sisters separated. Angelica checked in with Mariana while Tricia headed to her own desk. For the time being, she was acting as the Chamber's office manager. She didn't mind the work, but she missed her store. She missed interacting with her employees on a daily basis. She missed her *life!*

Not that she didn't see her assistant, Pixie Poe, and her part-time employee, Mr. Everett, on a regular basis. Angelica had been extremely kind to both of them by employing them either at her cookbook store, the Cookery; the little retro café she owned, Booked for Lunch; or the Chamber. Pixie usually waited on tables for part of the day and then put in a few hours in the Chamber office. She'd brushed up on her secretarial skills, and Tricia was half-afraid Pixie might decide that office work was more to her liking—and that she might find a clerical job that paid more or had more prestige. Still, Pixie seemed as pleased with the situation as one could be under the circumstances.

Tricia took her seat and woke her computer from its slumber. One of the first things she'd done after joining the Chamber's staff was take over the monthly newsletter, a task she rather enjoyed. It was considerably bigger than the one she produced for her store, and she'd learned a thing or two about graphics that were sure to give her own newsletter more pizzazz when she finally sent one out at the time of her grand reopening—whenever that might be.

"Ange, have you written your column for the newsletter?" she called.

Angelica looked up from the paper she'd been reading. "Yes. I'll e-mail it to you when I get home. It's on my laptop." She looked at her watch. "Goodness, I need to get going."

"I thought you didn't have to be in Manchester until lunchtime."

"I don't, but I'm going to talk to a prospective new member."

"I can do that for you," Tricia offered.

"You're already doing far too much. And besides, Mama needs a new pair of shoes. That could take an hour," Angelica said, and waggled her eyebrows playfully, reminding Tricia of Pete.

Tricia shook her head and shrugged. "Whatever you say."

"Before I go, I'll take Sarge for a you-know-what around the park. Later this afternoon, would you mind taking him for—" She paused and looked down at the dog. "W-a-l-k-i-e-s," she spelled, but Sarge could spell, too—at least that word—and he looked up from his little doggy bed, cocking his head to let her know it.

"Sure. Leave him here and I'd be glad to," Tricia said.

Angelica handed the paper back to Mariana. "I probably won't be back today, so we can go over the schedule for the rest of the month tomorrow."

"I'll have it updated and ready to go," Mariana promised.

Angelica walked over to her desk, retrieved Sarge's leash, and said the magic word. "Walkies!" Sarge shot out of his little bed and gave a happy bark. She turned back to Tricia. "If I think of anything else, I'll call or text you later."

"I'm going to see you again in less than ten minutes," Tricia said, and laughed.

"Sorry. My head is filled with so much clutter, I can barely think straight," Angelica said, and headed out the door.

Mariana shook her head. "I don't know how she juggles so many things, but I sure wish I had that ability—and her energy."

"It's sheer willpower on her part," Tricia said, turning back to her computer.

A few minutes later, Angelica dropped Sarge off and left for her shoe-buying and meeting expeditions. Tricia found enough to do to keep her occupied for hours. Mariana went to lunch, and by the time she came back, Pixie had arrived to put in her four-hour stint.

"Greetings, all," she called happily. She was dressed in her vintage waitress togs and an impossibly high pair of red heels, clutching a shopping bag, and a big alligator purse. She opened the purse, taking out a small bundle. Sarge welcomed her like an old friend as she slipped him a huge hunk of sliced ham from a napkin.

"Oh, Pixie, please tell me you didn't wait on tables in those shoes," Tricia said.

"Not to worry. I wore sensible flats for my shift at Booked for Lunch. But that doesn't mean I can't have style when I come to work here. Or at least I will when I change." She dumped her purse and a creased newspaper on her desk before heading for the first-floor bathroom. A few minutes later, she returned, her hair no longer restrained by a hairnet, her makeup refreshed, and dressed in a silk dress that was a riot of magenta and orange flowers. No doubt about it, Pixie could make an entrance. "Isn't this just the best day?" she called cheerfully as she strutted across the room to her desk with a hopeful Sarge trotting along behind her.

"So far so good," Tricia agreed.

Pixie sat down, but Sarge walked up to Tricia's desk, looked her in the eye, and cocked his head, gazing at her woefully.

"I suppose you want to go walkies," she said. Sarge's little tail happily thumped the floor. "I guess I could stand to stretch my legs, too," she said, and got up from her chair.

"I'll say. Did you even stop for lunch?" Mariana asked.

Tricia's stomach rumbled. "I guess I forgot. I'll grab something when I get back."

"I'll get started on labeling those envelopes for the new-member mailings," Pixie said, already pulling a box out from under her desk.

"And I'll be back in about ten minutes," Tricia said. "C'mon, boy."

Walking Sarge was never a chore, and he and Tricia headed down the sidewalk toward the town park, which was a perfect square, to do their usual two circuits. The lilac blooms and their lovely scent were long past, but thanks to the Board of Selectmen and Nigela Ricita Associates, there were stone containers filled with flowers at every corner, and on every street lamp hung a basket heavy with blossoms. All the benches had been painted, and now that the gazebo had been fully restored, the park was once again a destination. But on that afternoon there were no other people walking their dogs or strolling with baby carriages around the square.

Tricia hated to admit it, but her fondness for the picturesque Victorian gazebo had faded after the tragedy that had claimed her friend Deborah Black's life and killed the pilot of the plane who had crashed into the structure. She tried not to think about it, but if she was honest, she usually avoided going near the stone shelter, and even tried to avoid looking at it during her walks with Sarge.

She looked down at the dog, whose little tail wagged with joy as they rounded the corner and started up the walk on the park's western boundary. No such thoughts bothered Sarge, despite the fact that it had been his original owner who had caused the disaster.

While Sarge enjoyed his constitutional, Tricia thought about what Pixie had said. The weather was indeed sensational, and except for their encounter with that curmudgeon Earl Winkler, it had been a good day. If there was a man alive who had a more sour disposition than Earl, she had never met him. What was wrong with him? He represented the people of Stoneham. Couldn't he be happy for all that had happened in the village? She did a mental comparison of him to Pete Renquist. What a nice man—and fun, too. Not that she was attracted to him, though he made no secret of the fact he was available. He certainly seemed to flirt with every woman he came into contact with. Tricia had been doing her best to stop thinking of men and romance. It was a dead-end street, at least with the two men who seemed intent to pursue her: her ex-husband, Christopher Benson, and the local chief of police, Grant Baker. Instead, she thought about what Angelica had said before she'd left for her meeting. In the future, did she want to do other things besides just run her mystery bookstore?

Since the day after Haven't Got a Clue burned, Tricia had been buying up mysteries and had even rented a storage unit, which was quickly being filled. Some days she missed the store and her former life there so much that she'd break down in tears—but only late at night, when no one but her cat, Miss Marple, was around to witness it. But then there were days when she felt restless and eager to find something else to do with her life, no doubt exacerbated by the failure of her insurance company to settle her claim. Angelica was a crusading entrepreneur with her fingers in so many pies it made Tricia feel dizzy. Mariana had been right—it was a juggling act, but somehow Angelica made it all seem easy. And what other kind of business could Tricia run in addition to her beloved bookstore?

Open a restaurant? Heavens no! It was too much work with high overhead and low profits.

A day spa? Hands-on personal care wasn't her thing.

A cat rescue? Now there was an idea, but what if she became attached to her temporary charges? Crazy Cat Lady wasn't a title she aspired to.

Perhaps sticking to bookselling was her best bet.

They turned the corner heading east. At the first lamppost, Tricia noted the hanging basket had almost no blooms. She could have sworn the last time she and Sarge had walked around the park that the baskets had been exploding with colorful flowers. The leaves looked healthy enough, but where was the color? She'd have to mention it to Angelica. Perhaps she could arrange to have the baskets given a dose of fertilizer or—worst-case scenario—replaced.

Halfway down the walk, Sarge tugged on the leash. Angelica had trained him to do his business only in certain areas of the park, and of course, Tricia was prepared with a plastic bag to clean up after the little guy. And for that, she was glad Sarge was a bichon frise and not an Irish wolfhound.

With that taken care of, Tricia headed for the nearest trash barrel, which was located near the stone gazebo. Suddenly, Sarge began to pull at the leash and bark. Tricia held her ground, looking around for the squirrel the dog had no doubt seen but which she couldn't locate. Sarge barked even louder and fought to pull her toward the gazebo.

"Oh, all right. You can have a look. But when there's nothing there, you're going to feel pretty foolish," she admonished the dog.

But she'd been wrong. There *was* something in the center of the edifice.

Tricia halted, her heart skipping a beat when she saw the pair of rather worn leather loafers attached to a pair of jeans-clad legs. She hurried up the steps to see a man lying facedown. Crouching beside him, she held out a hand and forced herself to touch him. His skin was still warm. She stared at his chest and noticed he was still breathing. She grasped his wrist and found a weak pulse.

She let out a breath. Thank goodness this one was alive. She'd found more than her fair share of corpses during her tenure in Stoneham. Sarge had stopped barking and did what dogs do best—held a sniffathon, his nose taking in as much of the fallen fellow as possible, considering how tightly Tricia held the leash. She thought she recognized the clothes and the hair, and she scooted around the still form until she could see that it was indeed Pete Renquist. What on earth was he doing lying unconscious in the gazebo on such a lovely summer's day? He didn't seem to be bleeding. As far as she knew, he didn't suffer from seizures, but he obviously needed medical attention. Tricia pulled her cell phone from her slacks pocket and punched in 911. Seconds later, a voice spoke in her ear.

"Hillsborough County 911. Please state your name and the nature of the emergency."

"My name is Tricia Miles. I'd like to report an accident in Stoneham Square. A man's been hurt."

"Hurt how?" the dispatcher asked.

"I'm not really sure. He's lying in the gazebo and he's unconscious. He seems to be having trouble breathing. Heart attack maybe? His pulse is rather weak."

"Do you know his name?"

"Peter Renquist. He lives here in Stoneham."

"Do you know how to perform CPR?"

"I've never had to do it, but I think I could if necessary," Tricia said, her fear escalating.

"The Stoneham Fire Department's rescue squad has been dispatched." Sure enough, Tricia could already hear the squad's siren. "Please stay with the victim until they arrive."

The word *victim* made her shudder. "Of course I will."

She ended the call and spoke to the man beside her. "Pete? Can you hear me? It's me, Tricia. Help is on the way. I'm sure everything will be all right. Just hang on." She said the words with what she hoped was reassurance, crossing her fingers they'd be true.

Pete's eyes shot open, startling Tricia. His arm jerked up, and he grasped Tricia's arm with what could only be described as a death grip.

His lips moved, and she bent down to listen, but she couldn't hear what he was trying to say. "I don't understand," she said.

She bent lower so that her ear was close to his mouth.

"I never missed my little boy," he said, gasping. His eyes closed, and his grasp on her arm slackened as he fell into unconsciousness.

The rescue squad pulled up to the sidewalk, and the EMTs practically spilled from the vehicle. They paused to grab their gear before jogging to the gazebo.

Sarge's barking went back into overdrive. "Hush!" Tricia said, but she didn't have the same kind of control over the dog that her sister did. Sarge strained at the leash, and Tricia hurried down the steps to intercept the EMTs. She scooped up Sarge and his barking quieted; instead, he began to growl at the newcomers. "Hush!" Tricia told him again, still without results.

Tricia recognized one of the EMTs as Danny Sutton. "It's Pete Renquist," she told him. "I think he might have had a heart attack."

He nodded. "We've got it," he said, and he and his partner hurried up the stone steps to attend to their patient.

"Tricia!" Russ Smith called, running across the grass toward her. He'd no doubt heard the call for the EMTs go out on his police scanner. He had his camera slung around his neck and held his ever-present steno pad and a pen in hand.

Tricia stepped away from the gazebo, walking fast to close the space between them. "It's Pete. I found him."

"He's dead?" Russ asked, shocked.

"No!" Tricia asserted.

"Well, you're not known for finding live bodies," Russ said with irony.

Tricia glared at him. "It looks like he might have suffered a heart attack."

Russ looked toward the gazebo. "Poor guy. Did he say anything to you?"

"Nothing that made sense."

They turned their attention to the road, where an ambulance pulled up at the curb. Another set of EMTs hurried to join the firemen, hauling a gurney along with them.

Tricia and Russ edged away, yet remained close enough that they could hear the EMTs.

"He's gone into cardiac arrest," Danny said, and began CPR.

"Oh, no," Tricia said, feeling close to tears.

"Well, at least he *started* out alive," Russ said.

"Hey, don't count Pete out yet," she grated, glaring at him.

Russ just shrugged.

They watched as the EMTs worked in a fluid motion to transfer Pete to the gurney and whisk him off to the ambulance. By then they noticed a bunch of rubberneckers that had gathered around the edges of the park and were watching the show. Poor Pete.

Less than a minute later, the ambulance took off with its siren wailing. Sarge began to wiggle in Tricia's arms, and she set him down on the ground. The firemen packed up their gear, stowed it in their vehicle, and left the scene.

With the show now over, the gawkers began to drift away.

"That's it," Russ said. He cocked his head and addressed Tricia. "What were you doing in the park, anyway?"

She brandished Sarge's leash. "What do you think?"

He shrugged, looking back to the road, then at his watch. "Looks like Pete and I won't get to talk about that article after all. I sure hope the poor guy makes it."

Heavy-hearted, Tricia looked toward the road, where the ambulance had receded from sight. "Yes. Me, too."

TWO

Tricia returned Sarge to Angelica's apartment, stopping long enough to say hello to the Cookery's manager, Frannie Mae Armstrong, and Mr. Everett, who was working there part-time. Naturally, both asked about the ambulance and the ensuing commotion in the center of the village, and Tricia told them just the basics before she headed back to the Chamber office.

Pixie and Mariana had just as many questions, and Tricia told them the bare minimum, too.

"Boy, you've sure got the knack for finding stiffs," Pixie muttered, shaking her head.

"He wasn't dead!" Tricia turned to Mariana, forcing herself to speak calmly. "Have we heard from Angelica yet?"

Mariana shook her head. "She said she wasn't planning on coming back to the Chamber office today—remember?"

"Oh, that's right. I'm sorry. I guess I'm feeling a little rattled." Tricia settled into the chair in front of her desk, trying to decide if she was able to muster the enthusiasm needed to attack the pile of phone messages waiting for her attention. She'd catch up with her sister later. Angelica often came back to the Chamber office during the evenings to catch up with paperwork or make calls, sometimes bringing a makeshift dinner that she'd share with Tricia and Miss Marple.

Tricia found it hard to concentrate during the rest of the afternoon. In her mind's eye she saw poor Pete lying on the gazebo's cold concrete floor, barely holding on to life. She wondered if she ought to call St. Joseph Hospital to check up on him, but would they have information on an emergency case who hadn't actually been admitted?

Pixie had moved on from putting labels on envelopes to actually stuffing them. For the most part, she worked quietly while soft rock issued from the radio on Mariana's desk. Occasionally Pixie would sing along off-key, which caused Mariana to start clearing her throat as though she were choking on a bone. Though physically separated by the space between their desks, for the rest of the afternoon Pixie seemed to hover over Tricia, looking worried—even if she never moved from her chair.

At one point, a shiver passed through Tricia, and she looked up and, as expected, found Pixie staring at her. "What?"

Pixie looked away. "Nothing, I was just . . . staring into space."

A lie.

The Chamber was open until six o'clock, but Mariana only worked until five. At 4:59, she turned off her radio, grabbed her purse from the desk drawer, and rose. "I'll see you ladies tomorrow," she said, and headed for the door.

"Have a good evening," Tricia called.

"One more hour and it'll be our turn," Pixie said, and moved on to sealing the envelopes with a wet-sponge dauber. Without the background noise of Mariana's radio, the time seemed to drag. The battery-operated clock on the wall seemed to tick louder with the passing minutes, not unlike Poe's *Tell-Tale Heart*. Tricia couldn't seem to concentrate on any task she attempted, opening files only to glance at the screen and then close them once again.

Finally, Pixie glanced at the clock, which at last read 5:58. "Holy smoke, is that the time?" she said, and scooped all the envelopes into a box, replacing it under her desk.

"What's the matter? Have you got a hot date?" Tricia asked, and was surprised when Pixie actually blushed.

"Well, actually . . . yeah. I've got a boyfriend."

Boy? At Pixie's age? Hardly.

"Pixie!" Tricia called, feeling lighter than she had in hours. "When did this happen?"

"A couple of months ago. I didn't want to say anything. I mean, knowing how your love life is in the toilet and all."

In the toilet wasn't exactly true. *Flushed and long gone* was a better description. But it had been a conscious decision on Tricia's part. After losing her home and store, she didn't want to rush into any kind of relationship. She occasionally had lunch with her ex-husband, Christopher, but she was fairly certain she'd finally convinced him that any future relationship with him was out of the question. And while Chief Baker still dropped by on a regular basis, she thought of him only with friendship in mind—which was pretty much all their relationship had been based on, anyway.

"Don't be silly," Tricia chided her. "I'm thrilled for you. What's his name? What's he like? Does he—" She stopped herself.

"Know about my past?" Pixie finished for her. She nodded. "Yup. That was a difficult conversation, and things were a little tense for a while, but they're better now. In fact, they're terrific." She positively beamed. "His name is Fred Pillins—ain't that a weird name?"

"Pillins? I must say I've never heard of it before. It's unique," Tricia said. "Are you guys . . . serious?"

"When you're on the high side of fifty, everything had better be serious," Pixie said.

"Are you thinking about—?"

"Getting married?" Pixiee shook her head. "But shacking up ain't out of the question. It would sure save on rent and groceries and stuff. The way things are—I'm either at his place, or he's at mine."

"Where did you meet him?"

"At Booked for Lunch. He delivers the meat and cold cuts. We hit it off right away, and then one day he asked me out to dinner. The rest, as they say, is history."

"And you never said a word," Tricia muttered.

"Now that the cat's out of the bag, I'll talk your ear off about him," she said with a grin.

"I'd love to hear all about him," Tricia said sincerely.

Pixie consulted her watch. "But not today. I'm off." She withdrew her purse from the desk drawer and grabbed the garment bag with her waitressing clothes. Fingering a wave, she mimicked Angelica. "Tootles!"

"Have a nice evening," Tricia called after her.

Once the door closed behind Pixie, Tricia arranged the yellow Post-it notes chronicling the chores she needed to accomplish the next day in a line on top of her desk in the order of their importance.

As she passed Pixie's desk, she noticed a folded section of the morning newspaper on top. Tricia scooped it up, intending to toss it into the wastebasket, which she would empty before she closed the office for the day. She paused to look at it. Pixie had finished the crossword, but she'd only figured out three of the four scrambled words from the Jumble in the *Union Leader*. Tricia stared at the letters before her. U-G-E-H-N-R. She thought about it for a moment. H-U-N-G-E-R. That was easy enough. She thought about the lunch she'd never gotten around to eating. No wonder she felt so empty inside.

Her gaze traveled over to a wrinkled brochure, which also sat on the desk. It was for NRA Realty, a division of Nigela Ricita Associates.

Suddenly the letters of one of the words rearranged themselves in her mind and she smiled. R-I-C-I-T-A rearranged was T-R-I-C-I-A.

Her smile faded as a wave of cold passed through her—like someone walking on her grave. *No, it can't be*, she thought, her insides seeming to do a summersault. She studied the letters in the other word. There weren't enough letters in N-I-G-E-L-A to spell out Angelica. Still . . .

Tricia went into the kitchen to get a trash bag, then emptied the four wastebaskets and tossed the newspaper into it as well. For some reason, she couldn't stop thinking about those jumbled letters. Surely it was coincidence. Angelica *couldn't* be Nigela Ricita.

But, like Clark Kent and Superman, Nigela and Angelica had never been seen together. Heck, besides Antonio Barbero, no one in the village had ever met the elusive Ms. Ricita. Antonio did all the talking for his boss. She communicated with her employees via e-mail. That was certainly an effective way of keeping any questions about her identity at bay.

It can't be.

Tricia stared at the headline once more. The words *Angelica Tricia* seemed to jump off the page.

Since Nigela Ricita Associates had come to town, they'd invested in the Brookview Inn, the Happy Domestic, the Sheer Comfort Inn, the Eat Lunch rolling food truck, and the local pub, the Dog-Eared Page. They'd bought the building that now housed the Chamber of

Commerce. And, lucky for the Chamber, NRA had made improvements despite the fact that they intended to raze the building in the not-too-distant future, and charged the organization far less than the going rate for rent. The company also subsidized the flowers that festooned Main Street, which pleased not just the tourists but the shopkeepers as well.

These—all its—investments had been good for Stoneham and for its citizens, too. Nigela Ricita Associates had created not only jobs, but greater prosperity. Angelica was far too selfish to be behind all that altruism.

Tricia frowned and felt instantly ashamed. Maybe she'd felt that way about her sister in the past, but no longer.

Angelica had hired Frannie Mae Armstrong, who'd blossomed as the Cookery's manager. She'd given an ex-con the chance at a better life when she'd hired him to be a short order cook at Booked for Lunch. He'd moved from that lowly position to that of head chef at the Brookview Inn. Angelica had been the force behind Tricia giving Pixie a chance to excel, working for her at Haven't Got a Clue, and with the skills she'd picked up working for the Chamber of Commerce during the past six months, she could probably look for a better-paying job. Angelica was also responsible for Michele Fowler getting the job as manager of the Dog-Eared Page. She'd done a lot of good these past few years. Nigela Ricita Associates had done even more.

It can't be, Tricia told herself more sternly.

Angelica had an ego the size of Montana. Surely if she was responsible for all the improvements that had taken place in the village, she'd be shouting it from the top of the newly rebuilt village gazebo. What was served by her hiding behind a shell company?

But then Tricia remembered something Angelica had said months before when she'd spilled the beans about the dead brother Tricia had never known about. "You'd be surprised how good we are at keeping secrets in this family."

But the idea was absurd. How could Angelica be the head of a development company and not tell anyone—especially Tricia—about it? Her life was an open book.

Wasn't it?

There was only one way to find out.

Tricia reached into her pocket and pulled out her cell phone, intending to call her sister, when she noticed she'd missed a text message from Angelica. *Free for dinner? Come over at 6:15.*

Tricia glanced at her watch. It was six ten. Oh, yes, she had every intention of crossing the street and confronting Angelica with her suspicions.

It took only a minute for Tricia to leave a bowl of kitty treats for her cat, lock up the Chamber office, and leave the quaint little house. As she walked briskly down the sidewalk heading for the Cookery, she rehearsed various conversational openers.

So, are you Nigela Ricita?

No, too blunt.

Anything you need to tell me?

No, too subtle.

Would Angelica laugh and deny the accusation? Would she break down in tears and beg Tricia's forgiveness? Somehow, Tricia couldn't see either of those scenarios playing out. It didn't matter. Tricia was determined to find out the facts, and if what she now suspected was true, she would—

Tricia stopped dead in the middle of the empty sidewalk.
She had no idea *what* she would do.

Tricia unlocked the big door to the Cookery and entered, locked it behind her, and crossed the shop to the stairs to Angelica's loft apartment. The layout of this store and her own were so similar that she felt a pang of loss cut a little deeper into her soul every time she entered. When she reached the third floor and opened the door, Sarge bounded toward her, practically apoplectic with joy, despite the fact he'd seen her only a couple of hours earlier that day. "Calm down, calm down," she chided as the dog bounced up and down as though on a trampoline as they headed up the hall and into the kitchen, where the aromas of onions and garlic wafted.

"Honestly, Sarge," Angelica chided from her position at the stove, "put a sock in it."

Tricia looked around on the floor for something to distract the dog. Sure enough, she saw what had once been a knee-high white sock that had been tied in knots and given to the dog as a toy. Tricia picked it up and tossed it to Sarge, who caught it in his mouth, where it stayed, effectively silencing him.

She glanced over at her sister, who was standing over the stove stirring what looked like a pot of spaghetti sauce, still undecided as to what she felt—admiration or total fury. No doubt about it, had Angelica wished for a culinary career, she would have been one of the best. She often said she was happiest with a wooden spoon in her hand. The fact that she did it so well had been a boon for Tricia, who didn't like to cook and, before Angelica's arrival, had basically lived on a diet of yogurt and tuna salad, which was convenient but not particularly healthy. But right now food was the last thing on Tricia's mind.

"I've got a pitcher of martinis in the fridge—as well as a couple of glasses chilling. Why don't you pour us each a drink?" Angelica suggested as she grabbed a pot from the cupboard, no doubt for the pasta.

Tricia was going to need a hardy swig of that alcoholic rocket fuel to get through the upcoming conversation. She opened the fridge and found everything sitting on a tray. Even the skewered olives sat in the glasses. While Angelica filled the pot with water and put it on the stove, Tricia moved the tray to the counter and poured. She handed one of the glasses to Angelica, who barely looked up as she lit the burner.

"What shall we drink to?" Angelica asked, grabbing a spoon and giving the sauce another stir.

Ah, the perfect opening. "Why don't we drink to Nigela Ricita?" Tricia suggested.

"Why would we want to do that?" Angelica asked diffidently.

"She's changed the lives of everyone in Stoneham, wouldn't you agree?"

Angelica shrugged, her back still to Tricia. "I guess."

"In fact, she's got to be the best thing that ever happened to Stoneham."

"Oh, I wouldn't go that far," Angelica said, and took a sip of her drink.

"You can't deny she's brought a lot of changes to the village."

"So have you."

"Me?" Tricia asked, stunned.

"So has everyone who opened a store and managed to keep it afloat. The dialysis center has brought in a lot of new blood, too. Oh, my, that was a good pun, wasn't it?" Angelica said, and laughed.

Tricia didn't join her.

"Let's talk about something different. For instance, me," Angelica suggested.

"If we're talking about Nigela Ricita, we *are* talking about you," Tricia said, unable to keep the anger out of her voice.

Angelica's back stiffened, but she didn't face her sister. "I don't know what you mean."

"Of course you do. I finally figured it out, and I feel really stupid that it took me all this time to do it."

Angelica finally turned to face her. "And just what exactly did you figure out?"

"That Nigela Ricita is an anagram for Angelica and Tricia."

Angelica frowned. "Aren't you a couple of letters short?"

"So you fudged it. I want to know why."

Tricia studied her sister's face, and for a few seconds she thought Angelica might burst into tears, but then her eyes narrowed and she smiled before tipping her glass back and taking another sip. "Damn, I make a fine martini."

"You haven't answered my question."

"What do you want me to say?" Angelica repeated.

"Admit it! Admit that you've been living a lie."

"What lie?"

"A lie of omission—for keeping the truth about your secret identity to yourself."

"You make me sound like Clark Kent, although I think I'd prefer to be Diana Prince."

"Who?"

Angelica let out an exasperated breath. "Wonder Woman!"

"Oh, please," Tricia groused, and took a slug of her drink. Her mind was awhirl with chaotic thoughts that bordered mostly on anger.

Angelica turned back to the stove.

"Aren't you going to say anything?" Tricia demanded.

"What do you want me to say?"

"Sorry would be a good start."

"But I'm not sorry."

"Can't you at least be sorry for not telling me?"

Angelica stirred the pot. "Not really."

Again Tricia's mouth dropped open, but she was absolutely speechless.

Angelica tested the sauce. "Another triumph," she declared, and took another sip of her drink.

"I can't believe you," Tricia started, but Angelica turned and held up a hand to stop her.

"Look, I'm sorry I didn't tell you—"

"Who else knows?" Tricia demanded.

"Less than you'd think," Angelica said under her breath.

"Who?" Tricia roared.

"Antonio. My lawyers. And Christopher."

"Christopher?" Tricia cried, anguished. "You told my ex-husband but you didn't tell me?"

Angelica took another long pull on her martini and then set down the glass. "I went to see him the summer before I moved here to Stoneham."

Tricia looked at her sister, remembering that Angelica had gone to a fat farm in Aspen not long after she'd broken up with her fourth husband. Aspen wasn't all that far from where Christopher had gone to live after their divorce. "So, he gave you financial advice?"

"Yes. He advised me to set up my corporation in New Jersey, and helped me pull together some financing for a loft conversion I was about to undertake."

"You told my ex-husband, but you didn't tell *me*," Tricia angrily accused.

"It was just a lark. The whole thing was just supposed to be fun."

"Fun?"

"Yes. Serious fun."

"And what about Antonio?" Tricia asked.

Angelica's eyes lit up and a smile erupted across her lips. "He's the light of my life. The best thing that came from my marriage to Rod—come to think of it, the best thing that came from *any* of my marriages."

"You have what amounts to a son and you never told anyone about him?"

"Of course I told people. You just don't travel in the same circles."

"Do Mother and Daddy know?"

"Yes," Angelica grudgingly admitted.

"And you never told *me*?" she cried again, devastated.

"Well," Angelica hedged, "we weren't exactly close for a long time."

And I'm so angry with you right now, we may never be close again, Tricia thought. "And this whole Nigela Ricita thing came about because . . . ?" she demanded.

"I wanted to give Antonio a job so he'd live nearby and I could see him every day if I wanted. I don't care who his biological parents were; he is *my* son and I love him as much as I love you."

"How can you say you love me when you've kept so much of your life a secret from me?"

"How did I know I was going to be so fantastically successful?"

"Yes, how did you manage that?"

Angelica shrugged, noted that the water was boiling, and took out a box of penne from one of the cupboards. "After my divorce from Gary, I bought some property."

"That was husband number three, right?"

Angelica nodded. "I held on to the building for a couple of years without knowing what I wanted to do with it. Then when Antonio said he wanted to return to the states, I offered to hire him as a general contractor. He learned a lot and we had a great time working together. We sold it, split the profit, and kept working together."

"And did you have some kind of master plan in mind when you came to Stoneham?"

"Yes, to be closer to you." Angelica dumped some of the pasta into the water. "You *are* my family."

"But you lived here for almost three years before Antonio came to Stoneham."

"We had a big, complicated project that took far longer to complete than we thought. But we made a modest profit and he learned a lot, so it worked out in the end."

"And now he manages Nigela Ricita Associates for you?"

"More or less. He's very good at his job, too. I'm so proud I could burst. And now I'm going to be a grandma. Don't I look in great shape for such a monumental milestone?" she said, and laughed, but Tricia didn't find the statement funny.

"Who besides me will know?" Tricia demanded.

Angelica frowned. "Well, I suppose we should finally let Ginny in our little secret."

"Little secret?" Tricia repeated. "Ginny's going to be just as angry as me."

"Maybe for a day or two," Angelica conceded, "but she'll get over it —just like you will."

"And what about the rest of the village?"

"Why do they have to know?" Angelica asked, and checked the pasta water, which had come back to a boil. She adjusted the flame.

Tricia had no answer for that. "It just seems wrong."

"Why? It didn't take long for me to discover that I can do far more for Stoneham and its citizens as Nigela than I can as me. And there's nothing illegal about what I've done."

"But don't you want the credit?"

"I've got it."

"Under a pseudonym," Tricia pointed out.

"So what?"

Tricia stared at her sister, openmouthed. "I don't get it. I don't get *you*."

"I like things the way they are. I get far more *cooperation* the way things are now. Do I have your word that you won't tell a soul?"

Tricia felt like slapping her sister, but instead she balled her fists. "You do, but grudgingly."

"Why? Don't you see how much easier it is for me this way?"

"Not really."

"Spoilsport."

"Diva."

Angelica smiled. "I'll take that as a compliment."

That wasn't how the jibe was meant to be received.

"Now, shall I tell you how my meeting went with the Chamber presidents this afternoon, or do you want to tell me what I missed this afternoon at the office?"

It took Tricia a few moments to remember what had happened just hours before. "Well, there was some excitement, but it wasn't at the Chamber. Sarge and I had an unfortunate encounter during our walk in the park."

Angelica looked down at her dog, who was resting with his head on the knotted sock. "Not with a skunk. I would have smelled that."

"No, but, Sarge found—"

"Not another dead body," Angelica practically wailed.

"Of course not. At least, he wasn't dead when we found him."

"Who?"

"Pete Renquist."

"Oh, no! Is he okay?"

"He was in cardiac arrest when the paramedics loaded him into an ambulance and whisked him off to the hospital."

"Oh, my! And he seemed perfectly fine this morning. Are you sure he had a heart attack?"

"I'm not sure of anything, but I didn't see any sign of trauma. The poor man. I'm afraid I didn't give the Chamber its money's worth this afternoon while I sat around thinking about him."

"Since we pay you nothing, I don't think you have anything to worry about," Angelica said kindly, draining her glass and turning to the fridge to pour herself another martini. She offered to top up Tricia's glass, but she hadn't yet finished the one she had. Angelica held her glass aloft. "To Pete. May he make a speedy recovery."

"To Pete," Tricia agreed, and took a sip of her drink.

She'd barely swallowed when Beethoven's "Ode to Joy" broke the quiet, and Tricia grabbed her cell phone from her pocket. She recognized the number: Russ Smith.

"Hello?"

"Trish? I hate to be the bearer of bad news, but—"

"It's about Pete?" she asked anxiously.

"Yeah. Sorry, but I just got word that he died."

Dead? Angelica mouthed.

Tricia nodded.

"I'm so . . . bummed," Tricia told Russ.

"Yeah, me, too."

"And here's something that will bum you even more. It may not have been of natural causes."

"What are you saying?"

"There was a suspicious bruise and a puncture mark on Pete's right arm."

"I don't like the way this conversation has turned," Tricia said.

"That yet another murder has taken place in Stoneham? No, I guess you wouldn't. And of course, *you* found him."

"I'll remind you he was *alive* when I found him."

"Tell that to your buddy, Chief Baker."

Tricia let out an exasperated breath.

"I gotta go. I'm still at the office and have to keep the line free in case Nikki calls."

"Thank you for calling. I'll talk to you tomorrow."

"Right."

Tricia stabbed her phone's off icon.

"I change my toast," Angelica said, raising her glass once again. "Rest in peace, Pete." She took a healthy slug. "But there's more, isn't there?"

Tricia nodded. "Pete may not have died of natural causes."

Angelica raised an eyebrow but said nothing.

Tricia took a sip of her martini. She wasn't sure she would ever really like them.

She hadn't told Angelica what Pete had muttered before losing consciousness, but she'd have to tell Grant Baker when he came to talk to her—and he would. Not that what Pete had said made sense. He'd died with his secret, and now no one would ever know what it meant.

Angelica sampled a piece of pasta, declared it al dente, and enlisted Tricia to set the table. She did so on autopilot, but she had no appetite. She'd been wounded to learn Angelica's secret and now shocked to hear of Pete's death.

She wasn't sure she could take any more shocks that day.

THREE

Despite Angelica's marvelous dinner, Tricia ate very little. Angelica had insisted she take home leftovers in case she was hit with a case of the munchies during the night, and Tricia carried the containers back to the Chamber in a plastic grocery bag.

She unlocked the door to the office and let herself in. Miss Marple sat in a patch of early-evening sunshine in the kitchen and greeted her with a scolding *"Yow!"*

"I apologize. But I did leave you kitty treats before I left. It's not my fault you were nowhere in sight before I had to go," she explained.

Miss Marple just glared at her.

No sooner had she put the cat's now-full dish on the floor when she heard a knock at the back door. She ignored it. Several times Chamber members had appeared on her doorstep after hours with some request or other—knowing the business was officially closed, but also knowing that she would be there and expecting her to be willing to honor their requests. She worked enough hours for the Chamber—and gratis, too—that she was determined not to let whomever it was infringe on her personal time—especially when she was feeling so unsettled.

The knock came again, but Tricia stood by the sink, waiting for whomever it was to go away. A minute had passed, and she was just about ready to mount the stairs for her temporary living space when a knock came at the kitchen window, startling her. She turned and saw the face of her ex-husband, Christopher, peering in at her.

"Open the door!" he called.

Tricia frowned. "What do you want?"

"To talk."

She sighed. She knew he wouldn't go away until she let him in, so she stalked over to the back door and opened it.

"Why didn't you answer?" Christopher demanded.

"I thought it was a Chamber member."

He smiled. "Well, I *am* a Chamber member. Why wouldn't you want to talk to me?"

"The office is closed, so if you've come about a Chamber matter . . ." she said, grabbing his elbow and attempting to push him back out the door, but his feet stayed planted.

"I heard about what happened."

"Yes, it's very sad that Pete died," she said, but she doubted he'd already heard that it was a suspicious death.

"I'm sorry you found him," Christopher said gently.

For a moment Tricia wasn't sure what he meant, but then . . . "Thank you." Then again, she wasn't about to cut him any slack. He owed her an explanation, and now was as good a time as any to demand it. She crossed her arms and glared at him. "Why didn't you tell me that Angelica is Nigela Ricita?"

He shrugged, his expression bland. "She asked me not to."

Tricia waited for more of an explanation but was disappointed. "That's it?"

Christopher nodded. "I'm a man of my word."

Except when it came to a marriage vow.

"Do we have to stand here in the doorway to talk? Can't we sit down? I've never seen your living quarters," he said.

And you aren't about to, either, she thought.

He pushed past her and walked into the kitchen. Miss Marple looked up from her bowl and almost seemed to smile. *"Yow!"* She trotted over to meet Christopher, winding around his legs and looking up at him with adoring eyes.

Traitor!

"You played dumb with me when you said you'd gone to Portsmouth for the job interview to work for her company."

"No, I didn't. I really did go to Portsmouth, where I was interviewed for the job working for NRA."

"Did Angelica interview you?"

"No, Antonio did. She let him make the decision." Christopher pulled one of the bistro chairs away from the table and sat.

"And he made it knowing you were my ex-husband?"

"I don't think we discussed it. He asked for my credentials, did some checking, and voila—I was hired. Your sister is a very generous employer. I'd like to say it's a family trait, but your spirit of generosity seems to have evaporated these past few years."

And he knew damn well why, too.

"Aren't you going to offer me a drink?"

She considered Miss Marple's water bowl on the floor. "This is a shared refrigerator. I don't keep wine or have any liquor down here."

"How about upstairs?" Christopher asked. Tricia's glare intensified. "How about iced tea?"

Tricia shook her head.

"Coffee?"

"I'm not sure you'll be staying that long."

"Tricia, why can't we be friends? I thought we were getting along a lot better lately."

"That was before I found out you knew Angelica's secret."

"For what it's worth, among the advice I've given her was that she should level with you. I knew you'd be upset. Hell, she knew it, too, but she felt the timing wasn't right."

"And when was the timing going to be right?"

"Looks like it was today."

"It wasn't. I figured it out for myself."

"I'm sorry."

Damn him for actually sounding that way. She moved over to the counter, picked up the coffee pot and filled it with water. As she measured the coffee into the filter basket, she glanced askance to see him smiling. Damn him!

She hit the switch and grabbed two clean coffee cups from the drain board. Pixie kept on top of everything during her hours at the Chamber. Tricia set them on the table and brought out and then filled a small pitcher with milk and set it and the sugar bowl and a spoon in front of Christopher.

"What will Pete's death mean for the Chamber?"

Tricia shrugged. "He worked closely with Angelica on the historical-plaque campaign. It's a shame he won't get to see any more of them go up around the village."

"What else did they have in mind?"

"The cemetery ghost walks were supposed to start in the fall. I suppose someone else from the Historical Society will work with Angelica or Mariana on that. It's a shame, because Pete was a walking encyclopedia when it came to Stoneham's founding fathers—and mothers."

Christopher looked past her toward the refrigerator. "I don't suppose you have any cookies or a stale doughnut hanging around. I haven't had dinner yet," he explained.

"The Bookshelf Diner is only a couple of doors down."

"Come on, Trish," he chided her.

She frowned. She was going to have deep-set lines in her face if this continued. "Angelica sent me home with a load of leftovers. I suppose I could toss them on a plate and heat them in the microwave for you."

"That would be heavenly. Thank you."

Tricia turned to the fridge and doled out the pasta and a bowl of salad. This was like old times, only their dining room in their Manhattan apartment had been far more elegant than the humble kitchen where they now sat. Still, the take-out containers hadn't looked too much different. The coffee was ready before the microwave went *ding*. Tricia poured, and then set the salad dressing, silverware, and a paper napkin in front of Christopher. Turning back to the microwave, she retrieved his makeshift meal.

He inhaled deeply. "This smells great. It's too bad you didn't inherit the same cooking genes as Angelica."

No, and she hadn't inherited the secret-keeping genes, either.

Christopher dug in, obviously enjoying his meal.

Now what could they talk about?

He swallowed. "Have you heard from the insurance company yet?"

Tricia shook her head. "Sometimes I think I never will."

"Made any headway with buying the building?"

Again she shook her head. "I'm sure Bob will be by to bug me about it any day now. Why is he so keen to dump it? Is he having financial problems?"

"He's not my client, so I can talk freely about him, and yes, that's the rumor that's going around." Despite what he'd just said, he didn't elaborate.

"It's no surprise that NRA Realty has encroached on his territory. Karen Johnson actually believes in customer service."

"She's sharp," Christopher agreed.

"I suppose even *she* knows Angelica's secret," Tricia groused.

Christopher shoveled another forkful of salad into his mouth, chewed, and swallowed. He shook his head. "Not as far as I know." He sipped his coffee.

"So, what's the scoop with Bob?" Tricia asked.

"Legal trouble," Christopher said succinctly.

Tricia knew all about that. Bob's fingerprints had been matched to those found in Stan Berry's ransacked house after his murder. And it came to light that Bob had been arrested for a foolish prank as a teen. He'd skipped town and never completed his community service sentence. Now he was up to his chin in hot water.

Neither of them spoke again until Christopher had finished his meal and set his fork down. "Boy, that was good. You ought to let Angelica give you a few cooking lessons. She's terrific—at just about everything she does."

Tricia pushed back her chair and stood. "I'm sorry you have to leave so soon."

"Who says I do?"

"Me. It's been a traumatic day. All I want to do is settle back in my easy chair with a good book and forget about real life for a few hours."

"It might do you good to experience more of real life—at least the good part of it."

"I have plenty of good things in my life."

As though on cue, Miss Marple said, *"Yow!"*

They both laughed.

Christopher pushed back his chair and stood. "Can I at least kiss you good-bye?"

"No."

He leaned forward and brushed a light kiss against her cheek anyway.

"Hey!"

"So sue me." Watching where he stepped, as Miss Marple seemed about to trip him, Christopher headed for the door. "Thanks for the dinner and the conversation. Can I come by tomorrow night?"

"No."

"Okay, see you then," he said, and let himself out, closing the door.

"That man," Tricia grated.

"Yow!" Miss Marple agreed.

FOUR

Tricia read far into the night—much later than she'd intended, and it wasn't as though she needed to finish Agatha Christie's *Death in the Air* since she'd read the book at least three times before. But she'd known that the troubling thoughts of the day were bound to haunt her unless she was good and tired before she turned off her bedside light.

Without a treadmill, Tricia was forced to take a brisk early-morning walk around the village. Thanks to a new pedometer, she'd figured out several routes to get in her usual four-mile walk, and she enjoyed admiring the neat homes and gardens—at least when it wasn't raining. She'd miss that when winter came again, but decided that walking outside was far more enjoyable than the tedium of the treadmill.

It was nearly seven thirty when Tricia returned to her temporary home, and she had just enough time to shower, change, and eat a yogurt breakfast before she turned the plastic CLOSED sign to OPEN and unlocked the front door. Once she did, the Stoneham Chamber of Commerce was officially open for business.

No sooner had she sat down at her desk when Bob Kelly entered. As far as she knew, Bob hadn't darkened the Chamber's new office before then.

"To what do I owe the pleasure?" Tricia asked, knowing full well why Bob had come to visit.

He let his gaze follow the contours of the room that had once acted as the home's living room. He took in the four desks. "The Chamber never needed more than one employee when I ran it," he groused.

"Membership is up over a hundred percent since January," Tricia said, keeping her tone even. "And as you know, I'm not taking a salary."

"What will they do when you go back to running your store?"

"Perhaps they'll hire someone else. If membership continues to rise, they'll be well able to afford it."

Bob glowered and quickly changed the subject. "Everyone around the village is talking about poor Pete Renquist—and how *you* found him."

"I wish I'd found him a few minutes sooner. It might have made all the difference in the world," Tricia said sincerely.

"Pete and I worked together a lot over the years," Bob bragged. That was certainly stretching the truth. Under Bob's leadership, Michele Fowler, manager of the Dog-Eared Page, had pushed the Chamber to team up with the Historical Society on establishing the cemetery ghost walks. That hadn't happened until Angelica had come on board. Bob's agenda hadn't included anything that didn't bring attention to his projects and his realty company. He'd rebuffed Michele's suggestion because it offered no monetary value to the Chamber or Bob personally.

"Did he say anything to you before he died?" Bob asked, his tone neutral.

Tricia studied his face. Now, why would he ask that? Russ had said Pete's death was suspicious. Could Bob have been responsible?

Bob was a lot of things, but Tricia had never considered *murderer* to be among them.

"No," she lied. "What brings you to the Chamber this morning? Looking for Angelica?" she asked.

The dig made him bristle. "Of course not. I've come with a fantastic offer you can't afford to turn down."

So far he'd cornered her at the Bookshelf Diner, the convenience store, and even on her way to the ladies room at the Brookview Inn, and none of his offers to sell the building that housed her store had been in the ballpark of what she was willing to pay.

"Bob, we've talked about this before."

"Yes, and I've taken your comments to heart. I'm willing to lower the price to a more comfortable level."

He handed her a slip of paper with a number written on it. It certainly wasn't a number she felt comfortable with. She handed the paper back. "Sorry, there are a few too many zeroes here for me."

Bob picked up a pen from the desk and crossed out that number, wrote another, and handed the slip back to her.

Tricia frowned and shook her head. "Still too high."

"That's the lowest I'm willing to go."

"Then we won't be making a deal." Again she handed the paper back. "If you let me out of my lease, you could put a for-sale sign on the property today."

"Not a chance. According to the lease, it's *your* responsibility to repair the building."

"And you know I can't do that until the insurance comes through."

"Well, how soon is that going to be?"

"I have no idea. It could be tomorrow—it could be six months from now. If you're strapped for cash, why don't you put another of your buildings up for sale?"

"Who says I'm strapped?" Bob asked sharply.

"No one," she lied again. "But you seem to be in a hurry to round up some cash."

"I am not. The way the real estate market has recovered, I'm just looking to score big."

Well, he wasn't going to score big with Tricia. Her lease still had over a year to go, and if they couldn't come to an agreement, she was prepared to move. She'd hate to lose a prime Main Street storefront, but the way the village was expanding, she was sure she could still make a go of the business in a less desirable location.

"Nigela Ricita Associates is primed to develop the north end of the village. Perhaps I'll wait until they do and lease space from them. Or, I could just buy a property and develop it myself."

Bob looked horrified. "Why would you do that?"

"Because I can. And then I'd have exactly what I want and wouldn't have to worry about a landlord who constantly raised my rent. And, as you pointed out, with the real estate market's recovery it would be a win-win situation." Tricia looked thoughtful. "I think I'll call Karen Johnson over at NRA Realty and see if she has a property I could look at."

"There's nothing else on Main Street for sale," Bob practically growled.

"Perhaps nothing with Kelly Realty, but who knows what Karen has lined up? She's only been here in the village six months and already has quite an inventory—and made plenty of sales." Karen had done quite well signing Bob's former clients, who seemed pleased with the deals she'd made for them.

Bob stuffed the paper into his Kelly green sports jacket. "If you aren't prepared to deal, then I'll just find someone who is."

He'd just said he wouldn't be able to sell the building in its present condition. Who did he figure would buy it?

"It was lovely to see you, Bob. Did you know you'd let your Chamber membership lapse? I'd be glad to reinstate you right now if you'd like to write us a check."

"I don't have my checkbook with me," he said tersely.

"Shall I send you a bill?"

Bob's mouth dropped open in indignation, but then he shut it. "Why not?"

Tricia schooled her features so she wouldn't laugh.

"I'm a very busy man. I have to go," Bob said, turned and left the office without a good-bye. Tricia was surprised when he didn't slam the door behind him. Shrugging, she got up, went to the kitchen, and made what was sure to be the first of many pots of coffee that day.

Tricia heard the side door open and was surprised to find Mariana coming through it. "You're here bright and early."

"I've got a dental appointment this afternoon. Angelica said it would be okay if I came in early I could leave early, too."

"That's fine with me," Tricia said, and stood to one side, waiting for the coffee to brew.

Mariana got the carton of milk from the fridge, grabbed a cup from the drain board, and poured. "There're more dishes than usual this morning. You must have had company last night."

"A friend dropped by," Tricia admitted, unwilling to say just who it had been, and made a mental note not to leave evidence on the counter again. Mariana handed Tricia the carton, knowing she'd be doctoring her own cup.

"I heard Pete Renquist died. It's such a shame. He was so nice."

"Yes, he was."

Mariana shook her head, poured herself a cup of coffee, then left the kitchen. She settled at her desk, turned on her radio, and jumped into her workday.

Tricia lingered at the kitchen counter, putting away the dishes before pouring herself a cup of coffee and heading down the hall for the office.

The front door handle rattled, and Chief Baker entered the office. "Good morning, ladies," he called.

Thanks to her being the last person to speak to Pete Renquist, Tricia wasn't at all surprised to see the chief. "Good morning, Grant."

"You can probably guess why I'm here."

"Oh, yes. But I don't think this is the appropriate place to talk," she said, eyeing Mariana.

"How about your quarters? I understand you've got a cozy living room upstairs."

"And how would you know about that?"

He shrugged. "I heard it . . . somewhere."

"I don't think that's the appropriate place to talk, either."

"Would you like to go down to the station?" he asked, his voice much harder than it had been.

"Why don't we go to the park?"

Baker let out a breath. "To the scene of the crime? That would be satisfactory."

"Mariana!" Tricia called. "I should only be gone for ten or fifteen minutes."

"I can hold the fort," she said.

Tricia took her coffee with her and led Baker to the front door.

They exited the building. Tricia was the first to speak. "I'm surprised you didn't call me last night," she said as they headed south on Main Street.

"I was on my way over, but then I saw you had company. I thought you and Christopher weren't dating."

"We're not."

"It looked like you were having dinner."

Tricia stopped dead. "Were you spying on me?"

"No, I . . . well, I will admit that I was on my way over and saw him enter the Chamber building. I came to the door, intending to knock, but then . . . I don't know what came over me. I walked around the side of the house and just happened to glance through the kitchen window."

Tricia hadn't served Christopher for some ten or more minutes after his arrival. How long had Baker stood there, watching them? And why hadn't they seen him?

Tricia wondered if Nigela Ricita Associates—rats! Angelica—would spring for a set of new blinds for the kitchen.

"I don't suppose it would do me any good to report to the police that I've got a Peeping Tom when *you're* the Tom."

"It was wrong of me. I apologize."

"Grant, you have to get over this jealousy."

"I'm not jealous. Just a little envious."

"It's the same thing."

"No, it isn't," he insisted. "I envy the fact Christopher and you are still friends."

"*We're* still friends—or I thought we were until about a minute ago. And I thought we'd set those boundaries quite some time ago."

"We did. I'm sorry. It won't happen again."

It had better not.

Tricia took a sip of her rapidly cooling coffee and started walking once again. It took only a few steps for Baker to catch up with her. "I understand Pete's death has been ruled suspicious," she said.

"Where did you hear that?" he asked, not at all pleased.

"Around." She didn't elaborate.

"There won't be a ruling until after the autopsy is complete, but the doctors found a suspicious needle mark and a bruise. Until we know why Pete died, we can't rule that it was a natural death."

"Jumping the gun, aren't you?" Tricia asked

"Let's just say that there have been too many suspicious deaths in this village to rule it out. I'll be talking with the medical examiner later today, and I want to be informed before I do."

Tricia paused at the corner and looked both ways before she began to cross the street. "What did you want to ask me concerning finding Pete in the park yesterday?"

"Where exactly was he?"

"I'll show you," Tricia said. Again, she had to fight a claustrophobic feeling as she mounted the steps and paused, pointing at the gazebo's concrete floor. "He was lying right there; his head faced west. As far as I remember, he had on the same clothes as when I'd seen him earlier in the day."

"When was that?"

"It must have been about nine thirty, at the unveiling for the first historical marker at By Hook or By Book. It was a photo-op for the *Stoneham Weekly News*."

"Russ Smith took pictures?"

"Yes."

"Who else was there?" Baker asked.

"Angelica, Mary Fairchild, and Pete."

"Anything interesting happen?"

"Not until Earl Winkler showed up." She shook her head in consternation. "He's not a very nice man."

"What did he say?"

"Oh, you know what he's like. He hates the fact that prosperity has returned to Stoneham."

"Did he have words with Pete?"

"I wouldn't say words, but you could tell they had differing opinions on the subject."

"What subject?"

"The upcoming ghost walks at the Stoneham Rural Cemetery that the Historical Society is sponsoring."

"Would you say Earl had an ax to grind?"

"With Pete? You mean personally?" She thought about it. "I don't think so. I didn't really know Pete well. I mean, I'd spoken to him a lot in the past few months because Angelica has cultivated a relationship between the Chamber and the Historical Society. But usually I was just taking messages and passing them on to Angelica. She knew him better than I did."

"Depending on what I learn when I speak to the ME, I'll probably speak to Angelica, Mary, Russ, and Earl, too."

"The discussion wasn't particularly pleasant, but it wasn't threatening in any way, either."

Baker nodded.

"I take it Pete was unconscious when you found him."

"I thought so, but he did briefly speak to me, and it was just gibberish."

"What did he say?"

She frowned. "'I never missed my little boy.'"

Baker's eyes widened, but then he frowned. "Have you mentioned this to anyone else?"

Tricia shook her head.

"Not even Angelica or—" He seemed to have to force himself to say the name. "Christopher?"

"No. I told you, it was gibberish."

"Perhaps," he said, "but I don't want you going around and repeating it—just in case. Promise me."

Tricia sighed, feeling foolish. "I promise." She took another sip of her coffee, found it tepid, and frowned.

"How did you come to find Renquist?" Baker asked.

"I took Sarge out for a walk, and he must have sensed something was amiss. He pulled me in the direction of the gazebo and, well, you know the rest."

"Not entirely," Baker said, and pulled out a small flashlight to scan the concrete deck and illuminate the dark corners. Tricia couldn't see anything but dried leaves, a few cigarette butts, and small bits of paper that had probably been blown there months before.

Baker looked thoughtful. "I think I'll call the Sheriff's Department to see if they can send out a lab team."

"Isn't that a little premature? You don't even know a crime has been committed."

"That's true, but if it has, I don't want the scene any more contaminated than it already is."

"You're the chief of police," she said, and shrugged. "Is there anything else you want to know?"

"Do you know if Pete spoke to the paramedics?"

Tricia shook her head. "He was in cardiac arrest when they hauled him away in the ambulance. Unless he regained consciousness, I doubt it. You'd have to ask them."

"I will."

Baker studied the gazebo floor once more.

"What do you know about Bob Kelly's legal troubles?" Tricia asked.

"Just that he has them," Baker said offhandedly.

"Was a warrant ever sworn for his arrest on the old charges against him?"

Baker nodded. "He was arraigned, made bail, and now it's up to the courts to figure out what to do with him."

How had Bob kept that quiet? Did Russ know about it? Surely he would have reported it in the *Stoneham Weekly News*'s police blotter, along with the missing hubcaps and homes that had been egged after the high school senior prank day back in June.

"I'd better get going," Baker said, then turned and trotted down the granite steps. "If I need to speak to you again, I'll call."

Tricia walked down the steps, paused at one of the trash bins, and poured her cold coffee inside. She started across the grass, but before she made it back to the sidewalk, she decided to make a detour. The Stoneham Historical Society was located on Locust Street, two blocks west of Main Street. Though the day was pleasant, Tricia felt anything but cheerful. She didn't know if Pete had any relatives in the area, so she intended to speak to his colleagues. Still, it was never a happy occasion to deliver condolences.

The society was housed in none other than the village founder's home. Hiram Stone had made his fortune in quarrying granite and had built himself a house that, while not a mansion, was certainly bigger and grander than the houses of the people who'd worked for him.

The society's hours were from ten until two, but she had a feeling she'd find someone in and the back door unlocked. Bypassing the grand front entrance, she walked along a stone path that led to the back of the building.

The Stoneham Horticultural Society had teamed up with the Historical Society and had done a marvelous job recreating the home's original Italianate garden. Tricia paused to take in the beauty of this outdoor extension of the home. Beds filled with summer flowers flanked a gravel path that led to the garden's first focal point, a fountain and lily pond. At the end of the path were the remains of what had been a stone temple, which now sported a round, trellislike structure that acted as a kind of placeholder until they could rebuild the structure. It was walled-in by imposing beech hedges that she'd been told were hand-clipped. She'd visited the garden on several occasions in the past and made a vow that she would not wait so long to visit this place of tranquility again.

"Tricia, is that you?"

Tricia turned at the sound of the woman's voice behind her. Janet Koch stood on the immense stone patio with steps that trailed from the door. The tall, dark-haired woman was dressed in black, which was unusual for a summer's day but appropriate under the circumstances.

"You gave me a start," Tricia admitted.

"I'm sorry. That's the last thing I want to do today—cause someone else to have a heart attack."

So Janet hadn't heard that Pete had died under suspicious circumstances.

"I came to offer my condolences."

"Thank you. Why don't you come in and we can commiserate?" Janet said, and with a sweep of her arm, pointed the way.

A large parlor overlooked the home's garden, but Janet led the way to an office off to one side, where Tricia could smell coffee brewing. "Can I offer you a cup?" Janet asked.

"Thank you," Tricia said. "As you can see. I brought my own."

Janet poured for them both, and they each doctored their coffee the way they liked it. "Won't you sit down?"

Janet sat behind a desk of dark wood that Tricia guessed might be mahogany. Although old, it didn't match the décor of the rest of the house.

"I feel rather strange sitting at Pete's desk. Until the board meets in a few days, I'll be taking care of the day-to-day activities." She swallowed hard and took a sip of her coffee, her eyes brimming with tears.

"I take it you and Pete were good friends."

"You could say that. We'd worked together for the past five years, but of course Pete had been here much longer, first as a volunteer and then as one of the staff. We had many a brainstorming meeting right here in this office as we struggled to get funding—that is, until Nigela Ricita made a generous donation."

"Did she, now?" Tricia asked, her interest piqued.

Janet nodded. "We sent a letter, just our regular yearly solicitation, and were shocked when she sent us half a million dollars."

Tricia choked on her coffee. "She did what?"

Janet nodded. "That nice young man, Antonio Barbero, brought the check himself."

"But I never heard a thing about it."

"And you won't, at least not officially."

"Ms. Ricita also made a generous contribution to the Horticultural Society. They hope to rebuild the stone temple at the end of the garden with it."

Angelica had her fingers in many more pies than she'd let on. But

Tricia didn't want to discuss the further adventures of Nigela Ricita—at least not at that moment.

"I didn't know Pete well," she said, changing the subject, "but we'd spoken many times since I came to work at the Chamber. Did Pete have family here in Stoneham?"

Janet shook her head. "He'd been divorced for many years, and as far as I know had no contact with his ex-wife for at least a decade."

"He mentioned he was a dad."

"I believe he had a daughter, but they weren't close. She lived with her mother in California."

So Pete had a daughter. Then why had he said he'd never missed his little boy? "Just the one child?" Tricia asked.

Janet nodded and sipped her coffee.

"What will happen—I mean, as far as any arrangements?" Tricia asked.

"Pete once told me he wanted to be cremated and his ashes spread in the garden out back. Of course, the board would have to approve it, but I think it would be a lovely memorial after all the time he spent here, and I know it would have pleased him."

"When did you say the board would meet next?"

"Our next regularly scheduled meeting isn't for three weeks, but they'll have to convene an emergency session to figure out how we move forward." Janet's frown deepened. "Pete had a *joie de vivre* that attracted people. It worked well for him in this job."

"So, he had no enemies?"

Janet looked surprised by the question. "No." Then she seemed to think better of it. "Well, he was a terrible flirt, which annoyed many a husband, but the rich older ladies always enjoyed the attention. And, of course, Pete and Earl Winkler weren't exactly friends, but I wouldn't call them enemies."

"Does Earl Winkler have *any* friends?" Tricia asked.

Janet almost managed a smile. "It would be hard to believe. I'm still in shock he ever got elected to the Board of Selectmen."

"So am I."

Janet's gaze wandered to the wall where a group shot of people, including Pete and herself, hung. She sighed. "I still can't believe he's gone."

"Did you know I was the one who found him in the park?"

Janet looked up. "No, I didn't."

"Did he often leave the office and go for walks during the middle of the day?"

"Sometimes. He said it helped him clear his mind. Nobody minded. He put in many more than the forty hours a week he got paid for. He loved this house. He loved the gardens. He was very enthusiastic about the upcoming ghost walks at the Stoneham Rural Cemetery and at St. Rita's church. He'd been researching the people buried there, interviewing people, reading old books, and writing up various scripts."

"He really enjoyed the work," Tricia stated.

"You bet." Janet shook her head, sadness etched across her features. "We'll figure out a way to carry on. I know the ghost walks will be a success."

"Had you or Pete ever spoken to Michele Fowler about volunteering? It was she who first suggested the ghost walks."

"I've only met her once, at one of our fundraising cocktail parties. Do you think she'd be interested?"

"I know she works a lot of nights at the Dog-Eared Page, but I'll bet she'd be game. And you know, that English accent of hers would be a hit with anyone who came on the walks."

"I noticed people do tend to pay attention when she speaks. Would you be willing to put a bug in her ear?"

"I'd love to."

"Thanks." Janet rummaged in the desk and came up with a business card. It was Pete's. She crossed off his name, writing in her own. "I'll have to get new ones made, but the phone number is good."

Tricia pocketed the card and drained her cup. "I'm keeping you from your work."

"And I'm keeping you from yours," Janet said with what almost passed as a smile. She stood.

Tricia stood, too, and on impulse walked around the desk to give Janet a hug. "I'm so sorry you lost your friend."

"Me, too," Janet said, her voice breaking. "Me, too."

FIVE

Angelica arrived at the Chamber office at precisely nine forty-five, dressed to the nines—business style—and looking ready to take on the world. For a moment, Tricia felt a kind of flash of déjà vu—seeing her sister à la Auntie Mame, with a zest for life and a take-charge attitude that could move mountains and shift whole continents. And not for the first time, she felt a stab of jealousy.

After greeting Mariana and Tricia, Angelica grabbed a cup of coffee from the kitchen before joining them in the office, where she sat down at her desk. Angelica could have used the downstairs bedroom as a private office but had chosen instead to have a desk right in the living room with the rest of her staff. She definitely hadn't played the diva card since assuming the Chamber presidency, insisting that, since she didn't spend the majority of her day at the Chamber office, there was no need for her to take up so much real estate. Instead, the bedroom had become a small conference room. "What have we got on tap today?" she asked.

"The grand opening of the Antiques Emporium."

Angelica nodded. "I love these ribbon-cutting events. Do you realize this is the sixth new business to open since I took over as Chamber president?"

"Did you have anything to do with bringing them here?" Tricia asked.

"Not me, personally, but Karen Johnson from NRA Realty worked tirelessly to court them. They've already got twenty vendors and have space for another ten. Karen's pretty sure they'll rent the space within a week or two."

"Lucky them," Tricia said.

Angelica turned a jaundiced eye on her sister. "Don't you want to see Stoneham thrive?"

"Of course I do. I just don't like attending ribbon-cutting ceremonies."

"Why not?"

"Because *I'm* the one who has to tote the fake oversized scissors and the big roll of red ribbon to these affairs. It makes me feel like a dork."

"It's not like they're heavy," Angelica said.

"Then I stand around while you get to pose and look important."

"Darling, I *am* important!" Angelica sighed. "If you'd prefer to stay back here at the office, I'm sure Mariana will accompany me. But I'd much rather you come."

"Why?" So she could show off in front of Tricia?

"Because it gives us more time to spend together."

"We already spend two or three hours a day together," Tricia said.

"Oh." Angelica said the word oddly, as though she was surprised and yet hurt.

"I'm sorry, Ange. I do like to spend time with you, but I'm worried that people will think you're using all these photo-ops to grab attention and that it'll reflect badly on you."

Angelica looked thoughtful. "That's a good point. Okay, how about I carry the scissors and ribbon and you be my stand-in for the photo?"

"No, that's not what I meant."

"But you're right. I want the villagers to see the Chamber as an organization that can promote the area—and its members, of which you are one. It's vitally important that the Chamber grow, but I don't want to overshadow the organization like—like my predecessor did." Angelica seemed to go out of her way not to criticize her ex-lover, Bob Kelly, which was commendable. But the truth was, she'd done more in her brief tenure than Bob had done in the previous five years.

"Okay," Tricia said. "Perhaps we can get Russ to take the picture with me in it and have the caption say I'm representing the Chamber. But won't the business owner want to be photographed with the head of the Chamber and not just a volunteer?"

"We can do both. I'm sure if I buy a little extra advertising, Russ will do anything I request. Nikki won't get jealous if he takes your picture, though, will she?"

"I don't think so." Russ and Tricia had been an item for a while—but that was before he and Nikki had gotten together. At first she'd been jealous whenever Tricia's name came up, but she seemed to have gotten over it.

Tricia studied her sister and shook her head.

"What?" Angelica asked, looking down at herself. "Did I spill coffee on my blouse?"

"No. I just can't get over how you've changed."

"Sorry, Trish, but it's not *me* who's changed. It's your *perception* of me that's changed."

"I guess you're right," Tricia said, and swallowed down the lump that had suddenly appeared in her throat. "Okay." She looked down at herself. "Do I have time to change clothes?"

Angelica waved a hand in dismissal. "You always look beautiful. Now, let's grab our stuff and get over there. We don't want our newest member to feel we've neglected them."

Tricia watched as Angelica strode over to the storage cabinet and grabbed the prop scissors and big roll of red ribbon. Angelica had been right. She was still the oversized personality that had always seemed to dwarf Tricia all those years ago, but somehow the traits that used to bug her so much almost seemed endearing now. Almost.

Less than a minute later, the sisters left the Chamber office and headed up the street on foot.

The Antiques Emporium was housed in what had previously been Everett's Grocery. The long-empty cinderblock building had been spruced up on the outside with paint and some landscaping, and its inside had been divided into stalls. Those closest to the large bank of windows up front had been stuffed to the gills with the flotsam and jetsam of years past. Not everything was a certifiable antique, for the booths held Fiesta china, old Bakelite radios, vintage clothing, and anything one could imagine—from salt shakers to bone china, and doilies to damask. Pixie would probably go nuts shopping there.

Russ Smith had dutifully shown up with his Nikon and snapped photos of Angelica with the owner and several of the vendors, as well as Tricia and the same group of people. They'd sort out the details of the photos and captions later.

After the preliminaries were observed, Angelica, Tricia, and even Russ were invited inside to partake of refreshments that were laid out on one of the sales counters. Lemonade, punch, and more than a dozen different cookies had been made by the Emporium vendors. Tricia accepted a paper cup of lemonade and grabbed a snickerdoodle. Her grandmother had made the same crisp, cinnamon-laced cookies, and one bite brought back a host of wonderful memories.

"Thank you for coming," said the Emporium's owner, whose name Tricia had somehow missed.

"I'm glad I could be here," Tricia said.

"Toni," the woman said, offering her hand. "Toni Bennett."

Tricia struggled to keep from giggling. "Really?"

The woman laughed. "Really. My folks were big fans of the singer Tony Bennett and, well, here I am. And the worst thing is, I can't sing a note."

"It's a wonderful name. I'll bet most people don't forget it."

"It does come in handy," Toni admitted. She looked around at the customers who'd already entered. "What a beautiful day for our grand opening. I'm only sorry my favorite vendor couldn't be here today."

"Oh?" Tricia said.

"Pete Renquist." Toni shook her head sadly. "I was crushed to hear he'd died. It was Pete who encouraged me to open the Emporium. He was the first to sign up for a booth. He and I brainstormed on numerous occasions on a variety of subjects. He had so many wonderful ideas, so much knowledge, and such a zest for life." Her voice cracked and her eyes filled with tears that she quickly tried to wipe away. "I still can't believe he's gone."

"I feel the same way," Tricia admitted. Did Toni know she'd been the one to find him? Tricia wasn't going to mention it. "Did you know him a long time?"

Toni cleared her throat and forced a smile. "Yeah. I've been a volunteer at the Historical Society for about ten years, but I'm not sure anyone ever really knew Pete. He was warm and genuine, but there was a big part of himself that he kept private. I don't know of any other way to explain it."

Tricia nodded. "What kind of articles did he have for sale?"

"I'll show you. Follow me," Toni said, and led the way to what was probably the booth with the best location. It was large and situated near the front of the store and had good light. Unlike most of the other booths, Pete's actually contained antiques—primitives: old milking stools, rough-hewn tables and chairs, and antique pottery, mingled with what looked like tin dishes, Sandwich glass, and butter churns. Antique oil portraits and landscapes hung on the wall, which was some six feet shorter than the height of the ceiling and divided his space from another vendor's.

Tricia eyed the price tag on one of the paintings and winced. "Pete's wares are a little more . . ." She wasn't sure how to express it.

"Higher-end than most of the other vendors' merchandise," Toni finished for her. "Yes. And I told him he could do much better in Nashua or Manchester, but he told me he'd bought most of them for a song and wasn't worried about making a profit because he never intended for them to sell. He priced them at what he thought they were actually worth. I think Pete just wanted to help me out until all the booths were spoken for, and then he would have quickly bowed out. Judging by his outrageous prices, I don't think he expected to sell one item. He was a collector, and this was a way to have his collection admired. Now I'm not sure what will become of it all. I don't know if he even had a will or an attorney. I can keep the stuff here and, if there are sales, give the money to his estate—but if things work out, there's going to come a time when I have to pack up everything and rent the space to someone who can actually pay."

"I'm sure Pete would approve of any decision you make. He seemed like a reasonable guy."

"That he was," Toni agreed. "That's why I was surprised the other day when he told me someone had threatened him."

Tricia blinked. "Threatened? How?"

"He wasn't really clear about that. He said he'd found out something while going through some of the Historical Society's old records, and when he asked someone—and he didn't say who—about it, was told to mind his own business. Or else!"

"And he didn't give you a clue who it was he'd confronted?"

Toni shook her head. "But it seemed like he was disappointed in the whole situation. That maybe he'd once considered the person who'd threatened him to be a friend."

And who was that friend? So far, no one Tricia had spoken to had admitted to being close to Pete. He had been a terrible flirt, yet it seemed he'd only felt comfortable being an acquaintance, not a true friend, to most of the people with whom he'd interacted.

Perhaps the person who'd threatened him had carried out a death sentence. If so, it had to be someone right here in Stoneham. Someone everyone knew. But that was the thing; most of the villagers *did* know just about everyone else in Stoneham.

"Toni," a voice called.

She looked toward the store's office. "Sorry. Duty calls."

"Thanks for showing me around."

Toni gave Tricia a quick wave and then hurried off.

Tricia stood in front of Pete's booth, staring at his wide range of merchandise. How sad that all he had collected—loved—would be sold off, and for probably far less than its worth by whoever benefitted from his estate.

Tricia reached for her cell phone and called Chief Baker. Voice mail picked up. She left a message relaying what Toni had told her, suggesting he give the Emporium's manager a call. Ringing off, she looked up to see Angelica approach. "There you are."

"Toni was just showing me Pete Renquist's booth."

"Oh." Angelica pointed to the booth before them. "This one?"

Tricia nodded. "Really old stuff. A lot different from the rest of the kitsch in here."

"I like kitsch in my café but don't want it in my home. I suppose it's fun to collect, and I want the Emporium to do well, so who cares about my opinion? Come on. We'd better get back to the office. I've got a lot to do today and no doubt so do you."

"Yes, ma'am," Tricia said, and saluted.

They collected the scissors and ribbon and, on their way out, thanked everyone in sight. Tricia made sure to give Toni a wave, wishing she'd had more time to pump her for information.

Pete had been a part of the Historical Society for a long time. And he'd been a longtime resident of Stoneham. Surely there were other people who'd known him well. And, as she and Angelica headed back to the Chamber, it occurred to Tricia that she knew a local close at hand who might have that kind of information.

S I X

 Angelica's spirits always soared after a successful Chamber event, and she chattered on about the various conversations she'd had after the ceremony, but Tricia only half listened, pondering what Toni had told her about Pete. She'd tell Angelica about it—when her sister finally wound down.

They arrived back at the Chamber office to find Earl Winkler impatiently waiting for them. "What took you so long?" he barked.

"I'm sorry," Angelica said. She spoke in that sickly sweet tone of voice again. "Did we have an appointment?"

"No," Earl admitted, "but your receptionist thought you should have been back long before this."

Angelica glanced at Mariana, who vehemently shook her head.

"I'm sorry for the misunderstanding," Angelica said politely. "Now, what was it you wanted, Earl?"

"Selectman Winkler, if you please," he insisted.

Tricia had to cover her mouth and clear her throat in an effort to keep from laughing, but Angelica merely smiled. "Selectman."

"I want it made clear, and in front of witnesses," he added, eyeing Tricia and Mariana, "that I had nothing to do with Pete Renquist's death."

"Does anyone suspect you of it?" Angelica asked.

"Well, no. But we had words the morning of his death—you were a witness to it—and I don't want the situation misconstrued."

"By whom?" Angelica pressed.

"The police, for one."

"Did they contact you about it?" she asked.

"Well, no. But it's well known that you—and your sister"—he looked accusingly at Tricia—"are always getting mixed up with the police when there's been a serious crime here in Stoneham."

"What does that have to do with Pete's death?" Tricia asked.

"Nothing. But I don't want the two of you suggesting that I might make a good suspect."

"*Do* you make a good suspect?" It was Tricia's turn to be annoyed at the jerk.

"Of course not. I *serve* the citizens of Stoneham, not *kill* them."

"Are you accusing anyone in this office of killing him?" Angelica asked pointedly.

"Well, no," Earl said yet again.

"Then I suggest you take your umbrage and return to your regular job."

"I'm semiretired."

"Then go home," Angelica said firmly.

Earl glared at her, pivoted, and then stormed from the office, slamming the door behind him.

Mariana looked scared. "Honest, Angelica, I never told him when you'd be coming back. He must have just assumed—"

"Don't worry, sweetie. I believe you. People like Earl are too busy being important to actually listen to what's being said to them, so they make things up as they go along."

Mariana offered a weak smile, obviously glad to be exonerated. She rose from her chair. "I think I need a fortifying cup of coffee. Can I get you anything?"

Both Tricia and Angelica shook their heads and watched as Mariana headed for the kitchen. Angelica was the first to speak. "So, what was that all about?"

"Obviously Earl thinks *we* think he'd make a fine suspect in Pete's death."

"They did clash on more than one occasion, but half the village has clashed with Earl at one time or another."

"They haven't turned up dead, either," Tricia pointed out.

"What does he want us to do? Tell Grant he's innocent, or point the finger at him?"

"Why would he want that?"

"To make *us* look bad. It seems to be what he tries to do most."

Tricia thought about it for a moment, but Angelica had turned back to the mail littering her desk. Why had Earl shown up when he had? Why had he insisted on speaking to them in front of Mariana?

"I didn't tell you what else Toni said," Tricia began.

Angelica snatched her letter opener and looked up. "About what?"

"Pete. She said someone had threatened him."

"But not Earl?"

"Pete didn't tell her who—or exactly why. Just that he'd found something suspicious in some old records and he'd confronted some-one about it."

"You should tell Grant."

"I already left him a message."

"Good. Then let him handle it," Angelica advised, and slit the enve-lope in her left hand.

"I am. But I wonder what kind of records Pete was going through and who he might have contacted about it."

"Not your business," Angelica sang, and pulled a letter from the envelope.

"What kind of records does the Historical Society keep, anyway?" Tricia asked.

"Anything old, I suppose."

"Deeds? Marriage certificates? Death certificates?"

"I would assume most of what they've got has been donated."

"Diaries? Maps?"

"Stop speculating and get back to work," Angelica said mildly.

"Aren't you even curious?"

"I would be, but I have too much to do and only so many hours in the day to accomplish it."

"Speaking of the Historical Society, I visited Janet Koch this morn-ing. She's taking over for Pete until the board meets," Tricia said.

"That's nice," Angelica muttered, distracted, her gaze still on the paperwork before her.

"She said the moon was made of green cheese."

"Uh-huh."

"And that she has swamp land for sale in Florida."

"How about that?" Angelica muttered.

"Janet also told me that Nigela Ricita made a generous donation to the society."

That got Angelica's attention; she looked up sharply.

"Half a million bucks," Tricia said.

"It was supposed to be anonymous," Angelica grated.

"For the most part, it is."

They heard a noise from the kitchen, where Mariana seemed to be making a fresh pot of coffee.

"We won't speak of this—or Ms. Ricita—here at the Chamber office."

"When *will* we speak about it?" Tricia pushed.

"If I have my way, never," Angelica said, and turned back to her work.

Tricia sat down at her desk. She'd much rather be reading a mystery. She opened her desk drawer, where she'd squirreled away *Death in the Air*. Her personal library may or may not have been ruined by the smoke damage after the fire in Haven't Got a Clue. She'd walked through the apartment twice since the fire. Despite the soot, it didn't look too bad, but the smoky odor had been nauseating. She had studied how to clean smoke-damaged books but wondered how many she could salvage. Most of them weren't worth the cost of restoration, and thanks to eBay, she'd done a good job replacing scores of her favorite comfort reads. Just about everything in the store had been ruined by flames, water, or smoke. Still, she'd lined up her original contractor, Jim Stark, to come in and repair the damage, and he'd been amassing supplies, like replacements for the tin ceiling and the classic molding. Tricia had found duplicate copies of most of the author portraits that had adorned the walls, too. They and the books she'd bought as replacement stock sat in a climate-controlled storage unit until the day they could replace their damaged counterparts.

On impulse, Tricia picked up her desk phone and called the number she'd memorized months before. "New Hampshire Mutual. John Martin speaking."

"John, it's Tricia Miles."

"Hi, Tricia. No news yet," he said, sounding quite cheerful. Sure, he didn't have his life on hold.

"I guess I don't have to remind you how exasperating it is to have to wait so long for a settlement."

"You and everyone else. But we're not dragging our feet. Just trying to dot all the i's and cross all the t's."

And strain my patience to the breaking point, Tricia thought. She sighed. "So you've said. Can you give me *any* hope that a decision will be made soon?"

"As soon as I hear anything, I'll call. I promise."

"Thank you," Tricia said, feeling anything but thankful.

"I'll talk to you soon," John said, and ended the call.

"Not soon enough," Tricia grumbled.

"Darling, Trish," Angelica said with sympathy, "you must distract yourself. Have you had a chance to finish the Chamber newsletter? I sent my column like you asked."

"I saw it. I did a little judicious editing, but I think it's fine. Do you want to read it now or wait until the layout is finished?"

"I trust that you only want me to shine for the Chamber, so I'm sure it's fine, and I'll look at it when I do the final read-through."

"I'll finish it by day's end and e-mail you a copy at home."

"Thanks." Angelica scooped up the papers on her desk and deposited them in a drawer. "There's nothing that's screaming for my attention, so I think I'll head on back to the Cookery. I have a ton of e-mail that needs attending to."

Of course. Not only did she have to run her own little empire, but Nigela Ricita's as well.

"Will I see you for dinner tonight, Trish? I'm making shrimp pasta salad."

"I'd love it."

"See you at the usual time, with martini glasses chilled," Angelica called, and headed out the door.

I'd prefer a glass of Chardonnay, Tricia thought, then remembered what Pixie had said the evening before. "Wait a minute!"

Angelica paused at the entrance to the hall.

"Did you know that Pixie had a boyfriend?"

"Oh, sure. Fred Pillins, the guy who delivers meat to the café. Nice guy, but not what you'd call handsome," she said, and winced.

"What does that mean?"

"He's got a little scar on his face. But what does that matter? Pixie is smitten. It's so funny to see them together. They get all shy and giggly."

Giggly?

"How long have you known about them?"

She shrugged. "Since the day they met. Gotta go. Tootles!"

Tootles. It seemed to be Angelica's new favorite word.

Tricia tapped the escape key on her computer and it came back to life. She pulled up the file for the newsletter and stared at the screen, thinking about all that had already transpired that day—and it was only 11:14. No wonder she felt exhausted.

Mariana came back into the office and settled on the chair in front of her desk, putting her cup down on the mouse pad.

Tricia stood and wandered over to join her. "I meant to ask you before this, did you know Peter Renquist?"

Mariana shook her head. "Not well. I talked to him on the phone when he'd call for Angelica. I'd see him in the grocery store. That kind of thing."

"Did he have a girlfriend?"

"That's a matter of opinion," she said coyly.

"What do you mean?"

"He flirted with everyone—well, women," she clarified. "Most of us kind of blew it off, but . . . not everybody."

"Oh?"

She shrugged. "For a while, a lot of people thought he and Toni Bennett might be having an affair."

Was that the reason Toni had shed tears when they'd talked about Pete?

"But?" Tricia pressed.

Again Mariana shrugged. "It wouldn't have been a good idea. Toni's husband is a big supporter of the second amendment. I've heard he's got an arsenal. If he'd thought Pete was messing around with Toni, he'd have shot him for sure."

"Toni said her parents had named her after the singer. I take it she didn't take her husband's name when they married."

"That's right. Not so many women do that anymore. It's a shame. Still, she belongs to *him*, and he doesn't let people forget it."

So, there was a jealous husband hanging around. But Pete hadn't been shot, he'd been shot up—quite a difference.

"What's her husband's name?"

"Jim Stark."

Tricia blinked.

Her contractor.

SEVEN

Angelica wasn't at Booked for Lunch when Tricia showed up for her usual tuna plate, so she took it to go, intending to return to the Chamber office and retire to her private quarters to eat it and think about all she'd learned that morning. But then she made her second detour of the day and entered the Dog-Eared Page. Its manager, Michele Fowler, stood behind the bar with a stack of what looked like order forms before her. She looked up as Tricia approached. "A bit early in the day for you, isn't it, love?"

"I wondered if you had a few moments to talk?" Tricia asked.

Michele looked around the empty pub. "All the time in the world. Can I get you something?"

Tricia placed her take-out lunch container on the bar and sat on one of the stools. "Iced tea?"

"Sorry, we don't serve it."

"How about ginger ale?" Tricia suggested.

"Coming right up." Michele half filled a tall glass with ice and poured the soda from a well trigger. She set a napkin down on the bar in front of Tricia before placing the glass on it. "Now, what's on your mind?"

"By now I'm sure everyone in the village has heard about what happened to poor Pete Renquist."

"Beer, with a chaser," Michele replied sadly.

Tricia blinked. "I beg your pardon?"

Michele smiled. "I always remember people by their drink orders. You're Chardonnay, and lately a classic gin martini."

"And what are you?" Tricia asked.

"Gin or Merlot, depending on the time of day and the company."

Tricia took of sip of her ginger ale. "You know that the Historical Society has been gung-ho to take on your suggestion of the cemetery ghost walks, right?"

"It'll be great fun. I intend to be there the very first night they hold it."

"How would you like to be the docent leading it?"

It was Michele's turn to look startled. "Me? A docent?"

"The Historical Society is always looking for volunteers. Pete was working on the scripts before he died. It would probably be just a case of learning the material."

"Me?" Michele said again, sounding incredulous.

Tricia nodded.

"I don't know. It sounds like lovely fun, but I work evenings."

"I happen to know that Nigela Ricita is eager to see these ghost walks take off. She feels it would keep the tourists in the village after sunset. That would be good for business for the Dog-Eared Page. Maybe the walks could even start here. It would be a great selling point."

Michele nodded thoughtfully. "That it might. But I don't know a thing about the local cemeteries."

"As I said, Pete Renquist did extensive research on all of them. All it takes is a little memorization of facts and the ability to spin a good tale."

"Well, I'm certainly good at that." Michele looked thoughtful, and a smile played at her lips. "When would they need an answer?"

"The walks aren't set to start until September, so you've got plenty of time to think it over."

"I'd need to talk to Antonio Barbero and get his okay."

The pub's door opened, and who should walk in but Antonio himself, looking dapper in a three-piece suit with a crisp white shirt and a dark-striped tie.

"Are your ears burning?" Tricia asked, smiling.

He frowned at her. "I speak pretty good English, but I don't know what that means."

"It means we were just talking about you," Michele explained dryly.

"I hope you were saying nice things."

"Of course," Tricia said. "What are you doing here?"

"I came to discuss a new linen vendor with Michele. And you are here because . . . ?"

"The Historical Society would like me to take Pete Renquist's place giving the upcoming ghost walk tours," Michele piped up.

"I told her I thought Nigela Ricita would think it's a marvelous idea," Tricia said enthusiastically.

Antonio looked uncomfortable. "Perhaps. Is this a decision you've already made?" he asked Michele.

She shook her head. "I've only known about it for five minutes, but it does sound rather fun. Do you think there'd be a problem with me helping out?"

"Probably not," Antonio answered, but his tone wasn't as convincing as his words. "We shall see."

"Would this be at the Stoneham Rural Cemetery?" Michele asked Tricia.

She nodded. "And possibly the cemetery at St. Rita's church."

"I haven't checked out that one, but there are some wonderful Victorian monuments in the Stoneham cemetery. I've visited a number of spectacular cemeteries in Western New York and Massachusetts. Some of them are like lovely old parks. In Victorian times, people would go there for picnic lunches."

"Sounds terribly morbid to me," Antonio said, his discomfort evident. "But you are right. My employer is eager to encourage the tourist trade to remain in Stoneham after the sun goes down. I will mention it to her the next time we speak."

"Thank you," Tricia and Michele said at the same time.

"I don't want to interfere with your linen conference, but do you have a few minutes?" Tricia asked Antonio.

"I always have time for you, dear Tricia. That is, unless Ginny calls to say the baby is on its way."

"It won't take more than a couple of minutes," she said.

"I have things to do in back," Michele said, and left the area, giving them some privacy.

Tricia picked up her foam take-out box and glass of ginger ale and led the way to a booth at the side of the pub, slipping into it with Antonio following.

They looked at each other for a long moment before Tricia said, "I know."

Antonio stared at her, looking confused.

"I'm a bit disappointed that you never told me," Tricia said.

"Told you?" he hedged.

"That Angelica is Nigela Ricita *and* your stepmother."

Antonio's eyes widened and he swallowed, yet he didn't confirm or deny what she'd said. Perhaps he thought she was baiting him.

"This isn't a trick. I figured it out and confronted her about it last night. I take it she hasn't spoken to you since."

Antonio wouldn't look her in the eye. "No."

That seemed odd. She'd have to ask Angelica about it later.

Finally, he looked up at her, looking sheepish. "I wanted to tell you. I've wanted to tell Ginny, but Angelica has been very specific about her wishes."

"I can understand that. The more people who know, the more likely it is that everyone in the village will find out—and for some reason she doesn't want that to happen."

"For myself, I don't see the problem, but I must respect her wishes. She has been very good to me over the years. Not just these past few years—since I was a child. When my mother was sick and dying, Angelica paid for the hospital and the doctors. She did not have to do that, but it is her nature to help where she can."

"It's a bitter truth, but until recently, I didn't know that." More poignant, Tricia might not have even believed it.

"Are you angry with her?" Antonio asked.

"I should be, but I suppose I understand. And I am very happy about one thing."

"And that is?" he asked.

"Well, we're kind of like family now. Angelica and you and Ginny and . . . now me. And the baby, of course."

Antonio beamed. "Our bambino could not have a finer aunt in you. But for now, it must be our secret, no?"

Tricia nodded and sighed. "Yes."

"Now that you know, I hope that Angelica will finally let my wife in on the secret."

"It's got to come from her, don't you think?"

He nodded. "And if Angelica warns me in advance, I will remove all breakables from the room. My sweet wife will not be pleased."

"No, I don't suppose she will. I wonder if I should be present, too. Maybe I can help soften the blow."

"I agree. Now to decide on the timing. I would like it to happen before the bambino arrives."

"I'm having dinner with Angelica tonight. I'll push her to do it soon—perhaps tomorrow."

Antonio nodded. "Perhaps we can all have dinner at the inn. It's a neutral location, no? We can use the private dining room."

Tricia blinked. "There's a private dining room?"

"Of course. It can be very romantic—but I will have a table for four put in there before we meet."

"Good idea." She smiled and realized that her former admiration for Antonio now caused her to feel something entirely new: affection. "Angelica loves you as if you were her own son."

"I love her, too. My mother is gone. I am a lucky man to have had two mothers."

Tricia felt a sudden twinge of jealousy. Neither she nor Angelica would have biological children, but Angelica had the next best thing, and what a rarity it seemed to be to have a stepchild who actually loved his step-mother.

"Well, either Angelica or I will be in touch about dinner. I just hope that things will work out."

"Oh, gee, I hope so," Antonio said, although he didn't sound all that optimistic.

Tricia stood and moved into the aisle. Antonio did likewise. Tricia leaned forward and gave him a hug and was happy that he reciprocated in kind. "I never had a nephew before. It feels rather nice."

"I never had an aunt before, either."

Tricia's grin widened. "I'd better let you get back to work. Angelica—I mean, Nigela Ricita—is a hard taskmaster."

"She is, but she's also fair and well compensates her employees," he reminded her.

"So I've heard," Tricia said. She picked up the foam container, headed for the door, and gave a wave.

Outside, Tricia looked both left and right, glad to see so many tourists crowding the sidewalk. But then she caught sight of one of the hanging baskets of flowers and stopped dead. Like those in the park, the one before her was devoid of blossoms. She looked ahead, and every basket on the block was a mass of green—but no colorful flowers.

"Good grief," she muttered. "They've all been stripped!"

Mariana and Pixie were hard at work collating the inserts for the upcoming newsletter when Tricia arrived back at the Chamber office. "Did you notice anything unusual about Main Street when you went out to lunch?" she asked Mariana.

She looked thoughtful. "Now that you mention it, yes. There was a big black limo double-parked outside the Patisserie. I wondered if a rock star or maybe Nigela Ricita herself was in town today."

Knowing Angelica didn't travel around in a limo, Tricia muttered, "Probably a rock star. No, I meant the hanging flower baskets. I just walked past twelve of them on my way back from Booked for Lunch and not one of them had a flower in it."

"None?" Mariana asked.

"Where'd they go?" Pixie asked.

"That's what I'd like to know." Tricia looked at her boxed lunch. "I'll be in the kitchen if you need me."

"Sure thing."

Miss Marple jumped from Sarge's basket. Tricia figured she liked to leave her scent there to drive the poor dog crazy. Miss Marple followed Tricia into the kitchen, waiting patiently for a few cat treats, which Tricia had promised herself she wasn't going to give the cat on demand but always seemed to do so anyway. She poured herself a glass of iced tea and sat down at the bistro table with little appetite. She retrieved her cell phone and called Angelica, but got only her voice mail. She decided not to leave a message. The missing flowers were too big an announcement for that.

Picking up the plastic fork that came with her salad, Tricia picked at a piece of iceberg lettuce. She used to get annoyed when Angelica didn't immediately answer her calls. Now she realized that her sister must have to juggle a lot of responsibilities controlling not only her three in-village business plus all her Nigela Ricita obligations. Antonio was the public face of Nigela Ricita Associates, but Angelica was the mastermind. She'd even put her publishing aspirations on hold when she'd taken up the Chamber presidency. She didn't stop from the minute she got up until the minute she closed her eyes at night, and she was happier than Tricia had ever seen her. Somehow, working so hard seemed to be her preferred method of relaxation.

Tricia stabbed a hunk of tuna, shoving it into her mouth. She felt so ineffectual—as she had for a good portion of her life. Of course, Angelica wasn't doing it all alone. Her solution had been to hire really good people and pay them accordingly. Meanwhile, Tricia had one store with two employees and sometimes felt overwhelmed. Of course, if she was honest with herself, those times usually came after a sudden, violent death.

Of course, she knew why she felt so powerless. It was the seemingly endless wait for the insurance company to make a settlement on the fire damage to her store. She had no doubt that the minute the check came through she'd be feeling on top of the world. In the meantime, she, at least, had her volunteer duties for the Chamber.

But what Mariana had told her earlier came back to haunt her. She'd enjoyed working with her contractor, Jim Stark, during the initial renovation at Haven't Got a Clue and had thought him easygoing. Now to find out he was a jealous kind of guy—who collected a variety of firearms—and that he may have believed his wife had had an affair with a man who had just been murdered . . . Well, it was a bit too much to take in all at once. Preposterous as it would have seemed scant hours before, Tricia now wondered how her future would be affected if Jim actually had done the deed.

Would anyone mention to Chief Baker that Stark might have had a motive for murdering Pete? If no one volunteered that information, should she? And how would Stark react to her betrayal? There were other contractors in the area, but everyone agreed Stark was the best. He came highly recommended, he came up with cost-saving solutions when the reno ran into problems, and he and his men did good work on schedule. Tricia wanted to go home as soon as possible. Stark had promised that, when the insurance company finally came through with a check, he would make her renovation a top priority. Would he even deal with her if she dared mention his name in connection with Pete's death?

How badly did she want to return to her home and workplace?

Pretty damn bad.

Tricia set her fork down and closed the carton on the salad. She'd had enough.

Feeling terribly depressed, she placed the foam container in the fridge and headed back to the office without making a decision on what she should do with what she now knew.

EIGHT

Once again, the Chamber did not get a full day's worth of work from Tricia. Why was she obsessing over a rumor—and that's all it was—that her contractor may have been jealous of the attention another man paid his wife? Much as she tried to distract herself with Chamber work, she could not concentrate.

What she wanted to do was haul out her book and read. When life got tough, she could always count on getting lost in a mystery novel, but since Pixie was getting paid by the hour, Tricia couldn't very well rub her nose in the fact that an unpaid volunteer had leeway to goof off on a whim. That Tricia had allowed Pixie to read on the job at Haven't Got a Clue had been a perk her assistant had practically wallowed in. And yet, Pixie wasn't afraid of work. She seemed to look at every task as a chance to excel—and she did.

At 5:57, Pixie began to gather her purse, shoes, and waitress uniform in preparation for leaving.

"What have you got on tap tonight?" Tricia asked.

"Fred's coming over to my place to barbeque some steaks. His boss gives him the stuff that's just about to turn."

"Oh, how awful," Tricia said, appalled.

"No, it's not. Fred's dad was a butcher. He said you have to hang meat for it to get full-flavored. They don't do that nowadays and the meat tastes like sh—" She paused and seemed to think better of her descriptor. "Crap. I asked Mr. E, and he agreed. He used to be a butcher, you know."

Yes, she did know.

"What are you having?" Pixie asked.

"I'm going to Angelica's. She said something about shrimp pasta salad."

"That sounds like lunch."

"I prefer to think of it as *light*," Tricia said. *If carb heavy.* "It doesn't matter what she makes; it's always good."

"No doubt about it. She's good in the kitchen. She's shown me a few tricks over at Booked for Lunch. She said your grandma taught her."

"That she did."

Pixie frowned. "My granny ran a brothel. Is it any wonder I ended up the way I did?"

Tricia wasn't sure how to reply to that piece of news. Luckily, Pixie continued.

"We're having a salad and baked potatoes. Making them is gonna be my job, so I'm off to Shaw's in Milford to get the stuff."

"Have a good evening," Tricia called as Pixie headed out the door. Once she was gone, Tricia locked the office and immediately headed to the Cookery for dinner with Angelica. She had a lot to tell her—and really felt the need to unload. She just hoped Angelica would be in a receptive mood.

As usual, Sarge was ecstatic to see Tricia. It had been almost twenty-four hours, and he let her know that her absence had been keenly felt. She rewarded him with two biscuits that she slipped him, which did not go unseen by his mistress.

"He'll get fat if you keep indulging him," Angelica scolded her.

"They're small biscuits," Tricia said in her own defense.

Angelica scowled and turned back to her cutting board, which was covered in good-sized cooked, peeled shrimp she'd been in the process of cutting into bite-size pieces.

"What else is on tap tonight?" Tricia asked, swiping one of the tails before Angelica had a chance to stop her.

"Besides the shrimp pasta salad? I'm almost finished making it. I snagged a few of Nikki's snowflake rolls from the Patisserie. I just have to mix the shrimp with the pasta, mayo, and veggies, then let it cool for a while. Meanwhile, the martinis are already chilled."

"Why don't we drink wine anymore?' Tricia asked.

"Don't you like martinis?" Angelica asked, sounding surprised.

"Not particularly."

"Not even *mine*?"

"No."

"Oh. Does that mean I have to drink the entire pitcher myself?"

"I didn't say that," Tricia said, and retrieved the crystal pitcher, chilled glasses, and olives from the fridge. She poured and gave Angelica a glass before reaching for another tail. This time Angelica was ready for her and slapped her hand. Tricia backed off, retreating to the kitchen island with her drink. She commandeered a stool.

"So, how was your day?" Angelica asked conversationally, putting the now-finished salad in the fridge.

"Awful."

"What happened?" Angelica asked, concerned.

"Where do you want me to start?" Tricia asked, and took a sip of her martini. It wasn't horrible. It wasn't great, but it wasn't horrible, either. She must be getting used to them.

"Chamber business, if that's what's got you so down."

Tricia sighed. "Who takes care of the hanging baskets around the village?"

"The Milford Nursery, why?"

"Because just about all of them are devoid of flowers."

"What?" Angelica cried, horrified.

"You heard me."

Angelica dropped her knife and rushed to the bank of windows that overlooked Main Street. "They can't all have died."

"The greenery looks very healthy, but where are the flowers? Surely they couldn't all have fallen off at one time, either."

"Vandals!" Angelica cried, and turned back to face Tricia. "Oh my God! I hope the committee for prettiest village in New Hampshire has already been through to check us out. Otherwise, we're out of the running for yet another year."

"I thought they came through last month."

"I'm not sure of the timing. If all they saw was green, we're toast!"

She turned back to look at the vast sea of greenery where days before there had been a riot of color. "Perhaps now that we have a police force, we can catch whoever is doing this. Not like when someone was smashing all those pumpkins a few years back, although that seemed to stop after a while."

"There's a reason it stopped. I caught the culprit."

Angelica turned back to face her sister. "You did? You never said anything."

"At the time, I didn't think you'd want to know."

"Know what? Who was behind it? Why wouldn't I want to know?"

"Because it was Bob."

Angelica turned back to face her sister. "No! I don't believe it."

"Believe it. He was jealous that Milford's Pumpkin Festival was so successful and drawing the tourists away from Stoneham, and he took out his anger on the free pumpkins he was giving away to those who listed with Kelly Realty."

Angelica looked thoughtful. "At the time I did think he must have had a rush of clients, as the pumpkin pile did go down rather quickly." She shook her head and shrugged. "Do you suspect Bob of denuding the hanging baskets?"

"Could be. He's got a lot on his mind right now and none of it appears to be pleasant. But I would hope he'd think twice about doing something else that could get him in trouble with the law."

"I'll call the nursery first thing in the morning to find out what it will cost to replace the flowers. Maybe they can give the village a deal as it's getting late in the season."

"What if it happens again?"

Angelica frowned. "After we eat, we can go look at one of the baskets. I want to make sure it *is* vandalism and not just some horticultural blight. Are you game?"

"Sure. I've got nothing else to do."

Angelica returned to the island and picked up her drink. "Have you heard anything else about Pete's death?"

Tricia shook her head, deciding not to yet share what Mariana had told her about Jim Stark. "Grant came to the Chamber office to ask me about finding Pete. He said he couldn't really start an investigation until he knew what the actual cause of death was. But he was also going to have a lab team search the gazebo and the area around it for clues."

"Clues to what?"

Tricia shrugged. "To see if there was anything suspicious."

"You said there was a needle mark and a suspicious bruise on Pete's body, which would mean somebody injected him with something. What's obtainable that could stop someone's heart—and do it pretty quickly? Or what about an air bubble in the blood?"

"I've seen that threatened on TV and in movies, but I don't know if you could actually kill someone that way."

"You could look it up online," Angelica said, and looked toward her computer.

"I'm about to eat dinner, and that kind of information could have a negative effect on my digestive system," Tricia said.

"I've seen you eat while reading a book featuring a graphic autopsy," Angelica said sourly.

"Well, I don't want to look it up right now."

"What else could kill someone so quickly?" Angelica pressed.

"Poison, I suppose."

"How about arsenic?"

"It isn't a fast acting poison. Generally the victim is fed the substance over a long period of time."

"You mean like feeding them a steady diet of apple seeds? Are there any orchards around here?"

"It wouldn't have to be an exotic poison. Maybe something as simple as a vial of super-strength vinegar."

"Ya think?" Angelica said.

"I'm guessing." It was time to change the subject. "I also spoke to Antonio today."

Angelica lifted an eyebrow. "Did you?"

Tricia nodded. "I told him I'm very glad he's a part of our family."

Angelica's smile was tentative. "Thank you. What did he say?"

"Not much. But he made sure I understood that he respected your wish to keep your secret quiet."

"I'm thankful for that."

"It's time to tell Ginny—and before the baby arrives, especially if you want to be its grandma."

Angelica let out a long breath. "I suppose I'll have to. And as she's Antonio's wife, it really should come from me."

"Agreed. And she will not be pleased."

"Neither were you, but you seem to have gotten over it much quicker than I would have guessed."

"What choice do I have?"

"And what choice does Ginny have, too?"

"Very little."

"Antonio suggested we all have dinner soon at the Brookview Inn's private dining room."

"That would be lovely. I'll set up a menu tomorrow and call him."

"Why don't you let him decide on the menu. I'm sure he'll pick something Ginny is particularly fond of—you know, to get her in a receptive mood."

"Great idea."

Tricia eyed her sister critically. "You know, it almost seems like you have some kind of master plan in mind for all of us. Would you care to share it?"

"You make me sound like some kind of dictator or puppeteer," Angelica said.

"I'm afraid that's how some of the villagers view Nigela Ricita."

"I haven't done anything that didn't benefit Stoneham in one way or another, and I wish you'd stop trying to make me feel guilty."

"I'm sorry, Ange. I guess I still feel hurt that you kept it from me for so long."

"I admit, it was a mistake, and I'm sorry, but there's nothing I can do to change the past. Can't we just move forward and accept the present?"

"We will. But you didn't answer my question."

"What question?" Angelica asked, her expression blank.

"Do you have some kind of master plan for all of us?"

"Well, of course I do," Angelica answered matter-of-factly.

Tricia started.

"Oh, don't look at me like I'm some kind of megalomaniac. I want us all to be healthy and happy and successful. Period."

"And who does this theoretical *us* entail?"

"You, me, Antonio, Ginny. Grace, Mr. Everett, Frannie, Pixie, Mariana, Bev, Tommy—everybody."

"And how do you propose to deliver that magic pill?"

"No pill. People who are happy in their work are happy in life. It's as simple as that. And I want the people who arrive in this beautiful little town in New England stressed and careworn to leave happy and uplifted."

"You hope."

"So far, so good."

Tricia couldn't argue with that.

"What are you plotting for the future?"

"Not plotting, considering. Now that you know, you could be a wonderful sounding board. In fact, it would be oodles of fun if you and Antonio and Ginny and I all sat down and made a wish list for the village: things we'd like to see happen. Stores and services we'd love to see arrive. Needs that aren't yet being met."

"Like a shoe store?" Tricia suggested.

Angelica shook her head. "That's been on my wish list for years. We're much too small for a chain store, and a boutique would be too expensive for the residents." She shook her head. "It's a pipe dream."

"A tea shop?" Tricia suggested.

Again Angelica shook her head. "Not enough trade to keep one in business through the lean times. But I have thought about offering afternoon tea at the Brookview Inn during the summer months. Maybe just on weekends to start. We also need more daycare. Ginny wants to go back to work after the baby arrives, and my grandchild must have the very best."

"You wouldn't hire a nanny?" Tricia asked.

"Children need to interact with other children. It's good for them."

"What makes you the expert when it comes to child care?"

"Google is my best friend," Angelica said wryly.

"What about the ghost walks?"

"They could be great fun—and quite lucrative, not only for the cemetery, but for the Dog-Eared Page and the Bookshelf Diner. Before Pete died, he sent a report to NRA looking for backing."

"Did you give him any money for them?"

"It was included with the check Antonio gave them."

Tricia nodded. "When I spoke to Janet Koch at the Historical Society this morning, I suggested Michele give the talks."

"What a great idea!"

"Of course, her boss would have to okay it," Tricia said.

Angelica's smile was more a smirk. "I'm sure I can arrange it. Anything else happen today I should know about?"

Tricia hesitated, then shook her head.

Angelica considered her empty glass. "We'd better not have another. Not if we're going to check out those flower baskets."

Tricia downed the last of her drink, then placed the olive in her mouth, slid it off the pick, and chewed.

"You set the table and I'll get the food ready," Angelica said, heading for the fridge.

Tricia carried her glass over to the sink, then scooped flatware from a drawer and placed it on the table, her thoughts straying back to the subject of Jim Stark. The idea of her store renovation possibly being derailed had her feeling disheartened and depressed.

Don't think about it. Don't think about it. Don't think about it, she ordered herself.

She just wished she could pay more attention to that little niggling voice inside her brain that advised her to look at worst-case scenarios.

Sometimes she hated that stinking little voice she called her conscience.

It wasn't quite dark, but unlike in years past when the streets of Stoneham had emptied at six o'clock, several cars still lined the south end of Main Street. The Dog-Eared Page was the draw, but farther down the street a few cars were also clustered near the Bookshelf Diner. "We really need more eateries here on Main Street," Angelica said as they, along with Sarge, headed north on the sidewalk. "We need at least one fine dining restaurant here in the village."

"Where would it go?" Tricia asked.

"It could go where the Chamber office is currently located, but that's a bit close to the eyesore that is Kelly Realty."

"You'd think Bob would have done something to the outside of that building to spruce it up. Gray-painted cinderblock has no curb appeal and is not at all conducive to the ambiance he's always tried to encourage from the people he rents to."

Angelica didn't comment.

They continued down the block, passing more and more denuded hanging baskets. "What we need is a ladder so we can look into the baskets to see if the blossoms have been broken off or cut."

"Does it matter?" Tricia asked. "None of them have flowers."

"I guess you're right," Angelica groused.

A few other people ambled down the sidewalk, and the sisters greeted them with smiles but didn't bother with conversation. Tricia rather enjoyed the walk, and Sarge certainly did. However, Angelica was far too quiet.

They walked as far as the Antiques Emporium, crossed the street, and headed back south toward the town square. Every single hanging basket had been hit. "This kind of petty vandalism makes me so angry," Angelica muttered.

"The police station is just ahead. Do you want to report it?"

"Yes, I do." Angelica sped up, and Tricia and little Sarge had a hard time keeping up with her. "Do you think Grant is working late tonight?"

Tricia had seen his car parked in the municipal lot when they'd passed minutes earlier. "Probably. He doesn't have much to do in the evenings, either."

Arriving at the station door, Angelica grabbed Sarge, tucking him under her arm, and they entered.

Polly Burgess, the station's elderly dispatcher and receptionist, was also working late. She eyed Sarge with disdain. "No dogs allowed. You'll have to take *it* outside."

"He's a he, not an it—and he's my service dog," Angelica said.

"What kind of service can a dog that small perform?" Polly demanded.

"He's my emotional support."

"Where's his service vest?"

"In the laundry. Now, we'd like to speak to the chief, please."

"He's off duty."

"But he *is* here," Tricia said.

"Yes."

"Would you please tell him we're here?" Tricia asked.

"We'd like to report a crime," Angelica chimed in.

Polly looked at them with suspicion. "What kind of crime?"

"Vandalism."

Polly sighed and pushed the intercom button. "Chief. There are a couple of citizens here who'd like to report vandalism."

"I'll be right there," came Baker's clipped voice.

Polly glared at the sisters.

Baker appeared from behind his office door, his eyes lighting up when he saw Tricia. "Hello. What's this about vandalism?" he asked.

"Can we talk in your office?" Angelica asked as Baker reached out to pet Sarge, who growled. He pulled his hand back.

"Sure."

The sisters followed him inside and took seats in front of his desk. Angelica set Sarge on the floor but kept him on a short leash.

"What's this about vandalism?" Baker asked again.

"Someone has clipped every flower in the hanging baskets around the village."

Baker frowned, as though that wasn't his idea of a major crime. "Is that all?"

"Those baskets cost nearly fifty bucks apiece. If we have to replace them, it will be a substantial cost," Angelica said.

Baker looked unimpressed. "Do you have any suspects?"

Angelica shook her head.

"Do you know when it happened?"

"No. Tricia noticed all the blossoms were gone just today."

"Maybe someone's got really bad allergies," Baker suggested and laughed.

"They've been hanging for over two months," Angelica pointed out.

Baker's smile faded and he frowned. "The baskets are still up, aren't they?"

"Yes."

"They haven't been smashed, right?"

"No."

"Well, what do you want me to do about it?" he asked.

"I'm reporting a crime," Angelica said. "I thought that's what good citizens were supposed to do."

"We've got more important matters taking up the bulk of our time just now," Baker said.

"Have you made any headway on Pete Renquist's death?" Tricia asked.

The chief looked uncomfortable. "We're pursuing all leads."

Which meant *no*!

"Did you have a chance to speak to Toni Bennett?" she asked.

The name caused Baker to start, as though he had to remember it was the owner of the Antiques Emporium and not the singer. "Yes."

"And?" Tricia pressed.

"Hearsay."

"Oh, come on. Surely you're going to try to find out who threatened Pete."

"Of course, but hearing he was threatened without any corroborating information isn't much of a lead."

She supposed not. "Who else have you spoken with?"

"You are not a part of the investigation," Baker pointed out, obviously annoyed.

Tricia shrugged. "I spoke with Janet Koch at the Historical Society this morning—to convey my condolences," she quickly added.

"I've spoken with her, too. She wasn't much help."

"Have Pete's next of kin been contacted?" Angelica asked.

Baker nodded. "No help there, either."

"But you're doing everything you can to solve Pete's murder," Tricia stated, though it didn't seem to be much.

"Of course."

Tricia again debated mentioning what Mariana had told her earlier in the day. If she didn't name names, she could at least make a suggestion—just to get Baker thinking along a different line of reasoning. "It's well known that Pete liked to flirt with women. Is it possible a jealous husband or lover could have come after him?" she asked.

"Anything's possible."

Sure. Pigs flew on scheduled routes. The moon *was* made of green cheese. And a bridge in Brooklyn was sold just about every day.

Angelica picked up Sarge and stood. "I suppose we'd better let you get back to it." She didn't sound impressed with the chief's progress, either.

Tricia followed her out of the office.

"Keep me informed about those flowers," Baker called after them.

"If I can be bothered," Angelica muttered.

"Good night," Tricia called to Polly as she passed the receptionist's desk. The woman ignored her.

"Now what?" Tricia asked once the sisters were out on the sidewalk again.

"It's been a long day and I still have a ton of work to do. We may as well go home," Angelica said, and they started off. They walked in silence until they came to the Chamber office, where they paused.

"I'll see you tomorrow," Tricia said, and gave Angelica a hug. Sarge barked. "I'll see you, too," she said, and bent down to pat the dog's head.

"Why did you tell Grant about Pete's flirting?" Angelica asked.

Tricia shrugged and avoided her sister's penetrating gaze. "I just want him to investigate all possibilities."

"Did you have someone in mind?"

Tricia kept scratching Sarge's ears. "No."

Angelica didn't press the issue. "Well, good night."

"Night." Tricia called, and hurried up the driveway. She had no proof against Jim Stark. A part of her wanted to pursue that line of inquiry. What was worse, a bigger part of her—the part that wanted to go back to her old life and home—didn't.

NINE

Her room was still dark when Tricia awoke with a start the next morning. Her heart pounded and she was drenched with cold sweat. The crippling nightmare had returned, although it no longer haunted her sleep every night as it had during those first bleak days after the fire. Flames had poured from Haven't Got a Clue's shattered display window, while firefighters in assault gear directed the full force of their hoses on the fire—and the stock inside. Tricia had felt as though she were being slowly smothered as she'd watched helplessly from the street, held back by many arms that refused to let her go back to save her beloved store.

Of course, it hadn't actually happened quite that way—but it was close enough. The terror she'd felt when she thought she'd lost Miss Marple had been the worst. Then the realization struck that she might have lost everything else she valued. Still, at the time she'd felt lucky, and her friends—and most of all Angelica—had rallied to support her. She would never forget the kindness she'd been shown. Even strangers had stopped her in the street to express their regrets.

But as the days and weeks dragged on and still there was no settlement from the insurance company—and no end in sight for her enforced exile—she found herself growing depressed. She wanted to go *home*. To her *own* home.

Throwing back the covers, Tricia got up, disturbing Miss Marple, and quickly dressed for her morning jaunt. Could the soot-covered treadmill that still stood in her loft apartment be refurbished? She supposed she'd eventually find out. Going for a brisk walk was wonderful in good weather, but not so much fun when it rained. Thankfully the weatherman had predicted fair skies for the next few days. Tricia tied her running shoes and took off. She had a lot to think about as she followed her usual route, speed-walking along Stoneham's residential streets.

After she'd completed her rounds, Tricia usually ended up at the Coffee Bean for her first brew of the day. Coming back to her rooms at the Chamber office was always made a little more pleasant when she had a really good cup of coffee to kick-start the rest of her day.

However, on this day Tricia headed over to the Cookery. Outside the door, she pulled her cell phone from her pocket and called Angelica.

"Hope I didn't wake you," Tricia said.

"Are you kidding? I've been up for hours. What's new?"

"I'm outside the Cookery. Can I come up?"

"Of course."

"See you in a minute," Tricia said, and stabbed the end-call icon. She unlocked the door and quickly disabled the alarm system, then headed up the stairs.

As usual, Sarge made a wonderful welcoming committee, jumping up and down and barking enthusiastically.

"Want some coffee?" Angelica called as Tricia started down the hall that lead to Angelica's kitchen with Sarge scampering ahead.

"I've already got some," Tricia said.

"How about some toast?"

"Sounds good," Tricia said, taking a seat at the kitchen island.

Angelica put two slices into the toaster and turned for her own breakfast. "I've got some bad news."

"Another death?" Tricia asked, horrified.

"No! I called the Milford Nursery. They had a big sale over the weekend. Their stock has been decimated. They can't replace the hanging baskets."

"Oh, no! The flowers are such a draw for the tourists. What are you going to do?"

"I could call all over the state, but the cheapest and easiest solution just might be silk," she said flatly.

"You mean . . . fake flowers?" Tricia asked, aghast.

"Some of them look very lifelike," Angelica said optimistically.

"Yeah, the expensive ones. What's your budget?"

"There is no budget. It's coming out of Nigela Ricita's pockets."

"At least they're deep."

"I'm just worried that whoever decapitated all those petunias and pansies will just yank out the silk replacements."

"It's a possibility."

Angelica looked thoughtful but said nothing more.

"Who's going to scour the local craft stores?" Tricia asked.

"I've got to be in Portsmouth by ten, and I have a meeting in Manchester after lunch. How about Pixie?"

Tricia shook her head, remembering the cheesy Christmas decorations Pixie had fallen in love with and had wanted to use to decorate

Haven't Got a Clue the previous holiday season. "Her heart would be in the right place, but I don't think she's a good judge of such things."

"Would you have time to shop?"

"Only if you think the Chamber can spare me."

"Yes," Angelica said emphatically. "Can you go this morning?"

"I guess. I have a lunch date today, but I can check out the big craft store on Route 101 before then."

"Even if we can only decorate the baskets lining Main Street, it would at least be welcoming to the tourists when they get off the buses."

"And when is redecorating the baskets going to happen?"

Angelica grimaced. "Tonight."

"And who is going to do it?" Tricia asked, already knowing the answer.

"Why, you and me of course."

"Of course. What about Antonio?"

"You can't expect him to leave Ginny late at night with the baby due to arrive at any moment."

No, she didn't.

"Couldn't Nigela Ricita Associates pull someone from the Brookview Inn to do this?"

"And let it get out that we're replacing the real flowers with silk?"

"Somebody's bound to notice."

Angelica's lips pursed.

"Okay. Do I even have to ask who's going to be climbing the ladder?" Tricia asked.

"You know I'm afraid of heights," Angelica said, appalled at the idea.

Yes, she did.

Tricia drained her cup. "I have just enough time to shower and change before Mariana reports for work at the Chamber."

"If I haven't told you lately, I really appreciate all the work you're doing for the Chamber. I don't know what I'll do when you go back to your real life, and it *will* be all too soon."

Not soon enough, Tricia thought. "I'm happy I can take on some of the work to make it easier on you."

"The Chamber is now big enough that it needs a dedicated employee to run it—not a part-time volunteer, and that's where I'm going to steer it. The membership has already grown faster in the past eight months than I'd considered it would during my two-year tenure."

"It's your leadership," Tricia said. Angelica shook her head in denial, but she did look pleased at the sentiment. "I've gotta go," Tricia said, getting up from her stool and pausing at the sink to rinse her paper cup before placing it in the recycling bin.

"I'll see you later," Angelica called as Tricia headed for the stairs.

As Tricia closed the Cookery's door behind her, she pondered the kind of personality that could deprive the villagers and tourists of the beauty the flowers had brought. Could it have been Bob? Her thoughts had immediately gone to him, but only because he'd been annoying her of late. The truth was that there were plenty of villagers who were unhappy with the changes that had come to Stoneham during the past five years and were quite vocal about it. They were the ones who'd elected Earl Winkler.

Why did the sourpusses in life want to ruin things for everyone else?

The big arts-and-crafts store on Route 101 was running a sale, and Tricia cleaned them out of silk flowers. The manager had come to the register to help bag the sale, pleased that she could put out the

Halloween and Thanksgiving stock that was already languishing in her storeroom.

It was getting close to noon when Tricia returned to the village and pulled into the municipal parking lot. Instead of hauling her purchases to the Chamber office, she left the bags of faux flowers in the trunk. They weren't going to wilt, even under the blistering midday sun.

She had just enough time to stop at Booked for Lunch to pick up the orders she'd phoned in hours before, then carried them two doors down to the Happy Domestic. Technically Ginny wasn't supposed to be working. She was officially on maternity leave, but staying at home with nothing to do but fret did not sit well with her. "I'd rather stay occupied," she'd said more than once.

Tricia entered the shop and the bell over the door jangled. The sound was like a knife thrust to her soul. It sounded so like the one at Haven't Got a Clue. Some days the sound didn't bother her, and others, like today, the pain from the loss of her store was almost too much to bear.

Ginny's assistant, Brittney, was helping a customer, but she gestured with her thumb, indicating the backroom. Tricia nodded and headed that way. "Hello," she called before pushing through the saloon doors that separated the retail operation from the much smaller storeroom that doubled as an office.

Ginny sat at the big beat-up desk with stacks of paperwork before her. She looked up and a grin lit her features. "Thank goodness you're here. I could eat a bear—raw!"

"And risk trichinosis?"

"I thought you could only get that from undercooked pork."

"Pork, bears, and other wild game infected with parasites. Do you really want to take the risk?"

Ginny looked down at her bulging belly. "No. Besides, I already know that you've got a BLT and a cup of the soup of the day. Which is . . . ?"

"Black bean."

"Oh, my favorite—except it hasn't treated me well since . . ." Again she looked down at her belly.

"More information than I needed to know," Tricia said, and laughed. She took the seat across from Ginny and doled out the foam containers, plasticware, and napkins. Instead of her usual tuna plate, Tricia had ordered a julienned salad. Miss Marple would love some of the excess slices of ham and cheese as an indulgent snack. Since she knew it was Ginny's favorite dessert, Tricia had also ordered a piece of Angelica's decadent carrot cake for the two of them to splurge on and share.

"It won't be long now," Tricia said.

"A week from today, if the calculations are right."

"What are your plans after the baby arrives?" Tricia asked, dipping a piece of lettuce into her dressing.

"I've been thinking a lot about that," Ginny said, her voice subdued.

"You've changed your mind about working?" Tricia asked, surprised.

Ginny dipped her spoon into the soup and stirred. "Not at all. But I might change my mind about *where* I work."

"You'd give up the Happy Domestic? But I thought you were happy here."

"I have been deliriously happy here, but I'm not sure the hours are conducive to a happy family life."

"Your boss seems quite amenable when it comes to flexible hours."

"I've been very lucky," Ginny admitted, taking a bite of her sandwich.

Tricia poked at her salad. She'd known things would change once the baby arrived, but the thought of not seeing Ginny on a regular basis caught her off guard.

"I've been thinking," Ginny said once she'd swallowed. "I might like to try my hand at management of another kind."

"Oh?"

"While I would love to work with Antonio either at the Brookview Inn or the office down the street, I don't think it's good for a couple to be attached at the hip day and night."

"Is there an opening at NRA?" Tricia asked. Angelica hadn't mentioned it, but then she hadn't gone into the details of how her business ran, either.

"I don't know. I think it could be fun to work on projects that have end dates, not just picking baubles, waiting on customers, and banking the receipts. Maybe NRA will open another business here in town. Maybe they'd let me manage a couple of different stores or other parts of the operation." She shrugged. "What I'd really like is a job with more regular hours—and weekends off would sure be a treat, too."

"Have you spoken to Antonio about that?"

"He doesn't have a problem with it."

"Has he mentioned it to your boss?"

Ginny shook her head. "I've asked him not to. Not just yet, at least. And I'd like to talk to Ms. Ricita directly."

And you'll get that opportunity sooner than you know, Tricia thought. She decided to move away from the subject. "Have you come up with names for the baby yet?"

Ginny nodded. "If it's a girl, Sofia, after Antonio's mother. If it's a boy, William, after my father and Mr. Everett."

It stood to reason Antonio wouldn't name his son after his own father. The man had abandoned him. It was Angelica who'd bought him clothes and paid for his schooling. "Mr. Everett will like that."

"As my folks live down south now, it's likely he'll be a bigger part of the baby's life."

"Will your parents come up to see the baby?"

"Oh, sure. They don't mind New Hampshire during the summer, but if our next one arrives in winter, they'd wait until spring to visit."

"How does that make you feel?"

She shrugged. "I'm okay with it. I've still got family here," she said, and smiled. "You and Grace and Mr. Everett. You're all like family to me."

"I'm glad you feel that way." *Because I do, too*, Tricia thought.

Ginny scraped the last of the soup from her container. "Oh, that was good, but I think I'll save the other half of my sandwich for later. Especially if we're going to make a dent in that piece of cake." She wrapped the sandwich in one of the paper napkins and returned it to the foam container. Struggling up from her chair, she deposited the container in the small fridge she kept under the table that housed the printer and other office supplies.

"We really need to convince Angelica to stop using foam take-out boxes at Booked for Lunch. They're horrible for the environment."

"You know, I'll bet if you pitched a cost-effective alternative, she would seriously take it under consideration," Tricia said, closing the container on the remains of her salad.

Ginny eyed her speculatively. "That's a good idea. She's been awfully nice to me lately. Well, ever since the wedding."

"Really?" Tricia asked, opening the container that held the slab of carrot cake.

Ginny looked thoughtful for a moment, then shrugged. She picked up one of the plastic forks but waited for Tricia to cut the cake in two. Tricia wasn't as fond of the sour cream frosting as Ginny, so she took the lower portion, settling it onto one of the paper napkins before pushing the other piece across the desk to Ginny.

Ginny sampled a bite, letting it sit on her tongue for a bit before chewing and swallowing—her usual routine.

"Well?" Tricia asked.

"Nobody makes carrot cake as good as Angelica. I especially like her maple icing."

"Maple?" Tricia asked. "Since when does she make it that way?"

"She's always made it this way." Tricia seldom ate cake and took a bite. It was good, and the maple frosting was a lot less cloying and sweet than that traditionally associated with carrot cake.

Ginny cut another piece but paused before eating it. "So, you found Pete Renquist."

"He was alive at the time," Tricia began in her own defense.

"So I heard."

"Did you know him?"

Ginny shook her head. "But I heard rumors."

"Oh?" Tricia asked, playing dumb.

"That he was a bit of a letch, but relatively harmless."

"Did he ever flirt with you?" Tricia asked.

Again Ginny shook her head. She ate another bite of cake. "He seemed harmless enough, and honestly, the guy was old enough to be my father. I heard he hit on older women."

"You mean like me?" Tricia asked with dread. Pete was always flirting with her.

"Heck, no. Older than you. Ladies in their fifties."

An age that was only five years ahead for Tricia.

"The ones who've got empty nests and time on their hands to volunteer at fudd-dudd places like the Historical Society. That said, I heard the old broads ate up the attention. Their husbands had long ago given up giving them compliments."

Was that how Toni Bennett felt? Though well preserved, she was probably fifty years old. She said she'd been volunteering at the Historical Society for at least ten years, long before Pete had become its president.

"Do you know anyone like that?" Tricia asked.

Ginny scraped some of the icing from what was left of her cake. "Julia Harrison is one of my regular customers. She's a widow who often comes in on a Saturday. She hates to drive to Nashua, so she does her gift buying here—lots of figurines and pretty whatnots for her granddaughter. Once she kind of hinted that she was interested in Pete and that they'd dated a few times, but that it didn't work out."

"Did she give a reason?"

"Nope." Ginny slid the last piece of cake onto her fork.

Tricia took a bite of cake. She thought she knew of the woman, half remembering an article that Russ Smith had run in the *Stoneham Weekly News* about the Historical Society's Italianate garden.

"Does this woman volunteer for the Stoneham Horticultural Society?" she asked.

"I think so. Why?"

"No reason." Tricia ate another bite of cake.

"Any word on the insurance coming through for the store?" Ginny asked. She was only being polite—showing interest in Tricia's problems—but it seemed that Tricia was asked that question at least ten times a day, and after six months it depressed the heck out of her not to have an affirmative reply.

"Not yet," she answered with a forced smile, and ate the last bite of cake.

"You must be sick of waiting."

"I was sick of waiting a mere week after the fire—let alone six months later."

"Well, it can't be much longer. In fact, I'll bet you five dollars you hear from them before the baby arrives," she said, and looked down fondly at her belly.

"If only," Tricia said wistfully. She gathered up the napkins and cutlery and tossed them away while Ginny shook her head at the waste. "I'd better get back to work."

"Same time next week?" Ginny asked hopefully.

"If you're not in the hospital."

"Hospital?" Ginny asked, confused.

"You are going to have a baby," Tricia reminded her.

Ginny laughed. "And, boy, will I be glad when it's over."

Tricia thought about the proposed dinner she and Angelica were to have with Ginny and Antonio. Since Ginny hadn't mentioned it, she decided she'd better not.

Ginny struggled to her feet, and Tricia moved around the desk to give her a brief hug. "If the baby comes early, I'll have Antonio call you right away."

Tricia pulled back. "I'll be waiting for his call."

"Thanks for lunch," Ginny called as Tricia left the office.

More customers had entered the store since her arrival, and Brittney waved to Tricia from her post at the register.

Lunch with Ginny was always a pleasure, and speaking with her had presented Tricia with a lead on one of Pete's ex-girlfriends/

paramours. Now all Tricia had to do was think of an excuse to meet Julia Harrison.

Mariana's radio was on when Tricia returned to the Chamber office. She kept it turned to a soft rock station, and though Tricia didn't dislike the tunes, she did get bored of the station's limited repertoire. She wondered if Pixie and Mr. Everett got bored of the CDs she'd played at Haven't Got a Clue—a mix of new age and Celtic-influenced music. They'd never complained, but then, she hadn't complained to Mariana, either.

As Pixie was occupied with the new membership directory, it was up to Tricia to take care of a few low-priority tasks in her absence before she grabbed the tri-town phone directory and looked up the number for the Stoneham Horticultural Society. Was there a chance Mariana knew Julia Harrison? She decided to ask.

"Mariana, do you know a woman named Julia Harrison?"

"Sure. We go to the same church."

"She works at the Horticultural Society, doesn't she?"

"I don't think so."

"Volunteers, then?" Tricia asked.

Mariana shrugged. "Maybe."

"She's a widow, right?"

Mariana nodded. "Her husband died a few years back. Car wreck. It was an icy night."

"That's so sad," Tricia said with sympathy.

"Yeah, he was a great guy."

The conversation waned.

Tricia didn't want to call the woman with Mariana listening, but she pulled up the online white pages website, typed in Julia's name, and got a message that said, "We did not find a match." Perhaps Julia didn't have a landline, or if she did, it was listed under her deceased husband's name. Tricia decided she'd call the Horticultural Society when Mariana was out of the office.

The phone rang and Mariana answered it. "Stoneham Chamber of Commerce. Mariana speaking. How can I help you?" She listened. "Oh, sure, she's here. Just a moment." She stabbed the hold button. "Tricia, it's for you."

"A member?"

"He didn't say."

Tricia picked up the receiver and pressed the blinking hold button. "Tricia Miles. How can I help you?"

"Tricia, it's Jim Stark."

Tricia clutched the receiver tighter. Her contractor. The man who may have been jealous of Pete Renquist's attention toward his wife. "Jim," she practically squeaked.

"Something wrong?" he asked.

"Uh, no." She forced herself to lower her voice to normal. "No. I'm just surprised to hear from you."

"I was wondering if you've heard from your insurance company yet?" That made about eleven times that day she'd been asked the question. "I've got a kitchen remodel to do, and the client wants it done ASAP. It's a two-week job."

"Two weeks?"

"I wanted to let you know that my team and I will be tied up 'til the first week in September."

"Oh, well. Thanks for telling me."

"I'll give you a call when I'm at the halfway point with the kitchen to see if you're ready to schedule my guys on your store."

"Thank you," she said.

"Okay, talk to you then."

"Wait!" Tricia said, her thoughts spinning. Did she dare ask him about Pete? Her thoughts raced. "I wanted to express my condolences for the loss of your friend."

"Friend?" Stark asked.

"Yes, I met your wife, Toni, yesterday, and we shared remembrances of Pete Renquist of the Stoneham Historical Society."

"Renquist was no friend of mine," Stark said bitterly.

"Oh?" Tricia asked in what she hoped was an innocent-sounding tone. "I know he had a booth in your wife's new antiques store. She was so upset at his passing, I just assumed the three of you were friends."

"In this instance, you assumed wrong. Look, I have other calls to make. As I said, I'll call you in a couple of weeks to talk about your store reno. Good-bye."

He hung up before Tricia had an opportunity to say anything more.

The conversation had not gone well, but at least she knew by the tone of his voice that Stark had held some kind of resentment toward Pete. The question was, could Tricia find out just what it was without alienating the contractor?

TEN

 Late that afternoon, Angelica phoned to say she was swamped with NRA business and could Tricia fend for herself for dinner?

She could.

"Eatin' alone tonight, eh?" Pixie asked.

"Looks like it," Tricia said.

"Too bad I made other plans, or I could hang out with you."

"What're you doing tonight?"

"Fred and me are going for burgers, and then he's taking me to the roller derby."

"Where?" Tricia asked.

"In Manchester at the JFK Memorial Coliseum. It's the Queen City Cherry Bombers versus the Petticoat Punishers. Aw, man, it's gonna be great."

"I didn't know you were into roller derby." There was a lot about Pixie she didn't know.

"There was a time I used to skate with the best. That was way too many years ago."

Tricia shouldn't have been surprised. After all, Pixie was a kick-boxer. She was husky but toned.

"Sounds like fun."

"Aw, you're just saying that. You'd be bored stiff."

"No, really. I should get out more. Do more interesting . . . stuff."

"Do you want to come?"

Tricia shook her head. "I wouldn't want to intrude on the time you get to spend with Fred."

Pixie's smile was dreamy. "He's awfully sweet."

"When will I get to meet him?"

"Maybe my next day off I'll bring him around," Pixie said, but her tone wasn't exactly positive. Was she ashamed of her new boyfriend, or did she think Tricia might look down on him? She hoped not.

"That would be nice," Tricia said, and hoped she sounded enthusiastic.

Pixie gathered up her things. "I'm off. See you tomorrow."

"Good night."

Once the door had closed on Pixie's back, the Chamber seemed terribly quiet.

Tricia shut down her computer and turned off the lights, and the Chamber was officially closed for the day. Miss Marple was again asleep in Sarge's basket, and she didn't even look up as Tricia left the office, went upstairs to grab her purse, and then left to find sustenance.

She got a salad to go from the Bookshelf Diner, brought it back to the Chamber, and ate it in the silence of the Chamber's small kitchen. It was only seven when she finished, but she didn't have to meet Angelica at the municipal parking lot until midnight.

It would be a long evening.

After finishing her meal, Tricia went up to her stuffy upstairs quarters, turned on the air-conditioning unit in her bedroom, put a CD in the one-disk player she'd acquired, and settled down in the sitting room with another Agatha Christie novel. This time she was in the mood to revisit Hercule Poirot and chose *Evil Under the Sun*.

The hours had flown by, and Tricia's eyes had grown heavy, when she set the book aside. She got up to look out the window that over-looked the street. All was quiet.

Though it had taken a while, after her divorce Tricia had learned to enjoy living alone with Miss Marple. However, since the fire, she found she sought out company more often. Besides her standing lunch date with Ginny, she often joined Mr. Everett and his wife, Grace, on a regular basis just to keep in touch. As a consequence of all these lunches out, she'd gained five pounds, which her daily walks—with or without Sarge—had not eradicated. But even that didn't bother her as much as it would have before that terrible day in February.

She turned back from the window and glanced at the clock. It was late, but she still had more than an hour to go before she was to meet Angelica. The idea of pacing the apartment or watching reruns held no appeal, and the truth was she felt starved for company. Even if it was also Christopher's favorite watering hole, of late Tricia often found herself patronizing the Dog-Eared Page, showing up for a game of darts or to compete on Trivia Night. Seeing her ex there couldn't be helped as, apart from the Brookview Inn's dining room, the pub was the only game in town when it came to social drinking. She enjoyed the Dog-Eared Page. Between the music and the conversations, sometimes she almost forgot about the fire.

Almost.

It was just after eleven when Tricia donned her light jacket, grabbed a pair of wire cutters from the Chamber's toolbox, and stuffed them into her pocket; she'd need them later. She locked the Chamber's side door and headed off on foot for the village pub.

Main Street was silent, but Tricia wasn't afraid as she walked past the darkened businesses. Still, the thought that one of her fellow citizens had probably killed Pete Renquist did cause her to listen carefully as she walked, and to keep a sharp eye out for movement in the shadows. Less than three minutes later, she arrived at her destination.

Though the pub was sparsely populated on that Wednesday night, a boisterous song issued from the hidden speakers in the ceiling. A middle-aged couple sat huddled in one of the booths, nursing half-empty beer glasses, while another, older couple played a game of darts in back.

Michele Fowler sat at the bar with a sheaf of papers spread out before her. She looked up when Tricia shut the door.

"Welcome, Tricia. Come sit down." She patted the empty stool beside her. Tricia gladly took it. "What can we offer you?"

"Truth be told, I'd really like a cup of coffee."

"How about an Irish coffee?" Michele offered.

A smile quirked the edges of Tricia's mouth. "I think I could be talked into that."

"I think I'll join you," Michele said.

Shawn, the bartender, who'd cocked an ear in their direction, nodded and turned to make their drinks.

"What have you got there?" Tricia asked, tapping a finger on one of the printed pages spread across the bar.

Michele frowned. "Janet over at the Historical Society has given me copies of all of Pete's notes on the ghost walks."

"And?" Tricia prompted.

"I don't understand some of the references."

Tricia thought back to Pete's last words. They hadn't made sense, either. Michele handed her one of the papers. Tricia looked at the words and frowned. *Cemetery real estate.* What did that mean? Probably cemetery plots. And for which cemetery? As far as Tricia knew, the two Pete had been dealing with were both still accepting—she almost winced—clients. Were all the cemeteries in the area doing the same?

"Which is the oldest cemetery in town?" she asked Michele.

"The Stoneham Rural Cemetery—although it's hardy rural anymore, but I suppose when it was established in 1838, it was."

"Had Pete found any ghoulish stories to share?"

"I wouldn't say ghoulish, more historical. But there are a few recent murder victims"—Tricia could name several of them—"as well as murderers buried there. But I don't suppose it would go over well to talk about those souls, although it would be easy to fabricate something about those long gone to give the visitors a shiver or two."

"Yes, I suppose it would."

Shawn delivered their steaming coffees in tall glass mugs topped with blasts of whipped cream. Michele raised hers in salute. Tricia did likewise and took a sip. Lovely. Tricia's gaze returned to the papers scattered across the bar, her expression pensive.

"You don't like talking about this, do you?" Michele asked quietly.

"Are you kidding? I've been reading murder mysteries most of my life. But I have to admit, I'm not really sure how I feel about ghosts."

"Oh, I believe in them completely. With so many of the houses in England being centuries old, it would be strange not to run into a ghost or two during a lifetime." She laughed. "Mine, not theirs."

Tricia nodded toward the papers. "Surely there's enough material for you to work with to come up with a twenty- or thirty-minute talk."

"Oh, I'm sure there is. I've even been practicing my patter on Shawn."

"And what does he think?" Tricia asked, taking another sip of her coffee.

Michele eyed the thirtysomething hunk, who was listening as he dried the glasses he'd just washed. "He's bored. Not at all a receptive audience." She turned back to Tricia. "Perhaps you'd be willing to help me with my presentation?"

"I'd enjoy it."

"Lovely. Shall we start later this week? The talks are due to begin less than a month from now."

"I've got nothing else on my calendar," Tricia said, and it was true. Except for dinners with Angelica, she had nothing scheduled and would probably make no long-term plans until she had a timeline for returning to her home and reopening her store.

"Brilliant," Michele said.

They spent the next half hour in pleasant conversation as first one, then the other couple finished their drinks and waved good night.

"Looks like I'm closing down the bar tonight," Tricia said, taking the last sip of her tepid Irish coffee. It was then she realized she hadn't brought her purse or any money with her. "Oh, dear. I can't pay for my drink. I feel like a piker."

"Don't worry, love, it's on the house," Michele said.

"Thank you," Tricia said, and donned her jacket against the chilly

August night air. It was almost midnight and time to meet Angelica. "Good night," she called as she left the bar.

She found her sister sitting in her car in the municipal parking lot with the engine running and little Sarge in the passenger seat, riding shotgun. Angelica hit the control and the power window rolled down.

"Am I late?" Tricia asked.

"No, I'm early," Angelica said. She closed the window, shut off the engine, and joined her sister.

Tricia opened her car's trunk and withdrew one of the bags. "I had hoped to find petunias, but they were in short supply. I don't know all that much about flowers, but at least I know that roses would not be appropriate in a hanging basket."

"Thank goodness for that," Angelica said, but as she pawed through the rest of the flowers in the bag, her frown deepened. "A lot of these are tropical flowers."

"I know, but they're colorful and pretty—or at least they will be ten feet off the ground."

"Maybe I should alert Russ Smith to the vandalism and ask him to write a short article for the *Stoneham Weekly News*. Maybe if I offer a reward to find the culprits, it might squash the impending outrage."

"*Outrage* is rather a strong term when it comes to the merchants' reaction to fake flowers, but I think you're right." Tricia withdrew a plastic stem that sprouted four red carnations. "I brought a pair of wire cutters." She took them out of her jacket pocket. "We can cut these off and stuff them into the dirt in the baskets."

Angelica sighed. "Oh, dear. I guess we should have cut and sorted them earlier this evening. It's going to take all night for us to get this done."

"Then we'd better get started."

They decided to empty all the bags and sort and cut the flowers there in the parking lot under Tricia's car's trunk light. Angelica chose a palette of colors for the baskets before retrieving Sarge. She wore the end of the leash like a bracelet over her left wrist and grabbed a big flashlight and several of the bags, leaving Tricia to struggle with the ladder.

The whole project had sounded like a lark, but Tricia had never done any flower arranging, and after far too many unhelpful suggestions from Angelica, it soon became apparent that her efforts weren't going to cut it, and she knew that unless Angelica did the arrangements herself, she wouldn't be satisfied. "Ange, you're going to have to conquer your fears and climb this ladder."

"Oh, but I can't!" she cried, suddenly panicked.

"Yes, you can," Tricia said firmly. "You're Nigela Ricita. You have accomplished the impossible," she bluffed. "You have two successful businesses in your own name *and* you're a published author who single-handedly transformed the Chamber of Commerce in a mere eight months. And you can climb this ladder and make beautiful floral arrangements to spread happiness and cheer throughout the whole village."

Talk about laying it on thick!

Angelica's eyes brimmed with tears, and she swallowed. "Well, I guess I could try," she said, her voice trembling. "Will you lean against my legs so I don't fall?"

"Yes, I will," Tricia said patiently.

Angelica blinked away her tears and straightened, taking a deep, steadying breath before handing off the leash. Slowly, she approached the ladder, grasped it, and carefully placed her right foot on the first rung.

"You can do it," Tricia encouraged her.

"Yes, I can," Angelica said, swallowed and pulled herself up. It took another minute or two for her to force herself up the next two steps. "Okay," she said at last. "Hand me a couple of the flowers."

It wasn't as easy a task as it sounded, since Tricia had to juggle the leash, the bags, and the flashlight, and after fumbling for nearly a minute, she hefted a bag in Angelica direction. "Take this. I can't do it all."

Angelica snorted an impatient breath and snatched the bag from Tricia's grasp. Tricia aimed the flashlight in the general direction of the basket. Soon, Angelica became absorbed in the work, and Tricia could feel the tension in her sister's legs subside.

After several minutes, Angelica called, "Well, what do you think?"

Tricia squinted up at the basket. "Looks a lot better than what I could have done."

"You could learn to arrange flowers. I could teach you."

"You're stretched too thin as it is," Tricia said, which was true.

"You're right." Angelica sighed. "Okay, how do I get down from here?"

Tricia stepped back and grabbed Angelica's left hand, helping her down. "I guess I'd better carry the ladder," Angelica said, and proceeded to fold it for transport.

Sarge, who'd been sitting patiently, was eager to take off, and he had to be restrained when they only went as far as the next lamppost. Angelica unfolded the ladder, took a deep breath, and climbed the first step. "I can do this," she muttered, and took the next step. Half a minute later, she was engrossed in her second floral arrangement.

By the time they'd finished the fifth basket, Angelica seemed to have forgotten her fear of heights. "You know, maybe Nigela Ricita Associates should open a floral shop here in Stoneham."

"You wouldn't want to hurt the Milford Nursery's bottom line, would you, especially after you encouraged them to join our Chamber of Commerce?"

"I guess you're right," Angelica said. "If it ever got out that I was Nigela, it could look like a conflict of interest."

They did another two baskets before they ran out of silk flowers.

"Oh, dear," Angelica said. "If you've hit all the local stores, what are we going to do about all the other baskets?"

"Maybe you could order some online and pay for express shipping?"

"That means we wouldn't see them until at least Friday."

"It beats bald baskets," Tricia said.

"I guess," Angelica said with resignation.

Suddenly Sarge's ears perked up and he began to growl, straining at the leash. Tricia looked up the road and saw a figure advancing toward them. "Ange," she whispered nervously, wondering, should the need arise, if they could defend themselves with the stepladder.

"Tricia!"

Tricia immediately recognized the voice: Christopher.

"What on earth are you two doing skulking around the village at this time of night?" he demanded.

"Replacing the flowers," Angelica said, and scooped up a still-growling Sarge before he could start barking and wake the neighborhood. "What are *you* doing up this time of night?" she asked, inspecting his attire: a jacket over what looked like silk pajamas.

"I was thirsty and got up for a drink. I looked out the window and saw you two."

"If you'd looked five minutes later, we'd have been gone," Tricia said.

Christopher looked up at the hanging basket above them. "Why did you need to replace the flowers?"

"Because someone has snipped every last bloom," Angelica explained.

"Then how—?"

"They're fake," Tricia explained.

"Silk," Angelica insisted.

Christopher again looked up to take in Angelica's handiwork and shrugged. "Oh."

"What are you doing here?" Tricia asked.

"I told you."

"Yes, but what compelled you to come down to check on us?"

"There's a murderer running around here. You girls shouldn't be out on the street in the middle of the night."

"We're women, not girls," Tricia reminded him.

"And we have Sarge to protect us," Angelica asserted, and the little dog growled in agreement.

"That little squirt? He's hardly protection," Christopher said.

"No, but he can bark up a storm if he feels we're threatened," Tricia said.

"Well, I'd feel better if you two would let me walk you home—that is if you're ready to call it a night."

"Since we're out of flowers, I certainly am," Angelica said.

"Me, too," Tricia agreed.

"Good." Christopher reached for the ladder, folded it, and then carried it as he led the way back to the Cookery. Angelica took out her key and unlocked the door. "Where do you want me to put the ladder?" Christopher asked.

"Just leave it inside the door. I'll put it away in the morning."

Tricia handed over the empty bags and the flashlight. "I'll see you at the Chamber office in the morning."

"If I remember correctly, we have nothing going on, so I might not make it in until the afternoon."

"I'll see you then," Tricia said, and gave her sister a brief hug before Angelica entered the Cookery and locked the door.

Tricia turned to find Christopher standing before her with a big dumb grin across his face. "I can walk back to the Chamber without an escort," she assured him.

"I don't get to play good guy very often these days," he said. "And I'll sleep much better if I know you're safe."

Tricia looked down the well-lit, empty street and sighed. "Suit yourself." She turned and started off at a brisk pace. Christopher had to jog a few steps to catch up.

"You've changed," he said.

"You think so?" she asked, not bothering to look at him.

"Yes. Ten years ago you needed me."

"Ten years ago I thought we needed each other."

"Ten years ago I was arrogant. Five years ago I was even more arrogant."

"And now?" she asked, looking askance at him as they walked.

"I hope I've learned humility."

"You? Humble?" she asked, skeptical.

"Yes. I thought I could move to the mountains and live alone, but all I could think about was you."

"Funny, it took several years before you contacted me."

"I was living in denial."

Tricia stopped suddenly. "You've got some nerve coming here, bugging me, suggesting we get back together."

"It's because I realized I still love you."

"I suppose it was a case of 'you don't know what you've got until you lose it'?"

"That's right. And now I want to do whatever it takes to get you back."

"Unfortunately, you can't go back in time and rectify things."

"And I can't keep apologizing for the biggest mistake in my life, either."

"Why not?" Tricia asked.

"It hasn't done much good so far."

She stared at him for a long moment before she started off again. At the corner, she looked both ways, even though no cars had passed by in more than an hour, and crossed the street with Christopher following.

They didn't speak until they approached the Chamber office. "I can take it from here," Tricia said.

"I'll see you in," he insisted.

As they approached the side door, the motion-detector light clicked on, blazing. Tricia fumbled in her jacket pocket for her keys, finding them and then selecting the proper one to unlock the door. "Thanks for walking me home."

"I'd feel better knowing there's no one inside. If you don't mind, I'll wait and make sure there's no one lurking in the shadows."

She sighed.

"A man was killed only two days ago," he reminded her.

"All right," she reluctantly agreed. Christopher followed her inside the house. Once inside, Tricia turned on the lights, first leading him into the kitchen, then showing him the empty conference room, and finally the living room. "There. I'm safe and sound."

"We haven't checked upstairs."

"I don't think we need to," Tricia said firmly.

"I insist," Christopher said, and before she could stop him, he'd pivoted, opened the door to the stairway, and headed for the second floor.

"Wait!" she called, but he ignored her, bounding up the darkened stairs. Once at the top, he fumbled for a light switch. The overhead light glowed.

"Christopher," Tricia called, pounding after him.

He was already in her bedroom when she arrived at the landing. "Get out!" she shouted.

"Nobody in there," he said, turned on another light and inspected the tiny bathroom. "Or there." He pushed past her, heading for her sitting room. He turned on the light and stood in the center of the room. Miss Marple had been sleeping on the room's only chair, a wingback decked in pastel floral upholstery. The cat blinked up at him, and said, *"Yow!"*

"Yes, it is late," Christopher told her. "But I just wanted to make sure you and your mom are safe." He turned back to face Tricia. "You can't blame me for that."

"I can blame you for forcing your way into my home," she said.

"I didn't force my way; you unlocked the door."

"To the Chamber's office. You are now trespassing in my personal space."

He peeled off his jacket and tossed it on the footstool. Before she could protest, Miss Marple stood and Christopher scooped her up, taking her place on the chair and putting her down on his lap, where she promptly settled, tucking her feet under herself. "A fellow could sure go for a cup of cocoa before he goes back out into the cold."

"It's not *that* cold."

"It is when you're wearing pajamas."

130

"Come down to the kitchen and I'll make you a cup," she said, seeking a compromise.

"But Miss Marple is so comfortable," he said, and sure enough, Miss Marple's eyes were closed in pleasure, and she purred like a buzz saw as he petted her head.

Traitor! Tricia thought.

"I'll be right back," she grated. *And so help me, if I find you in my bedroom, I'll call the police.*

"I'm not going anywhere," Christopher assured her, looking up at her with those green eyes that almost always made her melt inside. This time she was determined to ignore their often-mesmerizing quality.

Tricia turned abruptly, lest she lose her resolve. She stomped down the stairs, went into the kitchen, and grabbed a mug from the drainboard. She filled it with water, which she nearly spilled when she thrust the mug into the microwave, hitting the timer for a minute. While she waited for it to heat, she got out the canister of cocoa and a clean spoon, her anger reaching the boiling point faster than the water. She didn't wait for the microwave to count down the last twenty seconds and punched the door release. She didn't want Christopher to say the cocoa needed to cool, thus delaying his departure. She dropped some of the powdered cocoa in her haste to get it into the mug, and slopped more of it onto the counter when stirring. When most of the cocoa had dissolved, she poured a little into the sink. She didn't want to spill it on the floor or carpet.

Tricia ascended the stairs with more care and quiet than she'd descended them less than two minutes before. "Here's your cocoa," she called as she entered the sitting room, but Christopher sat slumped in the chair and was quietly snoring. Miss Marple appeared to be deep in dreamland as well.

"Christopher!" Tricia called sharply, but he didn't rouse. She shook his shoulder, but he only nuzzled his head deeper into the wing of the chair.

For a moment she was so angry she considered pouring the chocolate over him, but she decided she liked the chair too much to risk such damage, and she wasn't eager to frighten her cat half to death, either.

"I hope you get a backache," she grumbled, and switched off the light before heading for her bedroom. She set the chocolate down and undressed, still grumbling to herself.

At last she sat on the bed, considered the mug of cocoa, and decided to drink it. She was so upset, she needed something to calm her jangled nerves. She shouldn't have had the Irish coffee so late in the evening. And didn't cocoa have caffeine in it, too?

She drank the last of it, set the mug on the nightstand, and set her alarm for seven, an hour later than she usually got up. It was after three. If she could fall asleep fast, she'd get just under four hours of sleep.

Climbing into bed, she turned off the light. She lay there for a few moments, fuming, wondering if she should lock her bedroom door. What if Christopher got up in an hour or so and climbed into bed with her?

She'd scream, and then she would *definitely* call the police. She'd have Baker arrest him. Maybe she'd get a restraining order against him, too. Yes, that was it. Christopher needed to be restrained from caring about her. He'd given up that privilege when he'd asked for the divorce.

Tricia squeezed her eyes shut and willed herself to sleep, but blessed oblivion would not come—she was listening too hard for creeping footsteps approaching from the other room.

It was after four when she finally let her guard down and allowed herself to feel drowsy.

The nightmare returned with a vengeance. Flames licked the inside of Haven't Got a Clue, the smoke thickening until it choked her. "Miss Marple! Miss Marple!" she called as she crawled along the carpet, searching for her beloved cat.

But it was only a dream. She knew it—she'd saved the cat and herself, and soon she'd begin to rebuild and refurbish, but the sense of danger still seemed closed—as someone frantically called her name.

"Tricia! Tricia!" came the shrill cries.

Tricia opened her eyes to see light streaming in her bedroom window.

"Tricia!"

The voice calling her name wasn't part of a dream. It was real!

ELEVEN

"Tricia!" someone called again, and finally Tricia recognized Mariana's voice. She threw back the covers, jumped out of bed—again disturbing Miss Marple, who'd been sleeping on the end of the bed—and raced for the stairwell, bumping into Christopher.

"What are you still doing here?" she hissed.

"I guess I fell asleep," Christopher muttered, his eyes open at half-mast and his chin covered with stubble.

Tricia heard footsteps bounding up the stairs, and she pushed him back toward the sitting room. "Hide!" she implored.

"Tricia, are you all right?" Mariana called, sounding panicked.

"Yes! I'm fine," Tricia called from the top step. Mariana stopped midway up the stairs. "I was up late last night. Looks like I slept through the alarm."

"I was so worried. I rang the doorbell and you didn't answer. And when I found the back door unlocked, I got worried."

"It was unlocked?"

Mariana nodded.

"I'm sorry. As I said, I was up late last night. Go on down and put on a pot of coffee. I'll be there in a few minutes."

Mariana nodded and turned, heading back down the steps.

Tricia turned toward her sitting room, her anger growing once again. "Christopher!" she called in a harsh whisper.

He stood before her in his PJs, smiling, taking in her filmy night-gown. "You're the most beautiful sight a man could wake up to."

"Get out!"

His smile broadened. "Sure." He reached for his jacket. "Are you sure I can't stay for a cup of coffee?"

"No."

"I'll just say a quick hello to Mariana as I leave."

"You will not."

He shrugged, slipping his arms into the jacket sleeves.

She pointed toward the chair. "You will sit there until I can get dressed, and then you will sneak out like the sneak you are for sneaking in."

"I didn't sneak. You let me in."

"I am not going to argue with you," Tricia said, turned and stormed off for her bedroom, slamming the door and locking it behind her.

Ten minutes later, she opened the door damp around the edges but dressed and ready for the day, sure it was going to be daunting but ready just the same.

Christopher stood as she entered the sitting room once again.

"Can I borrow your bathroom? I really have to go."

"No, you may not. You will wait for me to give you the word, and then you'll quietly hurry down the stairs and get the heck out of here."

"Tricia, I'm wearing pajamas. It's almost eight thirty. Half the village is up by now."

She glared at him.

"I'll quietly hurry down the stairs and get the heck out," he promised contritely.

"Wait until I give you a signal."

"Okay, okay," he agreed, raising his hands in surrender.

Tricia turned and headed for the stairs. She could smell the intoxicating aroma of coffee as she reached the bottom, and she ducked her head into the tiny kitchen, but Mariana was nowhere in sight. She must have gone to sit at her desk. Tricia crept down the hall, and sure enough Mariana was already seated at her desk going through the Chamber's e-mails.

"I'll just get a cup of coffee and then I'll be right in," Tricia told her.

Mariana nodded but didn't bother looking away from her screen.

Tricia crept back up the hall, looked up the stairwell, and waved for Christopher to join her.

Then she heard the back door open. Startled, she looked up to see Chief Baker come through it. She slammed the door to her private quarters.

"Grant!" she practically squeaked as her heart pounded in her chest. "To what do I owe the pleasure?"

"The ME has rendered the cause of death for Pete Renquist. I thought you might like to know."

Tricia leaned her back against the door like a human barricade. "And?" she asked.

"A heroin overdose."

Tricia felt her mouth drop open. "Pete? Heroin? I don't believe it."

"Believe it," Baker said. He sniffed the air. "Any chance I could get a cup of coffee?"

Still reeling from what she'd just heard, Tricia nodded. "Sure. Come into the kitchen."

Baker followed her into the tiny kitchen, taking a seat at the bistro table. Mariana had evidently wiped up the spilled cocoa from the night before. Tricia made a mental note to retrieve the dirty cup still sitting on her nightstand once she had a moment to spare. She poured two cups of coffee and doctored them both. She hadn't forgotten how Baker took his.

She heard the old wooden floor squeak behind her and looked to see Christopher, shoes in hand, tiptoeing toward the back door. She wanted nothing more than to throw him a murderous glare, but she refrained, swallowed, and turned back toward Baker, grateful that he sat at the opposite end of the kitchen.

"Anything wrong?" Baker asked.

"I'm—I'm still shocked by what you just told me," she stammered, forcing herself to keep her gaze on him and not look back toward the door. She heard it quietly close, and she let out a breath. "Heroin?" she repeated, carrying their cups to the table and taking a seat.

Baker accepted the cup and took a sip. "But it wasn't self-administered."

"What do you mean?"

"He was right-handed. It looks like someone clobbered him, and then injected him in the right arm."

"Can just one dose kill someone?" she asked in disbelief.

"When you're a junkie who hasn't shot up in over twenty years, yeah—one dose would do it. The body couldn't tolerate it."

"But I've heard about an antidote—"

"A lot of police and first responders do come armed with Naloxone, but you'd have to know someone has overdosed to administer it. As far as I've been able to tell, no one knew about Pete's secret past."

Tricia placed her hands around the warm cup, willing it to thaw the chill that had settled around her soul. "Was it difficult to root out?"

"Not after what you told me his last words were."

"'I never missed my little boy,'" Tricia repeated. "What did it mean?"

"*Little boy* is often used as a euphemism for heroin. After we talked, I asked the medical examiner to test for heroin. It would have turned up, but we got our answer a bit faster."

Pete Renquist a heroin addict? What had turned him around? How had he ended up in Stoneham and at the Historical Society? So many questions she'd probably never have the answers to. And who in Stoneham would have known that Pete had once been a heroin addict?

Then she remembered her talks with Charlie, one of Stoneham's mailmen, who'd known the Chamber's former receptionist, Betsy Dittmeyer. He'd met her at an Alcoholics Anonymous meeting, and he'd told Tricia that once an alcoholic, always an alcoholic. Had Pete been going to Narcotics Anonymous meetings? If so, whoever else went to them would have known about his addiction.

"You're thinking what I've already thought about. That someone arranged to meet him at the gazebo and then killed him."

"It does seem logical. But why?"

Baker shrugged.

"Do you think this was some kind of revenge killing?" Tricia asked.

"It seems like most murders are a form of retaliation, for one reason or another."

Tricia sighed, feeling helpless. "I appreciate you telling me this, Grant."

Again he shrugged. "I thought you had a right to know. Then again,

I don't want you talking about it, although I'm sure it'll get around soon enough. These kinds of things always do."

"It's such a shame. He was such a nice man."

"Except for the ex-wife, we haven't come up with any next of kin yet, but I've got a line on some former employers; maybe one of them will be able to tell me more about Renquist's past."

Tricia nodded. He was certainly more willing to talk about Pete's death than he had been the other evening. She decided to keep pushing. "What will happen to the body?"

Baker shrugged. "If he had a will, it might state Pete's wishes. I've got one of my guys calling all the attorneys in the area. One of them might know. He didn't have a safety deposit box at the bank, and I or one of my men will have a look at his house."

"Can I come along?"

"No. You're done with snooping around, remember?"

"I figured it couldn't hurt to ask," she said, offering him a weak smile.

For a minute or more they sipped their coffee in solemn silence, then Baker finally spoke. "From what I've learned, Renquist leaves big shoes to fill over at the Historical Society."

"You don't think his colleague, Janet Koch, can fill them?" she asked, just a bit annoyed.

He shrugged. "She's got a real life and a husband. Renquist lived alone. From what I understand, his life *was* the Historical Society."

"You don't think a woman is capable of running a business—or a nonprofit organization—and having a life?" she asked, thinking of all that Angelica was successfully juggling.

Again he shrugged. "Man or woman—it doesn't matter. But having a significant other would draw far too much attention from the job that needs to be done."

Tricia's grip on her cup tightened. She wasn't sure she believed that. But perhaps that explained why Baker was divorced. He had chosen his job as a law enforcement agent over his marriage. He'd told Tricia that his ex-wife had initiated the divorce, and yet when she'd suffered from cancer, he'd chosen to stand by her during the rough months of treatment. Despite the time he'd taken to support her in her time of need, he'd still chosen the job over his wife.

Tricia still felt that it wasn't a mistake that she'd ended her relationship with Baker. He had many fine qualities, but *life partner* wasn't one of them. Still, she liked him and probably always would. She managed a smile.

He noticed. "What are you thinking?" he asked.

She shrugged and took another sip of her coffee. "Kismet."

He frowned.

"How life flows, or doesn't, for people like Pete. How sad that some selfish person had to cut his life short."

"I will find out who killed him and bring that person to justice," Baker declared.

You hope, Tricia thought.

Baker drained his cup and looked up at the clock. "I've got to go back to work."

"And I'm already late starting it," Tricia said.

"Still no word from your insurance company?" Baker asked as he stood.

Tricia shook her head. Soft fur rubbed against her foot. She hadn't yet fed Miss Marple, either.

"I'm sure you'll hear soon," Baker said.

Tricia stood and walked him to the door.

"We should stay in touch," he said.

"If I learn anything I think you should know, I'll definitely call." She'd known he'd meant that communication between them should go beyond news of Pete's death, but she didn't acknowledge it.

"No snooping!" he told her again, emphatically stabbing the air with his right index finger.

"Have a good day," she called as he headed out the door. She closed it and stood staring at it for a long moment. Miss Marple nudged the back of her calf, and said, *"Yow!"* She wanted her breakfast and fast!

Tricia hurried back to the kitchen, washed out the cat's food dish, and opened a can of pseudo salmon for her girl, set it down on the floor for her, then changed the water. Tricia wasn't exactly hungry, but she perused the fridge's contents. Yogurt. Again. What she really wanted was an egg-white omelet—with onions and peppers—but she didn't have any eggs and she was too lazy to walk half a block to the Bookshelf Diner. She much preferred the days back at Haven't Got a Clue when she had a fridge with only her own groceries in it and had the leeway to have anything she wanted for breakfast. As it was, this was another day she would have to put up with a situation not to her liking. And as she'd overslept, she knew she wasn't going to get her four-mile walk in, either.

While Miss Marple chowed down, Tricia consumed her nonfat yogurt and poured herself another cup of coffee. She was determined to have a much more substantial lunch and would try to remember to call Booked for Lunch to order something other than the tuna plate.

Tricia topped up her cup once more and, with head held high, made her way to the former living room, now office space, in the house. She sat down before her computer and hit the power button, ready to start her workday.

"So," Mariana said, her voice level, "who was that guy who snuck out the back door after Chief Baker arrived?"

Tricia's heart froze. "Guy?" she bluffed.

"Yeah. A hunky guy in pajamas," Mariana said, and her lips quirked into a smirk.

Tricia let out a breath. "If you must know, it was my ex-husband. Angelica and I were out late last night. Someone clipped all the blossoms in the hanging baskets around the village, and we replaced them with silk flowers."

"And?" Mariana asked.

"Christopher walked me home."

"So why was he still here at eight in the morning?" Mariana pressed, still smiling.

Did Tricia really owe this woman an explanation? The fact was, nothing untoward had happened between her and her ex, but Mariana sat there with what amounted to a shit-eating grin plastered across her face.

Tricia glared at her. "He stayed for a cup of cocoa and fell asleep in my sitting room."

"If you say so."

"I do. And I'm sure you have better things to do than further speculate about my personal life."

At last Mariana looked away. "I'm sorry. It's none of my business what you do on your own time."

"No, it isn't," Tricia replied, but that didn't help her case. She knew Christopher leaving her temporary home in the early morning was sure to be the subject of gossip no matter how she tried to defend herself. She decided to ignore it and pulled her chair closer to the desk.

Mariana switched on her radio. No doubt she'd waited to do so until Baker had left so she could eavesdrop.

Stop it! Tricia ordered herself. Mariana was not Frannie—and as far as Tricia knew, Mariana hadn't succumbed to idle gossip. At least not yet.

Tricia checked her e-mails and found one from Angelica.

Looks like I'm busy all day with you-know-what business—and of course trying to track down silk flowers for the hanging baskets. I heard from Antonio—and we're on for dinner tonight. Will meet you at my place and I'll drive, then later tonight we can finish replacing the flowers? Tootles.

Terrific. Another late night. If Christopher showed up again, Tricia decided she would decline his offer to walk her home. She turned her attention to her own calendar. *Coffee with Mr. E.*

Her outlook suddenly brightened. She always enjoyed spending time with Mr. Everett. If the weather was fine, they'd stop at the Coffee Bean, buy a cup to go, and walk to the park, making sure to sit far away from the gazebo—the site of Deborah Black's death. Now, with Pete Renquist's death, they had even more reason to do so.

She glanced at her watch. It was almost nine. Mr. Everett would be arriving soon. She opened and answered several e-mails before the side door opened. "Hello!" Mr. Everett called.

"Come on in," Tricia called happily.

At the sound of the elderly gent's voice, Miss Marple ran up to greet him, winding around his ankles and telling him how much she'd missed him. He scooped her up and she nuzzled his chin, purring loudly.

"I'm always happy to see you, too, Miss Marple," he said, his blue eyes twinkling.

"We're going for coffee," Tricia told Mariana. "Can I bring you back anything?"

Mariana shook her head. "But thanks for the offer."

Tricia pushed back her chair and hurried to join Mr. Everett.

He set the cat down. "I'll see you later, my dear Miss Marple."

Miss Marple said, *"Yow!"*

Mr. Everett gestured for Tricia to precede him out the door, and they walked in comfortable silence to the Coffee Bean. Mr. Everett purchased cups of their respective favorite brews, and they headed for the park.

Tricia glanced across the street to look at the refurbished hanging baskets. From a distance, they looked pretty good. She'd try to get a closer view later in the day.

Mr. Everett noticed her staring. "Very odd, isn't it?"

"Odd?" Tricia asked, facing him.

"That most of the flowers are gone, and those across the street aren't the same as they were last week."

"It seems we have some kind of floral vandal in town," Tricia said as they paused at the corner, looked both ways, and crossed.

"Odder still that there should be lilies among them," he commented. "I've never seen them in a hanging arrangement before."

Tricia cleared her throat. "How's Grace?" she asked, desperate to change the conversation.

"Happy in her work," Mr. Everett said, "as am I. But I shall be overjoyed when Pixie and I can return to Haven't Got a Clue with you and Miss Marple."

"Believe me, I'm counting the days."

"Do you have a timetable?"

Tricia shook her head. "I'm still waiting for the insurance man to call."

They walked around the perimeter of the park, settling on their favorite bench. Tricia removed the cap from her coffee, blowing on it to cool it.

"It's terrible what happened to Peter Renquist," Mr. Everett said.

"Yes. I'm so sorry. I enjoyed working with him through the Chamber."

Mr. Everett nodded.

"Did you know him?" Tricia asked.

"He worked for me about twenty years ago at the grocery store, stocking shelves."

Tricia frowned. "Wasn't that an entry-level job? Pete must have been at least thirty at the time."

Mr. Everett nodded and took a sip of his coffee. "He was obviously overqualified but in desperate need of employment. He promised he would stick with the job for at least six months. During that time, he became a volunteer for the Historical Society."

"Did they hire him away from you?"

Mr. Everett shook his head. "He worked the full six months he'd promised me, then found a better-paying job at the library in Milford. The Historical Society hired him several years later." He shook his head. "Such a shame. He was a hard worker and was well liked."

"Not by Earl Winkler," Tricia said, remembering Pete's last conversation with the curmudgeon.

"Were I Peter, I'd have considered that a compliment."

"Why, Mr. Everett, I don't think I've ever heard you say a disparaging word against anyone."

"If ever there was a selectman who was against seeing the village prosper, it's Winkler. I will not go into details, but I once had an unpleasant encounter with him back when I still owned my store. That enough members of the electorate saw him as a fit candidate is a mystery to me."

Tricia knew better than to press him with questions about the incident. The memory must have been a bitter one for Mr. Everett to have even mentioned it. She decided to turn the conversation back to Pete. "Chief Baker wasn't sure what, if any, burial arrangements were being made. I wonder if the Historical Society will at least hold a memorial service for Pete."

"I'd be happy to contact them, find out, and pass along the word. I'd certainly be among those who'd like to show their respects."

"Thank you," Tricia said, and took another sip of her coffee.

"I saw Ginny yesterday," Mr. Everett offered.

"So did I. Angelica and I are going to have dinner with her and Antonio tonight at the Brookview Inn."

"That should be nice. I don't suppose Ginny will have much time to socialize after the baby arrives, which should be any day now. Grace and I can't wait to be his or her honorary grandparents."

Oh, dear. Would he and Grace be offended if Angelica stepped into what everyone would think was an honorary position as well?

"Will you be babysitting?" she asked.

Mr. Everett looked surprised. "I shouldn't think so. I would be frightened I might drop the baby." He shook his head. "I believe we'll just be around to spoil the child." He nodded and smiled. "I think I'll quite enjoy that."

"I'm looking forward to being an honorary aunt, as well," Tricia admitted. And now that honor hit a little closer to home. Honorary step-aunt? She frowned. Perhaps she'd just leave the step part out.

"Will you be babysitting?" Mr. Everett asked.

"I don't know. I've changed a diaper only once before, but I suppose with practice I could get good at it. I think I'd prefer to take pictures and bring gifts."

"You mean spoil the child—like Grace and me?"

Tricia laughed. "Definitely."

Mr. Everett drained his cup, then looked at his watch. "It's time for me to get to work at the Cookery. A lot of Internet orders came in late yesterday afternoon. As your sister uses the same software as you had at Haven't Got a Clue, I'll be up to speed to start fulfilling the orders on day one after we reopen."

"I've tried to keep up with the inventory as I've purchased books for stock, but I'm afraid it's gotten away from me."

"Not to worry. Between the three of us, we'll catch up before the grand reopening. I hope you don't mind, but Pixie and I have been drawing up a list of ideas for the celebration."

"Mind? I'm thrilled. Perhaps the three of us—and Grace, if she'd like to listen to shop talk—can get together for lunch to talk about it."

"That would be lovely," Mr. Everett said, and stood. He took Tricia's empty cup and disposed of it and his in one of the park's trash barrels.

They crossed the lush grass, heading for Main Street. "I'll see you soon," Mr. Everett promised, giving Tricia a nod.

"I'll look forward to it," she said, and they parted company, Tricia headed north and Mr. Everett went south.

As Tricia briskly walked back to the Chamber office, she pondered what Selectman Winkler could have done to upset Mr. Everett all those years ago, and wondered if she would ever know.

TWELVE

The rest of the morning flew past. Tricia made follow-up calls to at least ten numbers on her long list of outlying businesses. After much practice, her pitch was practically perfect, and of the ten calls, she'd convinced four to join, processing three credit card orders and with the promise that Bright Smile Orthodontics would be sending a check in the next day's mail. Angelica would be pleased.

E-mail seemed to have piled up while she'd been on the phone, but she decided to tackle it after lunch.

Even though Angelica wasn't going to be available, Tricia knew her sister would have made sure her usual tuna plate was ready as a to-go order at Booked for Lunch. So much for remembering to order something different. As she walked along Main Street, Tricia noticed several of the shopkeepers looking through their windows at her and waving, their faces covered in silly smirks. No doubt they'd heard about Christopher leaving the Chamber office in his pajamas—perhaps they'd even witnessed him walking down the street. He probably hadn't had the sense to take the back alley.

Still, Tricia walked on, her head held high. She had nothing to feel ashamed of. Christopher had been the jerk who'd pushed his way into her temporary home, and nothing naughty had happened. And even if it had, it was nobody else's business.

Booked for Lunch was packed with tourists, and Pixie was waiting on a table in back when Tricia arrived. Bev, the full-time waitress, refilled a customer's coffee, her smile broadening when she saw Tricia.

"Hey there, stranger. We missed seeing you yesterday, but then I guess you've been busy," she said, and giggled.

"I had lunch with Ginny yesterday. I picked up our take-out orders," she reminded Bev.

"Oh, yes—that's right. It's just that—"

"I have to get back to work," Tricia interrupted. "I'll just take my lunch to go."

Bev retrieved the salad from the small under-the-counter fridge and transferred it to a foam container. "Enjoy. And don't do anything I wouldn't," she said with a smirk.

Tricia said nothing and left the café.

This time, Tricia didn't look right or left as she trudged back up the street toward the Chamber office. Instead of eating at her desk, she choked down her lunch at the little bistro table in the small kitchen, just in case Mariana wanted a little more fun at her expense. Afterward, she went back to her desk to attack the ever-multiplying e-mails.

It was after two, and Mariana was on her way back from the storage closet with another ream of paper for the printer, when she said, "Pixie's late today."

Tricia glanced at the clock. Sure enough, it was nearly ten after two. "Booked for Lunch was packed a while ago. Pixie might have had to stay late to help clean up."

Her speculation was proved wrong when Pixie arrived at the Chamber office five minutes later, carrying a cardboard tray with the Coffee Bean's distinctive cups and one of their bags, no doubt filled with biscotti or muffins.

"Sorry I'm late, but I figured you ladies wouldn't complain if I brought a treat for all of us."

"Pixie, you spoil us," Mariana said, but she sounded pleased nonetheless.

"And it's fun to do," Pixie said, her smile wide, her gold canine tooth flashing. She passed out cups and napkins. The muffins were apple raisin, which pleased Tricia. She was becoming adept at convincing herself that anything that contained fruit *could* be considered healthy.

"Did you hear what happened last night?" Pixie asked, her eyes wide, practically gushing.

"You mean this morning?" Mariana asked, giving Tricia the eye.

"No, it was definitely last night," Pixie said with confidence. "Janet Koch over at the Historical Society was mugged. Mugged! Right here in Stoneham!" she cried.

"Mugged? Where did it happen?" Tricia asked, alarmed.

"I guess she was working late at the Historical Society and someone jumped her when she was leaving."

"Is she all right?" Tricia asked, aghast.

Pixie shook her head.

"She's not—" Tricia couldn't even bring herself to say the *D* word.

"No," Pixie said, "but whoever hit her *left* her for dead. She was found by the Society's groundskeeper this morning. She's at the hospital in Nashua in a coma with a fractured skull."

"Will she live?" Tricia asked, nearly on the verge of tears. She liked Janet.

Pixie shrugged. "I guess it's too soon to tell. Poor lady. Alexa"—one of the Coffee Bean's owners—"says she's a nice person."

"That she is," Tricia sadly agreed, looking down at her muffin. She'd lost her appetite. Poor Janet. And her attack, coming on the heels of Pete's murder . . . There had to be a connection.

"What have you got for me to do today, Tricia?" Pixie asked.

Before Tricia could answer, Mariana piped up. "I could use some help with the Member Appreciation Day invitations, if you don't mind, Tricia."

"Not at all," she said, distracted.

Tricia tried to go back to work, but her thoughts couldn't seem to stray from the the idea of Janet lying on the damp ground outside the Society's headquarters all night. She considered calling the hospital to get an update, but realized that the HIPAA laws would prevent her being told anything of relevance. Instead, she took her cell phone into the Chamber's small kitchen and called Grant Baker's personal number and was surprised when it didn't immediately roll over to voice mail. "Baker here."

"Grant, it's Tricia. I just heard about Janet Koch. What happened?"

"It looks like her attacker smashed her head into the stone wall. We found traces of blood on the side of the building. She was found by a coworker. The EMTs estimate she'd been lying on the ground outside the Historical Society's back entrance all night."

"But she has a husband. Didn't he worry about her?" Tricia asked.

"He's out of town on a business trip. One of their neighbors tracked him down. He's on his way back from Chicago and should get in this evening."

"What a terrible thing to come home to. What are Janet's chances?"

"I haven't gone to the hospital, but I did talk to a doctor in the ER. It doesn't look good."

Tricia's heart constricted. "She's such a lovely woman. I can't imagine anyone wanting to hurt her."

"It sure looks suspicious. First Renquist is killed, then his coworker is attacked. What's someone got against the Historical Society?"

"I can't imagine. They're all such nice people."

"I'm warning you, Tricia: don't use this incident as an excuse to go poking around," Baker said.

"Me? Poke around?"

"Yes, you. Someone means business, and you may have used up your store of good luck."

The village jinx having good luck? From the corner of her eye, Tricia saw Miss Marple enjoying her afternoon bath. Tricia had come so close to losing the cat in the fire. Yes, she did possess a lot of luck. But she wasn't willing to push that luck, either.

"I have no wish to be the next victim," Tricia said firmly. "I heard Janet is at St. Joseph."

"Yes. I've got a call in to see if I can get some protection from the Sheriff's Department, and if I do, she won't be allowed visitors. She'll need them more when—or if—she recovers."

If. It was a pretty big word when someone's life hung in the balance.

"Thank you for speaking to me," Tricia said.

"I'll let you know if we come up with anything."

"Thank you."

They said good-bye. No sooner had Tricia shoved her phone back into the pocket of her slacks when her ringtone sounded. She recognized the number and frowned: Christopher. She considered tossing her phone out the window, but as Beethoven's "Ode to Joy" continued to play, she stabbed the incoming-call icon. "What?" she demanded.

"Trish?"

"Yes!"

"Are you mad at me?"

"You mean you couldn't tell?"

Silence.

"What do you want now?" she asked crossly.

"To apologize. It didn't occur to me that—"

"That you might ruin my reputation?"

"That's a little strong," Christopher said reproachfully. "I mean, you *are* my wife."

"*Ex*-wife," she said with emphasis on the first syllable.

"And it's not like the village doesn't know about your past liaisons."

"Keep talking, Christopher. You're digging yourself in deeper and deeper."

"I'm sorry. I mean it. What can I do to make it up to you?"

"Please, just leave me alone," Tricia said wearily.

"You know that's impossible. I care about you."

Tricia indulged herself and rolled her eyes.

"Will you and Angelica be working on the flowers again tonight?" Christopher asked.

"Yes, but do me a favor—don't join us. Stay home. Don't even look out the window."

"But I worry about you. I'd never forgive myself if anything happened to you."

Yada yada yada.

It was time to cut the conversation short.

"I accept your apology. Have a nice day. Good-bye." Hoping he'd get the message and not call back, she broke the connection before he could go on (and on). To make sure, she switched off her phone. He could always call the Chamber directly, but she decided she'd let Pixie and Mariana handle all incoming calls for the rest of the afternoon.

With that decided, Tricia returned to her desk and refreshed her e-mail.

The phone rang. Pixie picked it up. "Stoneham Chamber of Commerce. This is Pixie. How can I help you?"

Tricia opened an e-mail from Dr. Wimberly's dental office inquiring about the monthly networking meeting.

"Oh, sure, she's right here." Pixie covered the mouthpiece and looked directly at Tricia. "It's for you."

"I'm not taking calls from Christopher Benson."

"It's from your insurance agent."

Tricia's heart skipped a beat, and she grabbed the receiver from the phone on her desk. "John? Please tell me you have good news about the insurance settlement."

"Sorry, but sometimes no news is good news."

That wasn't what Tricia wanted to hear.

"Is something wrong?"

"Not wrong, but . . . annoying. Bob Kelly has called me every day for the last week, hounding me to settle your claim. He wants you to buy his building."

Tricia sighed. "I'm sorry he's nagging you. He's been bugging me, too."

"He seems to think that the quicker we settle, the quicker you'll buy it."

"Mr. Kelly has an inflated opinion of the building's worth. According to the agent at NRA Realty, he's asking at least ten percent over market value. He won't come down, and I'm not going up."

"How long is it until your lease is up?"

"Another year. And, unfortunately, I'm still paying monthly rent, though I can't use the building or live there."

"We understand that, but as I warned you at the onset, these things take time. There's a lot to consider and—"

"Yes, yes," Tricia said, cutting him off. They'd been over this territory far too many times in the past six months. She didn't need to hear it again. "The next time I speak to Bob—and I'm sure it won't be long—I'll ask him to refrain from calling you."

"Thanks. And as soon as I hear anything, I'll call you—day or night."

"I'd appreciate that. Thanks, John."

They said good-bye and Tricia put the phone down. She noticed Pixie hovering.

"No good news?" Pixie asked anxiously.

Tricia shook her head.

"Don't get me wrong. I like working here and at Booked for Lunch, but I just want to go *home*."

Tricia felt the same way. "I'm glad you think of Haven't Got a Clue with such affection."

"Well, I'm not in a hurry for either of you to leave," Mariana said.

"Unfortunately, once the settlement comes through, we've still got to wait for the store to be refurbished. There was a lot of fire, smoke, and water damage on the first floor. It can be fixed, but it's going to take a couple of months."

"If nothing else, we'll be open for the Christmas rush," Pixie said, her gold tooth flashing as she grinned.

Tricia smiled. Pixie's faith gave her hope. "Yes, we will."

"Until then, we're a team, right?" Mariana asked.

"You bet your ass," Pixie answered.

"Then we'd better get back to work," Tricia said.

"Are you nearly done with the newsletter?" Mariana asked.

"Just waiting for Angelica's okay. Then I'll pass it along to you two for a final proofread." She pulled up the file but found it hard to concentrate with so many other subjects preying on her mind. Poor Janet lying in a hospital bed near death while Bob and Christopher kept concocting new ways to annoy Tricia, and the insurance company plotted to delay her check and keep her working gratis for the Chamber. And what would Ginny say when Angelica confessed that she was actually Nigela Ricita? Would the shock cause Ginny to go into labor?

Now you're not only being melodramatic, you're being silly, Tricia chided herself.

She scanned the first paragraph of Angelica's News from the President column and spied a typo. Oops.

Back to work, she told herself, but doubted she'd accomplish too much.

There was just too much going on to worry about, and at the moment she seemed best suited to do just that.

THIRTEEN

Afternoons at the Chamber office tended to drag. Much as she liked Mariana, Tricia enjoyed that final hour of the day with Pixie, even if they only spent the time in companionable silence. And since Pixie had gained a significant other, her life seemed to grow richer and more interesting each day, while Tricia's life had fallen into stagnation. She needed time to heal after the devastation to her store and her psyche that the fire had caused.

Tricia watched as Pixie gathered up her stuff. "How was the roller derby?"

"Great. I saw a couple of my old teammates. We all went out for a few beers afterward. We talked until past midnight. Man, those were the days."

"Will you be seeing Fred tonight?"

Pixie shook her head. "He's gotta get an oil change, so it's laundry for this old broad. How about you?"

"I'm going out to dinner at the Brookview."

"With a guy?" Pixie asked hopefully.

"Yes," Tricia said coyly.

"Who? Your ex? The chief?"

Tricia shook her head. "Antonio Barbero and Ginny."

"Aw, that doesn't count," Pixie said.

"It should be very interesting," Tricia said. And if Ginny exploded, the fireworks could be very entertaining, too.

"Well, I'm having a frozen dinner, so order something wonderful and think of me," Pixie said.

"I will," Tricia promised.

"See you tomorrow," Pixie called as she headed for the door.

After she'd gone, Tricia shut down her computer. She went upstairs, changed her clothes, and then fed Miss Marple before she locked the Chamber of Commerce. The air was blast-furnace hot and muggy as she started down the sidewalk heading south. She crossed the street at the corner and headed for the municipal parking lot and saw Angelica heading north to join her.

"What a day," Angelica cried in greeting.

"Tell me about it."

And Angelica proceeded to do just that. "You'd think that finding appropriate silk flowers would be an easy task, but I had to go all the way to Manchester, and I still don't know if I have enough." She glanced toward one of the baskets and an offending lily that now seemed to stick out like a sore thumb.

"I thought you were going to order them online."

"I didn't want to wait for delivery."

"Mr. Everett noticed the flowers—or lack thereof," Tricia said.

"Well, of course he would. He's as big a mystery hound as you are, and it's sure a mystery to me why someone would want to deprive the entire village—and our tourist guests—of their beauty," Angelica said as she unlocked the car and they got in.

"Hurry with that air-conditioning," Tricia said. "I feel like I'm half-cooked."

Angelica started the car and hit the control to let down the windows. "It probably won't even kick in before we get to the Brookview Inn. Getting back to my story, I bought the flowers and have already sorted them by color, and I have them separated so we won't need to spend as much time with it tonight."

Tricia sighed. So she *did* plan on repopulating the baskets that evening.

"What kind of a day have you had?" Angelica asked.

"One filled with startling news."

"Do tell," Angelica said, and waited for a car to pass before she drove out of the lot.

"Did you hear about Janet Koch?"

"Yes! That poor woman. Do you think she'll be all right?"

"I don't know, but I sure hope so. First Pete, now Janet. Speaking of Pete, Grant told me something in confidence—"

"Which you're about to spill," Angelica said with relish.

"Pete had a past."

"Was he a bank robber?" Angelica guessed.

"No! A former heroin addict."

"Pete Renquist a junkie?" Angelica repeated, incredulous, and braked at the corner.

"Apparently so. He died of a heroin overdose—that wasn't self-inflicted. Grant seems to think he hadn't been into the drug scene for many years."

"So why does someone wait half a lifetime to off the poor guy?"

"Your guess is as good as mine. The sad fact is, we may never know."

Angelica pulled up to the Brookview Inn and turned into the drive, parking in the back under a tree. "That wasn't all the news around the village. Frannie couldn't wait to tell me that Christopher was seen leaving the Chamber office early this morning in his pajamas. Are you two back together?" Angelica asked point-blank.

"No! After walking me home last night, the idiot barged in and wouldn't leave. He fell asleep on the chair in my sitting room with Miss Marple on his lap. Thinking he'd wake up and go home, I left him there. He didn't."

Angelica closed the car windows and gathered up her purse. "Well, if you do decide to start shacking up, please show a little discretion."

"Believe me, I have no plans to shack up with anyone."

Angelica shook her head sadly. "Well, that's too bad."

Tricia grabbed her own purse and got out of the car, slamming the door. Angelica got out, closed her door much more gently, and pressed the button on her key fob to lock it. An exhaust fan at the back of the restaurant's kitchen roared, and the mingled aromas of that night's dinner specials filled the parking lot.

They stood there for a moment, taking in the refurbished and majestic old inn. "How much of this place do you actually own?" Tricia asked.

"Ninety-five percent."

"You're kidding," Tricia said.

"No. The Baxter family didn't want to sell it outright, and it took a lot of negotiating, but in the end Antonio and I make all the decisions on what goes on. The family really only owns the name."

"Are they the same family that built the building where By Hook or By Book is housed?" Tricia asked.

"The very same. They're one of the oldest families still tied to the village."

Tricia looked back to the venerable old building before her. "Well, you've done a nice job updating the place."

"Thank you," Angelica said with pleasure. "The occupancy rate is up over fifty percent since NRA took over the day-to-day control. It's been a win-win situation for all involved."

She started off, and Tricia fell in step beside her as they approached the inn's back entrance.

"And none of the employees know?" Tricia whispered.

"No. And that's the way I want to keep it. It's Antonio's baby, and he's done a fabulous job." They climbed the steps and entered, walking down a well-lit corridor that led to the lobby. They paused at the reception desk, where the new night clerk, Missy Andrews, sat.

"Good evening, Ms. Miles. How can I help you?"

"Hello. Tricia and I are having dinner with Mr. Barbero and his wife in the private dining room."

"He just stepped out, but he said to expect you."

"Would it be all right if we went on ahead and waited for them?"

"Yes, go right on in," the pert blonde young woman said, smiling.

"Thank you."

Angelica led the way down the hall.

"Does this private dining room get much use?" Tricia asked.

"Actually, yes. It used to be a storeroom, but when we put in the new HVAC system, we found we could use part of the basement instead. It's worked out well." The door was ajar, and Angelica strode through it with Tricia following.

The décor was what Tricia expected: elegant yet understated. The only bling evident were the crystal sconces on the walls around a gas fireplace. The furniture was colonial, and the floor was dark hardwood with a large antique Oriental area rug. A table with crisp white linens and set for four sat in front of a window with sumptuous drapes that overlooked the inn's side garden. Closer to the door was a seating area that could comfortably accommodate six. Tricia sank into one of the upholstered chairs to wait.

Angelica hadn't seemed agitated until they'd entered the pretty private dining room and she'd begun to pace its confines. "You know, I'm much more nervous about how Ginny is going to react to the news about Nigela Ricita than I was about you finding out."

"Why's that?"

"I don't know. Maybe because she and I originally got off to such a rocky start when I first came to Stoneham. It's taken time to get her on my side. I don't want to lose that."

Tricia shook her head and continued to study the room, which was a delight. The walls were covered in a subtle rose-patterned wallpaper with a beige background, and original oil paintings of stately homes adorned each wall.

"Did you decorate this room, too?" Tricia asked.

"Of course. I did the refresh of the lobby and the guest rooms, too. It's amazing what you can order online these days."

Again Tricia shook her head, but this time in . . . wonder? Consternation? She wasn't sure which. "Will you please sit down?" she implored.

"My nerves are so jangled. I'm not sure how I can explain it to Ginny. She's going to *hate* me, I'm sure of it. I mean, doesn't everybody hate their mother-in-law?"

"She's not going to be happy, but I think *hate* is much too strong a word to describe her feelings."

"You are *so* optimistic," Angelica said, her face taut with worry.

The door handle rattled and Angelica jumped back, startled. The door opened, and Antonio ushered his very pregnant wife inside. "Ah, you're already here," he said.

"Oh," Ginny said, sounding surprised at seeing the sisters. "When Antonio said we were coming to the inn for dinner, I never expected to see you two."

"Sorry to disappoint you," Tricia said.

"Oh, no, it's not that," Ginny hastily explained, but she didn't go on. The three women looked at one another, all of them forcing smiles. "So, what's the occasion?" Ginny finally asked.

Tricia looked askance at her sister, who stood there with her mouth open but seemed unable to speak. "Why don't we sit down and have a drink before dinner?" she finally blurted out.

"Unfortunately, I'm only drinking sparkling water these days, but feel free to go ahead," Ginny said.

"Here," Angelica suggested, gesturing toward the most comfortable chair.

Ginny shook her head. "I might not be able to get up from there." She allowed Antonio to settle her at one of the chairs at the table. He then turned and pressed a button on the wall, which Tricia presumed would summon a waiter. She and Angelica seated themselves at the table, as well.

"How are things going?" Tricia asked, hoping her voice sounded normal, while Angelica continued to wring her hands.

"I can't wait to drop this kid," Ginny said, and exhaled a long breath. "I want my center of gravity back. I want my body *and* my life back."

"Ginny has had a long day," Antonio explained, looking sheepish.

"If you don't want to stay for dinner . . ." Tricia began.

"Oh, no!" Ginny said. "I'm here and I'm not about to give up a gourmet meal. If we were at home, we'd be having a bowl of soup and a sandwich or takeout."

They heard a knock at the door, and a white-coated waiter

appeared. "Hello, I'm James and I'll be taking care of you this evening. Can I get anyone a drink?"

"A dry gin martini with olives," Angelica said, sounding desperate.

"I'd like a Chardonnay," Tricia said.

"Campari on ice, and a bottle of Pellegrino *con gas* for my beautiful wife," Antonio said.

"Very good, sir. I'll be right back with your drinks and a selection of appetizers."

"Thank you, James," Antonio said.

The waiter gave a slight bow and retreated from the room. After he was gone, the four of them looked expectantly at one another.

"It's rather a surprise to see the two of you here," Ginny said again, taking in the sisters.

Angelica forced a laugh. "Well, we thought you could probably use a break from cooking."

"That's the truth. I don't think either of us has had a decent meal—unless we've eaten here—in the last month," Ginny said. "And I have a feeling we'll be eating yet more takeout for at least a week or two after the baby comes."

Angelica nodded vigorously, reminding Tricia of a bobblehead doll.

Nobody said anything for a long awkward minute or so, their gazes dipping to the floor and various corners of the room. Finally, Tricia was about to take the initiative and introduce the subject of why they had gathered, when Ginny spoke. "Antonio mentioned we'd be eating here in the private dining room, so I kind of assumed we were going to have one last romantic evening before the baby arrives. I have a feeling it could be years before that will ever happen again."

"Maybe not," Angelica said. "What you need is a willing babysitter.

Someone who loves you and is willing to watch over your little boy or girl as if it were her very own."

"Have you got someone in mind?" Ginny said, and laughed.

Angelica forced yet another smile. "Well, yes. Me."

Ginny's smile faded. "And why would you want to do that?"

"Because . . . because . . . Because I'm your baby's nonna."

"Nonna? That's Italian for grandmother," Ginny said, her eyes practically pinning Angelica to the wall.

Again, Angelica laughed. "Yes, I guess it is. You see, I'm—I'm—"

"Nigela Ricita," Ginny said without batting an eye.

Angelica swallowed, obviously taken aback. "Well, yes. I am."

Ginny waved a bored hand and reached for her water glass. "I've known that for months."

"You—you have?" Angelica practically squeaked.

Tricia frowned. "Has everyone but me known this not-so-secret secret forever?"

"Not forever," Ginny said, "but I was doing the Jumble puzzle one day and somehow the words Nigela Ricita popped into my mind and just unscrambled themselves."

"Me, too," Tricia said.

"You never said anything," Antonio said.

Ginny shrugged. "I assumed you were sworn to secrecy. And I know," she said, turning her gaze on Angelica, "that people don't cross Nigela Ricita."

Angelica's lower lip trembled and her eyes filled with tears. Suddenly Tricia felt terribly protective of her older sister. "She didn't mean any harm, Ginny. Everything she's done has been for the good of the village and its people."

Ginny's gaze softened. "And us." She reached across the table, offering her hand to Angelica. "Thank you for taking care of Antonio all these years. You were only his stepmother. Most women wouldn't have done what you did for him, especially after your marriage to his father broke up."

"Well, just like you, I fell in love with him, and I'm very pleased to still be a part of his life."

"A big part," Antonio said, with a wave to take in the inn at large.

Angelica squeezed Ginny's hand. "Well, will you take me up on my offer?"

"To babysit? Have you ever taken care of a baby before?"

"I have a dog."

"It's not quite the same."

"I suspect at this very moment that you and I have the exact same amount of experience when it comes to child care."

Ginny's lips quirked into a smile. "I'll bet you're right."

"Then perhaps we can learn together."

"I'm game," Ginny said, her grin broadening.

The waiter interrupted what could have become a love fest by arriving with a cart that not only held the drinks, but the promised appetizers, as well. He served them, pouring Ginny's sparking water. He handed menus all around. "Just press the button on the wall when you're ready to order," he said, and retreated, closing the door behind him.

Antonio picked up his glass. "To family."

"To family," the women chorused, and they all clinked glasses and drank.

Ginny set her glass down first. "I've been dying to talk to my boss about new opportunities within the NRA organization. Do you think she'd be interested?" she asked Angelica.

"I think she'd love it!"

FOURTEEN

"I'm so happy, I think I might explode!" Angelica gushed as she started her car and put it in gear.

"Calm down, girl," Tricia said, and laughed. It was well past eleven. The dinner—and the ensuing conversation—had gone on much longer than Tricia would have expected, considering how close Ginny was to delivering her baby. But everyone had been in such high spirits, no one had wanted the evening to end.

"I was so worried Ginny wouldn't accept me as her mother-in-law, and yet now I feel like we're really a family." Angelica looked both ways before pulling out of the Brookview Inn's parking lot, heading east. Antonio's car had already disappeared from view.

"Ginny seemed pleased, especially when you answered her question about her taking on more responsibility—and the possibility of opening a new day care center."

"A good employer makes sure her people are happy. If we were a bigger company, I'd have on-site day care."

"How big do you expect NRA to get?" Tricia asked. Did she have a megalomaniac for a sister?

Angelica shrugged. "That depends on Antonio and the next generation of Barberos."

"Do you want to make NRA a dynasty?"

"Why not?" Angelica said, and laughed.

"I hate to shatter your good mood, but we've still got to put silk flowers in the rest of the hanging baskets."

"Even that boring task couldn't upset me," Angelica declared, and she turned left onto Main Street.

Every other business except the Dog-Eared Page had long since shuttered its doors for the day. The pub's windows positively glowed, and Angelica slowed the car, hitting the power button on the driver's window. They could hear music and laughter. "I knew opening that pub would be good for the village," she said.

They rolled on past, and a few seconds later she turned right into the municipal parking lot. Angelica parked and they got out of the car. "We'll change clothes and then get straight to work."

But as they walked toward Main Street, Tricia looked toward the gas lamp nearest the entrance and her breath caught in her throat. "Oh, no," she cried.

"What?" Angelica asked.

"Look!" Tricia pointed to the hanging basket. When they'd left for the Brookview Inn, it was resplendent with silk blooms; now only the live greenery remained.

Angelica let out a breath that sounded like a sob. "No!"

Tricia snagged Angelica's arm, pulling her up the street. Every basket they'd worked on the night before had been denuded.

"How could someone have done this? Why didn't anyone see it happen?" Angelica cried.

"It's too late to call the police," Tricia said.

"Grant didn't take me seriously when I reported the vandalism in the first place—he's not going to care about the theft of the silk flowers, either." Angelica's voice broke on the last word, and tears filled her eyes.

"There must be something we can do," Tricia said, looking up and down the empty street. Up ahead and across the street, she noticed a light glowing at the *Stoneham Weekly News*. "Look, Russ must be working late. Let's talk to him. Maybe he can put something in the paper about it."

"I'll put a bounty on the head of whoever is responsible," Angelica threatened, and stalked off in the direction of the weekly newspaper. Tricia had to hurry to catch up.

Angelica banged on the big glass door. "Russ! Russ Smith! If you're in there, open the door."

It took a few moments, but finally Russ stuck his head out of his office door.

"Russ!" Tricia called.

He hurried for the door and quickly unlocked it. "What's the matter?"

"It's the flowers! They're gone!" Angelica cried.

"Calm down—calm down. Come on in and sit down and tell me what on earth is going on."

Angelica was so upset that her explanation made no sense, so Tricia took over.

Finally Russ waved his hands to end the tirade. "Okay, I got it, I got it. But it's too late to put an item in the paper. It's already gone to bed for the week."

"Oh, no!" Angelica wailed.

"Now, now—don't panic. I've got another idea," Russ said. "You say you've still got fake flowers you can put in some of the baskets?"

Tricia nodded.

"We can capture the guy on video."

"How?" Angelica demanded.

"Boris and Alexa Kozlov over at the Coffee Bean bought a camera when someone was filling their Dumpsters with trash. I'll bet if you asked Alexa, she'd be fine with loaning it to you."

"She loves the flowers—she's told me that many times," Angelica agreed.

"Maybe she could even get Boris to set it up for you."

"That's a great idea," Tricia said.

"I'll go over to the Coffee Bean the second they open in the morning and ask," Angelica said.

"But first we've got to beautify all those pots of greenery," Tricia said, starting to feel weary. Like Angelica, her good mood had evaporated when they'd found the flowers missing once more.

"There's no point in replacing the flowers until we get that camera installed," Angelica said, and stood.

Tricia and Russ stood as well. "I agree," Tricia said. She looked at Russ for a long moment. "By the way, what are you doing here at the office so late at night when your wife is about to give birth?"

Russ shook his head. "Nikki's not due for at least another week. I waited for her to fall asleep before coming here. If she wakes up, she knows where I am. I can be home in two minutes."

Tricia frowned. Two minutes could be a long time if you needed to get to the hospital fast. But that was Russ and Nikki's decision, and she wasn't about to voice her opinion on the subject.

Angelica reached the door and turned. "Thank you, Russ. I was so distraught, I don't think I'd have ever remembered the Koslov's had that surveillance camera. But even if they didn't, I'd pay big-time to get one put up so we could catch the vandal who's ruining our flowers."

"Keep me posted. It might make a fun story for next week's issue," he said before closing and locking the door behind them.

The sisters stood on the sidewalk outside the office. "I'm glad you saw Russ's light on. Maybe by tomorrow we'll have this mess with the flowers cleared up."

"You mean two days from now," Tricia complained, and shook her head.

"At least we'll get to bed at a halfway decent hour tonight," Angelica said. "For now, I'm going to put it out of my head and fall asleep and dream about my new grandchild."

"You. A grandma. And you look spectacular," Tricia teased.

"Don't I just?" They laughed. It felt good. "Okay, it's time for us to go our separate ways. I'll see you in the morning." Angelica gave Tricia a hug and they split up, with Tricia heading north for the Chamber and Angelica south for the Cookery. Tricia's footfalls echoed—something she never heard during daylight hours. Main Street was well lit, and she often walked home alone at night from the Dog-Eared Page without fear. But the hairs on the back of her neck prickled as though someone were watching her. She quickened her pace.

She was about to turn up the Chamber's driveway and walk to the back door when she saw one of the silk flowers lying on the sidewalk. She picked it up and looked around, but saw no one. Turning, she hurried for the door. The security light snapped on, bathing her in harsh light as she fumbled to unlock the door. Once inside, she double-locked the door and fought the urge to turn on every light in the place. Instead, she padded through the converted house to the darkened office up front and peered out the window. Across the way she thought she could see movement. Yes, someone dressed in dark clothing and a hoodie carried a large black garbage bag and skulked away.

Could it have been the late-night petal pincher?

FIFTEEN

Tricia hated the expression "slept like the dead," but that's exactly what had happened when she'd laid her head upon her pillow. And yet her sleep was not restful. Hours later, she'd awoken feeling foggy and somewhat disoriented. She was glad to give in to her usual routine of rising, walking, and buying coffee.

The Coffee Bean was between customers when she walked in. Alexa stood behind the counter. "Ah, the other sister," she called, and laughed.

Tricia glanced at her watch. It was only seven thirty. Had Angelica beaten her there?

"I take it Angelica has already been over to see you?"

"Yes, and we are thrilled to help her catch the felon ruining the flowers," she said with just a trace of a Russian accent.

A misdemeanor, maybe, but Tricia wasn't about to argue with the barista. "Thank you."

"Now, your usual brew?" Alexa asked.

A minute later, Tricia was on her way back to the Chamber to shower, dress, eat a modest breakfast, and feed her cat before starting the rest of her day.

The morning sun blazed through the Chamber's front windows, giving the office a kind of cheerful glow. Mariana arrived, made a pot of coffee, turned on her radio, and all was right with the world.

The phone rang at 9:32, and caller ID told Tricia it was none other than Mr. Everett. She picked up the receiver with pleasure.

"Hello, Mr. Everett. How are you this lovely morning?"

"Very well indeed," he said, and his voice conveyed his own pleasure. Oh, how she'd missed seeing the elderly gent on a daily basis.

"What's up?"

"I've spoken with someone at the Historical Society about Peter Renquist's memorial service. Naturally, they're just as upset that Ms. Koch was assaulted. They would prefer to wait several weeks for her to recover—"

If she recovers, Tricia thought to herself.

"—before they plan any kind of service for Mr. Renquist. As she knew him best, they feel she should speak for the Society."

"That does seem reasonable," Tricia admitted.

"However, I did learn that there will be a gathering of Peter's friends and some of his colleagues at the Dog-Eared Page this evening at about eight o'clock. I knew you would want to attend."

"I certainly do."

"Peter's friends are invited to share their memories of him."

"Will you?" Tricia asked.

"I fear that my association with Peter was so long ago that it would be irrelevant. But I do want to pay my respects."

"Of course," Tricia said.

"Very good. Grace and I will see you then."

"Thank you, Mr. Everett."

"I must get back to work. Frannie has a big box of books for me to inventory. It's great fun, I must confess. I'll see you this evening."

"See you then. Good-bye."

Tricia replaced the receiver, staring at it for a long moment, but then the phone rang again. She picked it up. "Stoneham Chamber of Commerce. This is Tricia. How may I help you?"

"Hello, love. Are you available for lunch?"

Tricia smiled at the sound of the voice with the lilting English accent. "Why, yes, I am. What did you have in mind, Michele?"

"The weather is spectacular, and I think it would be brilliant to have a picnic lunch. Are you game?"

Tricia couldn't remember the last time she'd been on a real picnic. "Sounds wonderful. Where?"

"The Stoneham Rural Cemetery."

"Oh!" Tricia said with a start.

"I want to do a preliminary scout to get a feel for the place, and as you're going to be my study-buddy, I thought you might enjoy a ramble through the graves. It'll be great fun," she insisted.

Tricia tried to sound positive. "If you say so. Where shall we meet? What should I bring?"

"You don't need to bring anything. We can meet right in the parking lot at the cemetery's front entrance. Unless there's a funeral, there shouldn't be a crowd." She laughed.

"What time?"

"Is one o'clock too late?"

"It's just fine," Tricia said. "I'll see you there."

"Brilliant. Cheerio."

"Bye." Tricia put the phone down.

"Got a hot lunch date with that hunky guy?" Mariana asked eagerly.

Tricia's expression soured. "No. I'm picnicking with a friend."

"Going anywhere romantic?" she asked slyly.

"The cemetery."

"Oh," Mariana said, startled.

Tricia tried not to smile, with limited success. She had no problem confounding Mariana.

The short ride along Stoneham's back roads to the Stoneham Rural Cemetery was pleasant and treelined. The humidity had dropped, and as Michele had said, the weather was spectacular. As Tricia pulled into the nearly empty parking lot, she recognized Michele's car. Michele sat behind the driver's wheel, speaking into her cell phone. Tricia parked, got out of her car, and approached Michele's. Across the way a middle-aged woman and a much older man stood over a grave. The woman was arranging a colorful bunch of flowers in an urn attached to a headstone while the old man wiped tears from his eyes. A picnic seemed so frivolous when others were in pain.

Still, Michele was here to celebrate the lives of the cemetery's historical denizens—or at least bring attention to some of its more noteworthy occupants. Noteworthy if not infamous in some capacity.

Michele saw Tricia, waved, and quickly finished her conversation. She put the phone away and got out of her car. Key fob in hand, she popped the hatch of her Mini Cooper. "I hope you brought your appetite. The Brookview Inn is very generous with their portions."

"I'll try to make a dent," Tricia promised.

Michele lifted a straw picnic basket out of the trunk, and Tricia shut the hatch.

"Hmm, it's heavier than I thought," Michele admitted. "It must be the iced tea—or maybe the cold packs. Would you mind?" she asked, offering Tricia one of the basket's handles. It was a bit awkward, but the basket was indeed heavy. "There's a bench under a tree not far from here."

"Lead the way," Tricia said.

The sun beat down on them as they made their way down the narrow ribbon of asphalt that wound through the cemetery. As it was older than the other cemeteries in the area, this one still allowed headstone monuments instead of flat markers. The monuments near the front of the cemetery were older, some of them wind-worn, chipped, and difficult to read.

"I wonder what these tombstones are made of," Tricia said idly.

"Primarily granite, marble, and limestone," Michele said, and gave a small laugh. "I've already started my research."

"You really enjoy this, don't you?" Tricia asked.

"I think the ghost walks will be great fun and a wonderful fund-raiser for the cemetery. It costs money to maintain these old graves, and these monuments are all that's left for the world to know about the generations of people who lived and died here in Stoneham."

"Sounds like you've adopted the village—and its predecessors."

"I enjoy living here. When I was offered the job of managing the Dog-Eared Page, I wondered if I'd miss living in a larger city, but I don't. I grew up in a small village in England, and while Stoneham is nothing like it, it's a slower pace, and I'm at a time in life where I enjoy that."

Tricia looked ahead to where a line of white oaks made a barrier not far from the black wrought iron fence that was the cemetery's east border. As Michele had indicated, there was shade and a wood-and-metal bench painted forest green. In a minute, they'd made their way over to the bench and sat down. Michele opened the basket and removed a thermos and two plastic cups, setting them on the bench between them, then withdrew two square foam containers, handing one of them to Tricia.

Tricia opened her container to find two pieces of fried chicken, a small scoop of potato salad, two deviled egg halves, and a small plastic container that held what looked like pickled watermelon rind. "Oh, how lovely," she said.

"Very American," Michele said, pouring tea for them both. It was unsweetened with lemon, just what Tricia was used to.

"What did you take on a picnic in England?" Tricia asked, accepting the paper napkins Michele handed her.

"Cornish pasties. Scotch eggs. Grosvenor pie. Cheese-and-pickle sandwiches, or perhaps sausage rolls. I must make a batch soon—I've had a hankering for them for a while now."

"I don't think I've ever had them."

"Then you're in for a treat. I'll save you some."

Tricia tasted the potato salad. It needed salt. As though anticipating her request, Michele dug through the basket and came up with a shaker. She opened the lid and handed it to Tricia.

"I must say, I prefer to salt my food myself, don't you?" she asked Tricia.

"Yes." She sprinkled a little on the salad. Perfect.

They ate for a minute or two in silence, enjoying the quiet as a gentle breeze caused the leafy branches above them to sway.

"You're probably wondering why I asked you to come here today," Michele said at last.

"It had crossed my mind."

"I'm concerned about what happened to Janet Koch."

"You mean you think that her accident and Pete's death are connected?"

Michele nodded. "I'm very interested in the history and the upkeep of dear old cemeteries such as this, but I must admit, I'm a bit worried about doing the ghost walks—at least until your friend Chief Baker catches the person responsible for the attacks."

"I can't say I blame you," Tricia said, and took a bite of chicken leg.

Michele shook her head. "I'm probably just being paranoid, but for now I've decided not to talk about it to anyone."

"Have you told the Historical Society that you've changed your mind?"

Again she shook her head. "I still want to do the talks—and will prepare for them—but for the time being I would prefer not to advertise the fact. Now that Janet is out of commission, I'm not sure who to speak to at the Society."

"I'm pretty sure Mr. Everett knows everyone there. In fact, he told me this morning that there's to be a wake for Pete Renquist at the pub tonight. He and his wife intend to attend."

Michele nodded. "I'll ask him then. I've asked my bartender Shawn not to mention the ghost walks, and I'm asking you to do the same."

"Of course."

"Thank you."

Michele picked at her potato salad.

"Are you afraid?" Tricia asked.

"I'm a Brit. Stiff upper lip and all that, but I am concerned. I shouldn't like to be the next victim."

Tricia looked down at her half-eaten lunch. She'd lost her appetite.

She closed the lid on the foam box. At least she'd have leftovers for another lunch or dinner. It was time to change the subject. "What have you got planned for Pete's pseudo wake?"

Michele shrugged. "Not much. Just a gathering where people can toast their friend and colleague. Nigela Ricita has authorized me to order eats from the Brookview Inn." She laughed. "Company discount and all that. I'm sure Pete would have approved."

Tricia would have to thank Angelica for that, too. Somehow she'd missed—or ignored—seeing Angelica's softer, more thoughtful side, and felt a bit ashamed.

"You will be there," Michele said. It almost sounded like a commandment.

"Of course."

Michele smiled and nodded, then she, too, looked at her unfinished lunch and closed the lid. "I think I've had my fill for now. Would you like a brief tour of some of the older headstones and the stories I've learned about those buried beneath them?"

"Why not," Tricia said.

They repacked the picnic basket and stood. Michele led the way.

They walked for several minutes in companionable silence until they came upon a stately granite obelisk. "I know who's in this grave," Tricia said. "Hiram Stone, founder of Stoneham."

"You've got that right. I'm wondering what to say about him. I read the Founder's Day pap on the official Stoneham website."

"And you don't agree?"

"Oh, the facts are mainly right, but they've painted the man as a saint, and he was far from that."

"What's the dirt?" Tricia asked, intrigued.

"The man was a notorious drunk and a letch who was enamored with the local temperance leader."

"You made that up."

"No, I didn't—I promise you," Michele said, smiling. "He was so bad, the village leaders thought it best to try and marry him off. That didn't work, of course, because he was a dedicated skirt chaser. He was engaged to several women—probably gold diggers—who ultimately dumped him because they couldn't stand his philandering."

"He looks like such a staunch community leader in the portrait hanging in the village meeting hall."

"I'll let you in on a secret not many know. That isn't Hiram Stone."

"Who is it?" Tricia asked, shocked.

Michele shrugged. "At some point the village board decided they needed to honor the man, but all they had was this monument," she said, indicating the tall pillar of granite before them. "One of the selectmen went on a trip to New York and bought the painting at an auction house. When he returned, the board announced finding a long-lost portrait of the village founder."

Tricia shook her head, smiling wryly. "It makes a good story."

"But I'm not sure the current Board of Selectmen would want me to tell it. Don't worry. My research isn't quite finished. I'll find other wonderful stories to tell about the old gent."

"I have no doubt you will," Tricia said, a smile tugging at her lips.

They walked deeper into the cemetery, Michele pointing out several of the more unusual monuments with a funny or poignant story to go with each of them. Saddest of all were the graves of a family of children who'd died as the result of a virus. It was so sad to think that the diseases of the past had taken such a devastating toll on those with no access to the wonder drugs available to protect today's children. How had their parents fared with such overwhelming loss? How had they carried on without those babies they'd loved with such tender care?

Finally, they wound their way back to the cemetery's front entrance and their cars. The lot was empty now, but in the distance Tricia saw a figure watching them from the far side of the graveyard. It was a man, or at least she thought so, but from such a distance she really couldn't be sure. And why was he staring at them?

Then again, maybe *she* was paranoid. The person was probably just facing in their direction, staring at a headstone, grieving for a loved one. She turned back to Michele.

"Thank you for a lovely lunch."

"Don't forget your leftovers," Michele said, opening the picnic basket and extracting Tricia's foam container, handing it to her.

"Thank you. I guess I'll see you later this evening."

"I'm looking forward to it."

"See you then," Tricia said, and got into her car. She started the engine and backed out of the parking space. But before she hit the accelerator to leave, she could have sworn she saw that the figure in the graveyard was still staring at them.

SIXTEEN

 By the time Tricia made it back to the Chamber office, Pixie had arrived for her afternoon stint, and Mariana was full of questions about the cemetery lunch.

"It wasn't that big a deal. We ate fried chicken and potato salad and did a lot of girl talk."

"About what?" Mariana pressed.

Tricia shook her head. "I don't know. I didn't record our conversation."

Mariana pursed her lips and went back to her desk, looking disappointed. Had her day been so dull that she wanted to live vicariously through someone's—anyone's—adventure, however dull?

"I think it's a cool place to have lunch," Pixie said. "I heard the Historical Society is going to have ghost walks this fall. I'm going to sign up. I wonder if they'll have a special Halloween ghost walk? Do you think they'd want people to come in costume? I love to dress up."

Tricia inspected Pixie's costume of the day, which was a navy-themed dress with white piping and a jaunty sailor's cap to top it off. For a stocky, dyed-redheaded, gold-toothed woman on the high side of fifty, Pixie looked quite cute.

Luckily, the subject was soon dropped, and the rest of the afternoon was lost to phone calls, paperwork, and envelope stuffing.

Mariana left right on time at five o'clock, which gave Tricia and Pixie time to talk, and it was then she realized she'd been waiting all afternoon to live vicariously through Pixie's new adventures in love land. "Are you spending the evening with Fred?" she asked.

"Yep. It's a big day for us. Our two-month anniversary. We're celebrating by getting tattoos."

Tricia gaped. "But . . . isn't it early in the relationship for that?"

Pixie shrugged. "We talked about that. So I'm getting the sun, and he's getting the moon. They're usually done together as one tat. Later, if things work out, I'll get the moon, and he'll get the sun. It's kind of like a promise we're making to each other."

Promise rings wouldn't be half as permanent.

"You ever think of getting a tat?" Pixie asked.

"I can honestly say no."

"Everybody gets 'em nowadays. You could get a little book on your arm or ankle. It would be cute, but you need to go to a place that does quality work."

"It sounds like you've done your homework on this."

"Ya gotta. Otherwise, you end up looking like an old rummy sailor who got drunk and went to a hack. I'm wearing this tat to the grave and it *has* to look good."

"You're braver than me," Tricia said sincerely.

Pixie waved a hand in dismissal. "Are you kidding? You've stared down killers. That's not something I could do, so a tattoo would be pretty easy stuff for a stand-up chick like you."

Stand-up chick, huh? Tricia liked the sound of that.

Pixie waxed poetic on all the tattoos she'd seen in prison and beyond, then segued into her latest pedicure and wax—more information than Tricia really wanted to know, but she listened transfixed nonetheless. No doubt about it, Pixie could spin a story. Maybe she'd be interested in volunteering to be a docent for the Historical Society, too, some day.

All too soon it was time for Pixie to leave. Tricia watched as she grabbed her things and headed for the door.

"Hey, wait a minute." Pixie paused. "When am I going to get to meet Fred?"

"You really want to?"

"Well, of course I do," Tricia said.

"Gee, maybe you could stop by Booked for Lunch around ten thirty some morning. That's when he makes his delivery."

"Sounds good. Maybe I could scrounge a cup of coffee from Angelica at the same time."

Pixie grinned. "I'll bet you could."

"All right. How about we plan it for some time next week?"

"Great." Pixie headed for the door once more. "See ya tomorrow. And I'll show off my tat as soon as I get in." And out the door she went.

Tricia frowned. Pixie hadn't mentioned just where this tattoo was going to go. Tricia just hoped it wasn't going to be on an embarrassing body part.

With time to kill before she was to meet Angelica at her loft apartment, Tricia went out back to water the perennials that some previous owner had planted along the west side of the house.

Distracted by thoughts of possible tattoos she might one day get, she was halfway through the job, facing away from the drive, when a noise from behind caused her to turn with a start.

"Bob Kelly, what are you doing here at this time of day?" Tricia asked, nearly watering his shoes with the hose. He took a step back.

"I need you to make a decision, and I need it now," Bob demanded, his tone formidable.

"Bob, what's gotten into you?" Tricia asked, turning so that the water ran into the grass.

"Do I have to spell it out for you?"

"Yes!"

"I need the money. I'm going to jail unless I can keep paying that shark of an attorney of mine."

"You mean because you ransacked your own property?"

"No, because I never finished my community service."

"I thought that all blew over."

"It didn't. I've tried to keep it quiet, but it looks like they're going to make me do time, and when I get out, I'll be on probation, and not only will I have to finish my community service, but I'll be stuck with even more of it."

Oh, what a tangled web, Tricia thought without pity.

"What about all the rent you collect? You own half the village."

"Make that past tense."

"You've sold some of your properties?"

"Not on Main Street, except for the lot where History Repeats Itself used to be. And now maybe your building, but only because it's a wreck and I might have to put a lot of money into it if you leave without fixing it."

"Don't think I haven't thought of that," Tricia said evenly.

"You've got the money," Bob said.

Tricia did have the money, but she didn't like being pressured. And she didn't want to pay more than fair-market value, either. He'd already stuck her for more than fair-market rent. "And how would you know about my financial situation?" she bluffed. Angelica had probably told him. It seemed like she'd shared an awful lot of information with him.

"I have my ways."

Tricia looked at him with suspicion. "Have you hacked into the bank's files?"

Bob looked away.

Nobody knew how Betsy Dittmeyer, the Chamber's former receptionist, had established so many bogus accounts in banks all over the country to hide her ill-gotten gains. Had she confided to Bob how she'd done it when she'd worked for him? Had they worked together? Probably not. If Bob could have gotten his hands on that money, he would have already done so. And once the accounts had been turned over to the district attorney, they were frozen so no one would have access to them.

"I haven't done anything illegal," he said at last.

"Since you vandalized Stan Berry's home you mean?"

"Yes," he said bitterly. "But I've considered doing something very stupid if I can't buy my way out of this conviction."

"And what's that?"

"I'm not about to tell *you*."

Was he bluffing, or was he actually that desperate?

Tricia studied Bob's face. The skin along his jaw was taut with worry, and the strain he was under was evident by his stooped posture.

"Come on, Tricia, buy the damn building." He reached into the inner breast pocket of his rumpled green sports coat and pulled out a sheaf of papers. "I've filled out the sales contract, all you have to do is—"

"No!" Tricia cried.

Bob slammed his fist against the home's shingles, and Tricia jumped back, dropping the hose, afraid he might hit her, too. She'd never before been afraid of Bob Kelly, but at that moment she was. She took a shaky breath. "You'd better leave, Bob. Now. I don't want to be forced to call the Stoneham Police Department to drag you away."

Bob shoved the papers back into his pocket. "You haven't heard the last of this, Tricia."

Tricia took another shaky breath but stood tall. "Are you threatening me?"

But Bob didn't answer. Instead, he pivoted and stormed off.

Still feeling shaky, Tricia realized the grass all around her was wet from the still gushing hose. Her hands were trembling as she turned off the water, coiled the hose, and replaced it on the rusty metal holder attached to the house. Taking a deep breath, she walked around the side of the building and walked up the ramp to the side entrance, which she'd left unlocked. For a moment she worried that Bob might have gone inside and was waiting for her, but Miss Marple sat in the middle of the hall leading to the office and didn't seem at all alarmed.

Tricia stepped forward and picked up the cat, which nestled its head against her chin and began to purr with enthusiasm. "Thank you for being here, Miss Marple. At this moment, I need a kitty hug." Miss Marple did not hug back, but her obvious affection helped Tricia to feel calmer.

All too soon, Miss Marple jumped down from Tricia's embrace. Just as well. Tricia was going to be late meeting Angelica. She grabbed her keys, made sure she left the outside light switched on, and left the house. It would be late when she returned from Pete's wake—or from replacing the silk flowers. Would Bob be waiting for her? She tried not to think about it as she made her way down Main Street toward the Cookery.

The store had been closed a good half hour before Tricia arrived. She unlocked the door and let herself in. By the time she climbed the stairs to Angelica's loft, she heard Sarge announcing her arrival with shrill barks and remembered that she'd forgotten to grab one of his dog biscuits before leaving the Chamber office. Oh well, she'd give him two the next time she saw him.

"Hello!" she called over the sound of barking. Once Sarge realized who the intruder was, his barking immediately switched from menace to welcome.

"Come on back to the kitchen," Angelica hollered.

Tricia cautiously made her way down the hall with Sarge bouncing along at her side. As they entered the kitchen, Angelica said, "Hush!"

The barking immediately stopped, and Sarge looked at Tricia with hopeful eyes, his pink tongue lolling out the side of his mouth. "I forgot his biscuit."

"You know where I keep them," Angelica said, and Tricia helped herself to one from the canister on the counter. Sarge sat up pretty and accepted the biscuit, then scurried off to his bed to enjoy it.

"What's for dinner?" Tricia asked as Angelica piped yolk mixture into half of an egg.

"Just leftovers from the café, I'm afraid. Salads mostly. And we had a lot of eggs left over, so I'm making deviled eggs."

"Quite a few. What's that, two dozen halves?"

Angelica nodded. "I thought I could take them to the Dog-Eared Page for Pete's wake later on."

"Good idea," Tricia said. "Who told you about the wake?"

"Nobody. I kind of suggested it."

"You did?"

"Well, Michele Fowler is the one who got the word around. I just put a bug in her ear."

"She said Nigela Ricita authorized eats for Pete's wake."

Angelica shrugged. "Sad people drink too much. We don't want anyone to get drunk, have an accident, and sue us."

That sounded like the words of a businesswoman, but Tricia didn't believe it for a minute. Angelica equated food with love. It was so like her to want to feed people—especially those who were grieving.

"What kind of a day did you have?"

"Busy. I had lunch with Michele at the Stoneham Rural Cemetery."

"Not my kind of lunch venue," Angelica said, wrinkling her nose.

"It was quite nice, actually. She already knows quite a bit of local history—and good gossip, too."

"And what was the occasion?"

"She doesn't want me talking to anyone about the ghost walks."

"And so you're telling me," Angelica said, looking up from her handiwork.

"You won't repeat it. She's worried that whoever killed Pete and came after Janet might mark her next."

"I can't say I blame her," Angelica moved on to another egg half. "Anything happen at the Chamber today that I should know about?"

"Everything's putting along just fine, but I did have a bit of a scare just before I came here. Bob came to visit me, and he wasn't friendly."

Angelica looked up. "What do you mean?"

"He shoved a sales contract for my building in my face, and when I wouldn't sign, he slammed his fist into the side of the house."

"Bob threatened you?" Angelica repeated incredulously.

Tricia nodded. "And he meant to frighten me. He's determined not to go to jail. He said he might be forced to do something stupid. What do you think that means?"

Angelica shrugged. "I don't know. Liquidate his assets?"

"I'm serious."

"So am I," Angelica said. "Bob's family had nothing. Everything he has he earned through hard work." She shook her head. "It upsets me to think he threatened you. I didn't think he would stoop that low."

"I'll admit, I was actually afraid."

"Have you told Grant Baker about this encounter?" Angelica said, and piped the remaining yolk mixture into the last egg half.

"No, it happened just before I left to come here. But maybe I should."

"What about Christopher?"

"No. And I don't want you telling him, either."

"It wouldn't hurt to have someone tall and imposing to act as your bodyguard for a few days or weeks," Angelica said, and bent down to retrieve paprika from her spice stash.

"No," Tricia reiterated.

"All right. I'll promise not to tell him, but only if you *do* speak to Grant. Now, promise me."

"I promise."

"Good. I'm sure we can get a couple of people to walk you home after the wake. Perhaps Antonio, if he shows up," Angelica said, and sprinkled a good measure of paprika over the eggs.

"Why wouldn't he come?"

"Oh, Ginny had an upset stomach this afternoon. He may not want to leave her . . . just in case it's time for the baby to arrive."

"Oh, dear. Keep me posted, will you?"

"Of course."

"I hear you spoke to the Koslovs about their camera."

Angelica nodded and pulled the plastic wrap from one of the drawers. "Boris wasn't keen to set it up, but Alexa is furious about the flowers being destroyed. She had him set it up right outside their door, so I thought we could start there with our replanting."

"Fine with me."

"Good." She covered the eggs and put them into the fridge. "Now, let's eat. We don't want to be late for Pete's wake. I'll pass the leftovers and you can choose what you want."

Tricia stood to receive the bounty and was nearly overwhelmed by the foam containers Angelica handed her—five in all. Tricia placed them on the big granite island and opened them. Angelica hadn't been kidding when she said salads. Egg salad, tuna salad, ham salad, chicken salad, and a leafy green salad.

Angelica supplied plates, serving spoons, forks, and a couple of rolls. "Dig in."

Tricia picked up a spoon and doled out greens, then topped them with a small helping from each of the other salads. "This is my second picnic of the day," she said.

"Picnics to me mean fun," Angelica said. "Nothing to do with the pressures of the day, just relaxation." She held up a finger. "Hang on, I forgot the best part." She reached into the cupboard behind her and bought out a bag of barbeque potato chips.

"Good Lord—the calories!" Tricia cried.

"You don't *have* to eat any," Angelica said, opening the bag and spilling some onto her plate.

"The hell I don't," Tricia said, and took the bag from her sister, dumping a small portion onto her waiting plate. Then she paused, staring at the bag and the bounty before her. "This reminds me of the time Grandma Miles took just the two of us to Cove Island Park."

"I remember," Angelica gushed. "Oh, we had so much fun that day. She brought along a couple of plastic bottles of bubbles, and we blew them at each other until we were both sticky."

Tricia smiled. "You know, I think that's my happiest childhood memory."

"Really?" Angelica asked.

Tricia nodded. "At the time, Grandma was the person I loved the best, and now it's you."

"Oh, don't be silly," Angelica said, and grabbed one of the rolls.

"I'm not. I'm being honest."

"I'm sorry to say that it took us both too long to appreciate each other. But you know, now that you know about my secret life, I think we could have a helluva good time together."

"You want to share it with me?"

"I thought I made that clear the other day. And now with Antonio and Ginny and their kids . . . Just think of the fun we all could have." She eyed Tricia with a sly grin. "Are you game?"

Tricia's mouth curved into a smile, and she remembered what Pixie had said. "You bet your ass."

SEVENTEEN

The Dog-Eared Page was quite literally hopping—or at least several couples were dancing quite energetically to the beat of music that blared from the pub's sound system when Tricia and Angelica arrived. Tricia held the door open for her sister, who carried a large tray with the deviled eggs and a full-sized carrot cake.

"Ah, there you are," Michele called over the cacophony issuing from the speakers. "You can set that down over on that table in the corner."

Angelica nodded and threaded her way through the crowd, which was at least three-deep at the bar. The eats table was loaded with platters of cold cuts, various rolls, condiments, pasta and potato salads, grapes, berries, and pineapple, different cheeses, and cookies. Nigela Ricita had been very generous.

Suddenly, the music ended, catching several people off guard, who'd been yelling to be heard. Looking sheepish, they lowered their voices. Within seconds an old Beatles tune—and much quieter—issued from the sound system: "In My Life."

The crowd stopped talking, listening to the haunting lyrics, growing somber. When the music ended, Michele raised her glass. "To Pete. God rest his soul."

"To Pete," the majority of patrons echoed, raising their glasses. Tricia didn't even know most of the people who'd come to pay their respects to Pete. She and Angelica snaked their way through the crowd to get to the bar, where they ordered drinks: a martini for Angelica and a glass of Chardonnay for Tricia. With glasses in hand, they again made their way through the crowd to a booth on the side where Grace and Mr. Everett sat across from each other. Tricia sat next to Mr. E while Angelica eased in beside Grace.

The music hadn't come back on, but the murmur of many voices made it difficult to hear.

"Glad you could join us," Grace practically shouted. Before her sat a half-finished glass of her favorite sherry. Before Mr. Everett was a tall glass of what looked like ginger ale.

"Did you have something to eat?" Angelica asked.

"Not yet. What did you bring?"

"Curried deviled eggs and a carrot cake."

Grace Harris-Everett's eyes widened in delight. It was no secret that, like half the village, she loved Angelica's carrot cake. "That sounds delightful."

Suddenly the air was pierced with the sound of someone hitting a glass with a spoon, which effectively cut through the din. The murmur of voices died to nothing, and Michele again addressed the group. "A few of Pete's friends would like to speak. First, his next-door neighbor, Sandra Marshall."

An elderly woman sidled up to the bar. There wasn't a sound in the room when she started to speak. "Ten years ago, Pete Renquist bought the house next to mine. My husband, Donald, had had a stroke and could no longer take care of our yard or driveway, but Pete stepped up to help. In the spring, summer, and fall, he'd cut my grass. In the winter he and his snowblower cleared my drive. I don't know what I would have done without him. I don't know how I'll manage without him. I'll miss his kindness. I'll miss his sweet smile, his generosity. I don't believe anyone ever had a better neighbor than Pete Renquist—" Her voice broke, and tears filled her eyes. She raised her glass, and everyone drank in Pete's honor.

"We have others who want to toast Pete, too," Michele said.

This time, a man of about thirty approached the bar. At Michele's nod, he spoke. "I'm sorry, I don't know a lot of you. My name is Rob Weber. I worked with Pete for the past two years at the Historical Society. He's been a mentor to me, a real friend. I didn't know a soul when I took the job and moved here, but he helped me find a place to live, even fed me for the first couple of weeks while I struggled to figure out a new town. He was a great guy." Rob raised his glass, and everyone toasted.

Michele nodded in their direction, and Angelica picked up her glass and stood, then made her way over to the bar. Everyone quieted down once again.

"As president of the Stoneham Chamber of Commerce, I was privileged to spend time with Pete Renquist these last eight months. During that time we formed a solid working relationship that brought benefit to not only the Historical Society, but the people of Stoneham and its merchants. Though at times Pete could have a bit of a sharp tongue, he was never a bully. Like me, he came to love our little adopted village and had only its best interests at heart. We shall miss him." She raised her glass. "To Pete."

"To Pete."

Angelica returned to the table. Michele nodded toward the back of the room, and a number of people stepped aside to let the next speaker move up to the bar. Tricia's eyes widened in surprise as she recognized Toni Bennett. She looked around, but the antique dealer's contractor husband was nowhere in sight.

Toni's face was flushed and her eyes were red-rimmed. She'd obviously been crying.

She spoke a few words too low for Tricia to hear. She cupped her ear as a male voice called out, "Can't hear you!"

Toni started again. "Pete Renquist was my friend." She stopped, wiping a tissue over her eyes, mopping the tears that leaked from them. "We worked together at the Stoneham Historical Society. He as an employee, me as a volunteer," she managed, her voice breaking.

"Her performance is a little over the top, don't you think?" Angelica whispered from across the table. Tricia held a finger to her lips and shushed her sister.

"I never met such a kind, considerate, and funny person," Toni continued.

Kinder, more considerate, and more fun than her husband? Tricia wondered. The hairs on the back of her neck prickled as Toni took a moment to collect her thoughts—and emotions—and Tricia turned to glance at the pub's front entrance, where she saw Jim Stark standing, his shoulders hunched, his lips pursed, his face flushed with what could only be anger. His gaze was riveted on his wife, who seemed oblivious to his presence.

"Pete had his faults—we all do—but I choose to remember only the good, and I hope you will, too," Toni said, and raised her glass.

Those all around her raised their glasses, too, and chorused, "To Pete."

This time, Tricia didn't raise her glass. She looked back to the pub's entrance in time to see that Stark was no longer there, and she heard the door shut with a bang.

"That was weird," Angelica said, just loud enough for Tricia to hear.

"You don't know the half of it," Tricia said.

"Will I?" Angelica asked coyly.

Tricia looked at the bottom of her rapidly diminishing drink. "Perhaps."

Toni drained her glass, placed it on the bar, and, without further adieu, headed for the exit. Tricia watched her go. By the time the door closed behind Toni, the next speaker stood before the bar.

They listened as four more of Pete's friends got up to give their heartfelt farewells. Afterward, Michele invited everyone to partake of the refreshments, and people swarmed the eats table.

"You'd better hurry if you want to get something to eat," Tricia encouraged her tablemates.

Angelica shook her head. "I'm not hungry."

"Nor am I," said Mr. Everett.

"I'd love a small slice of your wonderful carrot cake," Grace said.

"I'll go get you a piece," Tricia volunteered, and got up from the table. She made her way through the crowd, waiting for her turn. Out of the corner of her eye, she saw Bob Kelly standing at the back of the pub with a beer in hand. He didn't seem to be with anyone, and he had the expression of a hunted man. She turned away, only to find her ex-husband standing uncomfortably close.

"That was a nice speech Angelica gave," Christopher very nearly hollered over the din.

"Yes." Tricia didn't want to make eye contact and looked around the person standing in front of her, hoping there would still be cake by the time she made it to the table.

"I thought I might run into you here, Trish."

She said nothing, still staring ahead.

"I wanted to apologize again for the other night."

"I forgive you," Tricia said, still not looking at him.

"Can we talk?"

Finally she turned to him. "We are."

"I mean *really* talk."

"It seems like all we do is spar."

"We need to clear the air."

A man juggling a plate of food moved past them, allowing Tricia to step forward. Maybe she should just let Christopher talk and get it out of his system. Then maybe she could finally convince him that she wasn't interested in resuming any kind of relationship with him.

"Okay," she said at last. "I'm sitting with Grace and Mr. Everett. Once they leave, I'll talk to you."

Christopher immediately brightened. "Thanks, Trish. I'll leave you alone until then."

"Thank you."

Christopher stepped away, heading for the bar.

"What a crowd," the woman next to Tricia grumbled. "I had no idea Pete had so many friends." The woman was attractive, albeit a little overweight, but she knew how to dress to overcome that obstacle. Her hair was a pleasant shade of blonde, and the makeup she wore accentuated her pretty blue eyes, downplaying the wrinkles from years of smiles.

"Me, either," Tricia said.

"Were you a long-time friend of Pete's?" the woman asked.

Tricia shook her head. "I only met him in March. My shop burned down. While I wait for the insurance company to pay my claim, I'm volunteering at the Chamber of Commerce. My sister is its president."

"How nice. I mean about your sister. You must own the mystery store."

"Yes, I do."

"I met Pete during the restoration of the garden behind the Historical Society."

"It's lovely. I was just there the other day."

Several people peeled away from the eats table, and Tricia and the woman were able to advance two steps closer.

"It was a lot of work to get it back to the way it was when Hiram Stone lived in the house, and it will take a lot of work to keep it that way, but well worth it."

"It's very peaceful. Before her"—Tricia hesitated—"accident, Janet Koch said Pete's ashes would likely be scattered there."

The woman's smile was bittersweet. "He'd like that. He loved that house and the garden. I hope Pete rests in peace."

"Me, too," Tricia agreed with regret.

"I'm sorry. I should introduce myself. I'm Julia Harrison." The woman offered Tricia her hand, and they shook.

"Tricia Miles."

Julia Harrison—the woman Mariana had told Tricia about—just the person she had been hoping to meet. But how could she ask Julia about the relationship she'd never quite forged with Pete? She thought about it for a moment before an idea came to her.

"Pete was a sweetheart, but such a flirt," Tricia said, and shook her head, plastering what she hoped was a wry smile across her lips.

Julie laughed and shook her head, too.

Another few people—plates heaped with food—turned away from the table and sidled through the crowd. Tricia and Julia stepped forward once again.

"What's so funny?" Tricia asked.

"Pete. He was a great guy. Had a wonderful personality, but had an Achilles heel when it came to dating."

"Oh?" Tricia asked.

"I don't mean to speak ill of the dead, but—" Julia leaned closer and lowered her voice. "He suffered from ED."

For a moment Tricia was befuddled. *Ed?*

Julia seemed to note her confusion and whispered, "Erectile dysfunction."

Tricia's eyes widened. "Really?"

Julia nodded sadly. "Pete and I dated for a while. He was such a joy to be with. We could talk forever about the Historical Society, art, food, music—just about everything. But when it came to intimacy, we ran up against a brick wall."

"But there are medications for that," Tricia said.

"That's what I told him, but he wouldn't even consider it. He was too embarrassed to discuss it with even his doctor." She shook her head sadly. "I may have hit the big five-oh, but I'm not dead yet. It broke us apart."

"I'm so sorry."

"I was, too, but I got back into the dating game and met a great guy. I don't know if we'll end up together for the rest of our lives, but we enjoy each other's company and have fun—in and out of the sack." Julia giggled.

So, Pete's flirting was just an over-the-top attempt to make people believe he was some kind of lothario when in fact he was ashamed of a treatable medical condition. Tricia felt even sorrier for the poor man.

Finally, the last few people ahead of Tricia moved away from the decimated food table. Tricia was able to snag the last piece of carrot cake for Grace. She grabbed a plastic fork and some napkins while Julia scored a deviled egg, a roll, and a slice each of ham and cheese.

"It was nice to meet you, Julia."

"Same here. I'll make a point to visit your store when you reopen."

"Thank you," Tricia said, and turned, heading back for the table.

"Here you go," she said, handing Grace the plate.

"Thank you, dear," Grace said, and cut a small piece of cake. She sampled it and closed her eyes in bliss. When she swallowed, she said, "This has got to be the best carrot cake I've ever eaten. You are amazing, Angelica."

"I can't take credit for this one. Tommy, my short-order cook, took my recipe and bakes them on the side to make a few extra dollars. But don't tell Nikki Brimfield over at the Patisserie."

Grace smiled. "Your secret is safe with me."

"I didn't know Tommy baked, too," Tricia said.

"Yes. In fact, I'm worried that he'll soon leave me for another job. I'm paying him a lot, but if he'd be happier baking, then I don't want to stand in his way, either."

It was then Tricia remembered that Booked for Lunch's former short-order cook had been snatched up by the Brookview Inn to be its head chef. Angelica must have masterminded that, too, since she now owned most of the inn. Tricia frowned. It surprised her how many little good deeds Angelica had performed, and not only hadn't she flaunted her generosity, she'd managed to stay anonymous. Tricia smiled at her sister.

"What?" Angelica asked.

"Nothing."

"Shall I go get the car, dear?" Mr. Everett asked. "You'll be finished with your cake by the time I bring it around."

"Yes, why not?" Grace said.

Tricia got up from her seat so that Mr. Everett could leave.

"I'll say good night, ladies."

"Good night," the sisters chorused. They watched him leave. Other people seemed to have the same idea, and he was followed by several other couples.

Angelica turned to Grace. "You two are such a cute couple."

The elderly woman smiled. "We are rather cute."

"Mr. Everett is a dear. I know Frannie will be heartbroken when he goes back to work for Tricia."

"In the meantime, he looks forward to your coffee dates," Grace told Tricia.

"As do I." Tricia remembered Mr. Everett's assessment of Earl Winkler during their last conversation. If she asked, would Grace say what her husband wouldn't? "Mr. Everett and I talked about Pete the other day, and I mentioned Pete's little altercation with Selectman Winkler."

"William is no fan of Earl, and who can blame him?" Grace said.

"Oh?" Tricia said innocently.

"That man played a despicable trick on William back when he owned his grocery store."

"What did he do?" Angelica asked.

"As you know, Earl is an exterminator. His company handles all kinds of infestations, but he's been known around here as the rat killer."

"Rats?" Angelica asked, appalled.

"Are there really rats here in Stoneham?" Tricia asked.

"Not that I've ever seen, but I'm sure there are. Wherever there is garbage, there are rats," Grace said knowledgeably. "Anyway, one day some twenty or so years ago, Earl came into William's grocery store, and William actually saw him remove two brown mice from his coat and place them in the produce department."

"You're kidding," Angelica said, her mouth hanging open in disgust. Grace shook her head.

"Really? Did Mr. Everett confront him?" Tricia asked.

"Yes, but Earl swore William was lying, and you know that just isn't possible. William is incapable of even stretching the truth, let alone lying. But Earl swore his innocence and stormed out of the store. Needless to say, William set a couple of traps straight out of his hardware department, and in hours the mice were history."

"Did he call the police to report Earl?" Tricia asked.

"That's not William's way."

"Did he ever get his revenge?" Angelica asked.

Grace's lips quirked into a smile. "In a way. In those days William was a member of the Stoneham Businessman's Association, the forerunner of the Chamber of Commerce. Earl tried to join, but he was repeatedly blackballed."

"Mr. Everett blackballed him?" Tricia asked, surprised.

"That I don't know. I only know that Earl was not welcomed into the association."

"I know Earl's rebuffed every invitation we've made to invite him to be a member of the Chamber," Angelica said.

"He knows that some people in the village have long memories," Grace said. "I don't think he wants to take the chance of someone bringing up his past indiscretions."

"You mean he pulled that stunt on more than just poor Mr. Everett?" Angelica asked, concerned.

Grace nodded.

"I will *definitely* take him off our to-be-contacted list."

They heard a horn outside go *toot-toot!* "That will be William. I don't want to keep him waiting," Grace said, and gathered her purse and sweater. Angelica got up and let her leave the booth, and Tricia rose, too.

"I'm sorry we had to see each other on such a sad occasion, but it's always nice to spend time with both of you."

Tricia leaned forward and gave Grace a quick peck on the cheek. "See you soon."

She and Angelica watched their friend leave before taking their seats again.

"Mr. Everett said you were speaking with Christopher earlier," Angelica said.

Tricia pursed her lips and nodded.

"What's he want now?" Angelica asked.

"To talk. I told him I'd do that as soon as Grace and Mr. Everett left."

"Then I guess I'd better go."

"I don't mean to chase you away."

"I have a million e-mails I can attend to before you and I go on flower patrol once again. And it'll give me time to change, too."

Tricia looked at her watch. It was barely nine o'clock. "All right. I'll see you about eleven."

"Eleven it is," Angelica said, and stood. She hesitated. "Here he comes. You'll have to tell all later, and I want to know more about Toni Bennett, too."

"Don't worry. I'll fill you in on all the details."

"See you later," Angelica said, and stepped over to the bar to speak to Michele. Christopher wasted no time slipping into the other side of the booth.

"Hi. Can I buy you a drink?"

Tricia looked at her empty glass, but decided not to encourage him. "No, thank you. So, what did you want to talk about?"

"Our relationship."

"We don't have one," she reminded him.

"But we could again."

Tricia frowned. "Funny, when I made the same request six years ago, you didn't want to see a counselor, and discussion was definitely off the table."

"I was in a bad place back then."

"And I acknowledged that—time and again. But still, you didn't give much consideration for my feelings. What I wanted or felt meant nothing to you."

"I'm sorry. I couldn't see beyond my own pain."

His pain? He'd never uttered such descriptive verbiage in the past. Had he been talking to a shrink?

"You hurt me," Tricia said. She needed to be blunt if she was finally going to get her point across. "And saying you're now sorry doesn't do anything to change the past. Fool me once, shame on you. I'm not about to give you—or anyone else," she said, thinking of Chief Baker, "the opportunity to fool me again."

Christopher's frown deepened, and he shook his head in disapproval. "My, but you've become cynical."

Oh, how she wanted to unleash her ire at him, but she'd been brought up to keep those kinds of feelings suppressed. The Miles family had been so good at keeping secrets and feelings from interfering with life. And honestly, if Christopher didn't now understand how much he'd hurt her with his past actions, he never would.

Tricia wished she'd taken him up on his offer of a drink, for she felt like she needed something to fortify herself. Still, she charged ahead. "You divorced me."

"And you didn't contest it," Christopher accused.

"Because you were adamant about not going to counseling. You had your mind set to shed me from your life. Well, you don't get to have that life back just because you now find it inconvenient."

"Inconvenient?" he repeated in disbelief.

"Yes. If I didn't do the work myself, I had to hire someone who would. We both had careers, but mine took a backseat, and I had to make sure that our house was clean, our laundry was done, our bills were paid, and everything else that goes with running a home."

"You never cooked," he accused.

"And you preferred to go out to eat fat-laden steaks and drink too much."

"You always paint me as the bad guy."

"You left me," Tricia repeated succinctly.

"But not for another woman."

"And that's supposed to make me feel better?"

"Yes!"

Tricia looked away and sighed. "Which proves my point. You have no clue who I am or what I need. And why in God's name would you think I'd take you back?"

"Because you love me."

Those four words hit like a blow below the belt. "Sorry, pal, but that's no longer enough."

"What do I have to do to regain your trust?"

Tricia looked into her ex-husband's beautiful green eyes, and a pang of regret shadowed her heart. "Erase the past. But you can't do that. Nobody can."

"If I could erase the past, I would. All I can do now is apologize for my arrogance."

"And I accept that apology. But that doesn't mean I can forget."

"You make me sound like a monster."

"You're not a monster, but you're no saint, either. Believe it or not, I've made a life without you. It was difficult at first, and for a time it was lonely, but all in all, it's been satisfying."

"Are you content to be just satisfied when there's so much more to life?"

She answered honestly. "For now, yes."

Christopher looked down at his hands, folded on the table before him. "I'm sorry you feel that way. You'll never know just how sorry. Can we at least be friends?"

"We *are*," Tricia said truthfully. Just not destined to ever be *close* friends, and especially not friends with benefits.

"Are you and Angelica going to be replacing the flowers once again tonight?" Christopher asked

"Yes. We're meeting at eleven."

"What are you going to do until then?"

"Go home, change my clothes, spend some time with my cat."

"*Our* cat."

"She doesn't belong to you anymore."

"Miss Marple doesn't know that."

"Well, I do."

Tricia scooted across the booth and got up. "Well, it has not been fun, but good night."

"Wait. Can I walk you home?"

For a moment, Tricia remembered the feeling of being watched the night before but decided she must have been mistaken, since the figure in black had shown up after she'd gone inside the Chamber building. "No, thank you. It's only two blocks. I'll be fine."

He grinned. "Yes, you are fine."

Tricia did not smile. "Good night, Christopher."

And without a backward glance, she left the bar.

EIGHTEEN

Lights blazed inside the Cookery. Angelica stood behind the door waiting when Tricia arrived at precisely eleven o'clock. She unlocked the door. "So, spill," Angelica said eagerly.

"Spill what?"

"Your conversation with Christopher," Angelica said, and turned back to the counter to grab her hoodie.

"Basically the same thing he's been on about ever since he moved to New Hampshire. Can we get back together again."

"And you said . . . ?"

"No."

"Are you sure there isn't just a little spark of interest left?"

"Has Christopher tried to enlist you to his cause?" Tricia accused.

"Well, yes," Angelica admitted. "But I told him I would not interfere. See, I *will* be a good mother-in-law to Ginny!"

Tricia ignored the last part of that statement and addressed the first. "Thank you."

Angelica jerked her thumb toward the street beyond. "Let's not waste any time. We'll pick up the flowers from my car and then do the hanging planters in the middle of the village."

"It's a plan."

Angelica flicked off the lights and locked the door. They headed out of the Cookery with Tricia again carrying the ladder and ready to tackle the job once more.

Angelica headed north up the sidewalk at a brisk pace, and again Tricia found it hard to keep up. The door to the Dog-Eared Page opened and a laughing couple emerged. They turned south, away from Tricia and Angelica, who headed for the municipal parking lot and Angelica's car.

"It's going to take a good two hours, if not longer, for us to replace those flowers," Angelica said with a weary sigh.

"Then the sooner we get started, the sooner we can go to bed."

"Isn't it tragic that we'll both be going to bed alone?" Angelica said wistfully.

"I wouldn't say tragic," Tricia said, hoping the subject of Christopher wasn't going to come up again.

Angelica shrugged. "I've loved and lost, and I miss the companionship, but right now my life is too hectic for a relationship," she said reasonably.

"And mine will soon be hectic when I can finally get started on rebuilding my store—and my life."

They left the ladder on the sidewalk and entered the nearly empty municipal parking lot to retrieve the bags of flowers from Angelica's trunk. Back on the sidewalk, Tricia unfolded the ladder, and this time

Angelica didn't even blink at the thought of climbing it. Since she'd already sorted the flowers, Tricia hoped the job would go a lot faster.

"So, what precipitated that tearful speech from Toni Bennett?" Angelica asked as Tricia handed her a fistful of silk flowers.

"Toni and Pete may have been more than just friends, at least according to Mariana," Tricia said.

"Oh, yeah?" Angelica said, shoving a reasonable facsimile of a carnation into the basket's dirt.

"Did you know she was married to Jim Stark?" Tricia asked.

"No. So, she kept her maiden name? Good for her."

"Jim called me to ask if my insurance had come through, and I mentioned I was sorry Pete had died, suggesting he might have been a friend. He let me know in no uncertain terms that they weren't." She handed Angelica another handful of silk fakery.

"Do you really want to annoy the man who holds a big piece of your future in his hands on an unsubstantiated suspicion?" Angelica asked, placing a faux white lilac bloom next to a bogus pink peony.

"Don't think I haven't considered that. The minute I get the okay to start repairing my home and shop, I want to get moving."

"And yet, after all the time and money you put in, Bob will still own the property," Angelica pointed out.

"I told you how much he wants for the building. Karen Johnson advised me he was asking too much. I trust her. I've never trusted Bob. You're in the same boat. And you're still attached to a building Bob owns, too."

"Yes. NRA Associates has contacted Bob about selling the building, and his prices are off the charts."

"What will you do?" Tricia asked as Angelica descended the ladder.

"Punt."

"What does that mean?" Tricia asked while Angelica folded the ladder.

"It means when my lease is up I'm moving the Cookery and my home to the lot the Chamber office now occupies."

"It's a shame you're going to raze that lovely little house."

"I have no intention of doing so," Angelica said as they moved across the street to start on the empty baskets there. "I've already bought a lot on the outskirts of town. I'll move it there and sell it."

"Won't that be frightfully expensive?" Tricia asked.

"Not really. The money we found in all those boxes of junk that were left behind when we took over the property was almost equal to a third of the selling price," Angelica said as she set up the ladder once more. "It would have been an expensive lot, otherwise. I can at least break even on moving the house. I hate waste. I've listened to Ginny's lectures on the subjects of reuse and recycling. Why destroy a charming little home when some family might love it once again?"

Tricia smiled as she watched her sister climb the ladder once more. "I'm glad you think so. And Ginny will be happy to hear that, too."

"We should talk about *your* options for your store before you put too much into the reno," Angelica said, taking another bunch of flowers that Tricia handed her.

"My lease demands that I make the repairs."

"Yes, but if you don't want to overpay for the building or the next ridiculous rent increase that Kelly Realty demands"—once again, she didn't pin the blame on Bob himself—"then we need to find a property for you to develop."

"I've already thought of that," Tricia said as she watched Angelica place the flowers in a harmonious arrangement.

"Good."

"But I'm not sure I'm up for all that work."

Angelica grinned. "It can be a lot of fun!" she said in a sing-song cadence.

"Oh, sure, when you've got a big, strapping son waiting in the wings to do your bidding. I'm all alone."

Angelica looked down at her sister. "Oh, no, you're not. Not as long as there's breath in *my* body." She turned to her handiwork. "How does that look?"

"Perfect."

Angelica climbed down the ladder once again. As they collected their stuff, a couple of the pub's patrons passed them heading for the municipal parking lot. They said hello but acted as if placing fake flowers in baskets at such a late hour was a normal occurrence. If the couple thought it odd, the sisters were past caring.

They moved down the street.

"See the camera?" Angelica asked. She pointed to a spot over the Coffee Bean's transom. The device was trained on the hanging basket in front of the store.

"Boy, that's small," Tricia said, squinting.

"It is, but you'd be surprised how good the images are. And if our flower thief shows up, it'll nail him."

"What if it's a her?"

"I can't imagine a woman destroying flowers."

"Not all the people who complain about the village improvements are men."

Angelica nodded. "I guess you're right. But I know there are more tall men than women in this village, and it had to be someone tall to snip all those blossoms. Except for us, can you see any other woman hauling a ladder around at this ungodly hour to destroy the plants?"

Tricia shook her head.

They finished the basket and moved on to the next.

"Back at Pete's wake, when I got up to get Grace's cake, I met a woman who dated Pete for a while," Tricia said.

"The way he spoke, Pete seemed to think he was the reincarnation of Casanova," Angelica said, pushing a pseudo nasturtium into a pot.

"It turns out he was all bark and no bite," Tricia said.

Angelica's eyes widened in understanding. "Really? Nothing a little blue pill couldn't have cured."

"If he'd sought one out. He didn't."

Angelica shook her head. "The poor woman."

"She found someone else who could satisfy her."

"Then at least it worked out for her," Angelica said.

"But how sad for Pete," Tricia lamented. "That also means he and Toni probably weren't an item, either."

"Platonic friends?" Angelica asked. "I suppose it happens. Back in the day my best friend was a gay man. Drew was so jealous, but honestly, he was more like a best girlfriend."

"Are you still friends?"

Angelica shook her head sadly. "He died from AIDS."

"What was his name?"

"Jeremy. I wish you could have known him. He was a lot like you. He loved nothing better than to read a good mystery—*and* hang out in gay bars." Angelica finished decorating the basket and climbed down from the ladder. "Not many more to go."

The next flowerless basket was in front of the Dog-Eared Page, and Angelica was just putting the finishing touches on it when Tricia pulled the last of the silk flowers out of the bag. "Finally."

The lights in the pub winked out and Michele emerged, locking the door. She turned and nearly jumped. "Oh! You startled me."

"We're sorry," Tricia said.

"What on earth are you doing on the street so late—and with a ladder?" Michele asked looking up at Angelica.

Tricia proffered a silk fuchsia. "Trying to bring a little beauty back to the village."

"I did wonder what happened to all those glorious blossoms—and in such a short space of time."

"Someone has made it their life's work not only to cut off all the real flowers, but to remove the silk ones we've put up."

"I imagine it would be frightfully expensive to replace all the baskets."

"I'm afraid it's too late in the season to do so," Angelica explained. "This will have to do. And we don't even have enough flowers to do all them all."

"Oh, dear."

"We've got just enough for this one basket, and then we're calling it a night," Tricia said.

"Well, it's late. I won't keep you ladies any longer. You must be just as tired as me. I've got a date with my soaker tub and a glass of wine, and then I'm off to dreamland."

"Sweet dreams," Angelica said.

"Good night," Tricia called as Michele gave a wave and started down the street for the municipal parking lot.

Angelica climbed down the ladder and folded it while Tricia balled up the shopping bags and deposited them in one of the municipal trash bins. "And now, we wait," Angelica said.

"I'm hoping they're still in the baskets tomorrow morning."

"And if they aren't, I'm hoping that camera will capture whoever is ruining our baskets so I can call Chief Baker to make an arrest."

"What if it's just a kid's prank?" Tricia asked as they started back up the street.

"Then their parents should take responsibility and make restitution. I like the idea of community service, though. Make the kids pick up litter or dig a ditch or something so that they will learn to respect someone else's labor."

They crossed the street, heading for the Cookery. "Speaking of community service, did you see Bob at Pete's wake?" Tricia asked.

"No."

"It looked like he was trying to keep a low profile. Bob bragged to me that he and Pete were great pals and that he was the one who forged the alliance between the Historical Society and the Chamber of Commerce."

"I don't think so. As far as I know, the Chamber and the Historical Society didn't *have* a relationship until I came onboard. They were members in name only. Oddly enough, it was Pete who sought out the Chamber after learning of Michele's interest in someone starting the ghost walks."

A scream pierced the night.

The sisters looked up the street. "You don't think . . . ?" Tricia asked, panicked.

Angelica dropped the ladder, and the sisters started running toward the municipal parking lot. Tricia pulled her phone out of her jacket pocket as they ran and lagged a little behind, trying to stab 911 onto the small screen as Angelica charged ahead.

"Michele! Michele!" Angelica cried.

With very few cars in the lot, it wasn't hard to spot Michele's Mini Cooper.

"Help!" Tricia cried into the phone.

"Michele!" Angelica hollered.

A figure dressed in black with a ski mask to hide his face ran from the lot, jumping over the low metal barrier that rimmed the east side of lot, and bolted north up the alley.

Michele was huddled against the driver's-side door, clutching her throat and gasping for air. "He tried to strangle me," she managed between choked breaths.

Angelica crouched beside her. "Are you all right?"

"I think so," she managed, but her words came out in a sob.

"Yes, there's been an attack in the Stoneham municipal lot. Can you send someone?" Tricia demanded.

The 911 dispatcher asked what seemed like far too many questions, but in no time Tricia saw the flashing blue lights of one of the three Stoneham Police Department patrol cars as it approached. She stabbed the off icon as Angelica helped Michele to stand. Tears had muddied her mascara, giving her raccoon eyes where she'd rubbed them.

The cruiser pulled up alongside the women, and Officer Dave Hanson practically jumped from the car. "What happened?" he asked without preamble.

"A man tried to strangle her," Tricia said. "We saw him run off down the alley."

"Are you hurt, ma'am?" he asked, concerned.

Michele shook her head. "More frightened."

"I'll call for backup," Hanson said, turned away, and spoke into the small microphone attached to the shoulder of his uniform blouse.

"Did he try to take your purse?" Tricia asked.

Michele shook her head again. "I would have gladly given it up. I was about to unlock my car when he came up from behind me with some kind of a cord."

Tricia looked around but didn't see any cord. The man must have taken it with him when he'd fled.

"Would you like to sit down, ma'am?" the cop asked.

"I want to go home," Michele cried.

"You'll do no such thing. The best room at the Sheer Comfort Inn is empty tonight. You can go there. It has a wonderful soaker tub, and I'm sure we can wrestle up a nice bottle of wine," Angelica said, wrapping an arm around Michele's shoulder.

"Oh, please. I just want to go home."

"Before that happens, I need to ask you some questions," Hanson said.

"Can she do that in my store?" Angelica asked. "It's just a couple of doors down, and it's warm and much more comfortable than standing around this chilly parking lot."

"I'll walk you down there," Hanson said, and the four of them started off with Angelica and Michele in the lead, and Tricia keeping pace with the officer. "We heard her scream and came running. I don't know what would have happened if we hadn't scared the man away."

"You're sure it was a man?"

"Yes."

"Was it anyone you'd recognize?"

Tricia shook her head.

They arrived at the Cookery. Angelica already had her keys out and unlocked the door. Tricia paused to pick up the ladder when she heard footsteps running across the road. "Tricia? What happened?"

It was Christopher, of course, only this time he wasn't clad in pajamas.

"Someone attacked Michele in the municipal parking lot."

"And you were telling me earlier how you didn't need an escort," he said angrily.

"Angelica and I found her," Tricia said. "It's lucky we'd just finished the last of the baskets and were around to hear her scream." She turned away. "I can't talk to you now. I'm a witness, and I need to speak to the officer."

"All right. But I don't want you walking back to the Chamber office by yourself. I'm going to wait right here until you're ready to go home. No arguments."

"Only if you promise no funny stuff."

"I find nothing humorous about the situation," he said.

She believed him.

"It's cold and damp out. You may as well come inside and wait with us," she said.

He nodded and took the ladder from her.

As they entered the Cookery, Tricia had no doubt it would be hours before she saw her bed.

She was right. The police investigation took several hours—far longer than the actual attack. Angelica was not able to convince Michele to stay at the inn. Instead, the officer drove her back to her apartment in Milford, with Tricia promising to have Pixie drive Michele back to the village the next morning. She knew she could count on Pixie to give a helping hand in a crisis.

Christopher was as good as his word. He stayed out of the way during the police investigation, and afterward they walked back to the Chamber office in silence. Upon arriving at the house, he insisted on coming inside, making sure everything was safe, and then he said good night. No funny business, no begging for a kiss. Tricia wasn't about to admit it, but Michele's attack had rattled her. She'd felt safer with Christopher walking beside her.

After he left, Tricia poured herself a glass of wine from the small fridge in her sitting room and tried to read but was too distracted for even that. She settled on her comfy chair and was glad when Miss Marple joined her. It was only the sound of the cat's rumbling purr that seemed to soothe her jagged nerves.

Eventually Tricia felt settled enough to try to go to sleep. She changed into her nightgown, slipped between the cool sheets, and turned off the light, but thoughts of the evening's events kept circling through her mind.

Michele had anticipated some kind of attack, and it had come.

What did the man in black have against the Historical Society? And more frightening, how long after he was caught would it be before Tricia began to feel safe again?

NINETEEN

The phone rang far too early the next morning, but Tricia groped to pick up the receiver without opening her eyes. "'Ello."

"They're gone—they're all gone!" Angelica practically wailed.

Tricia opened her eyes and squinted to focus on the numerals on her bedside clock. "Ange, it's not even seven o'clock," she muttered.

"I couldn't sleep, so I got up to make myself a cup of tea. I looked out my kitchen window and could see that every one of the silk flowers we put in the baskets last night is gone. Only, this time, let's hope we caught on video the vandal who's been stealing them. I'll have that contemptible bastard thrown in jail for the rest of his miserable life."

"I doubt any judge is going to sentence whoever stole the flowers to life in prison," Tricia said reasonably.

"But that's what he deserves. As soon as I get dressed, I'm heading over to the Coffee Bean to see if their surveillance camera caught the felon."

Petit larceny was all the perp could be charged with, but it was no use arguing with Angelica when she was in one of those moods.

Again, Tricia squinted at her clock. Miss Marple had been sleeping at the foot of the bed. She was not pleased at being awakened this early, either. Still, now that she was awake, Tricia figured she might as well get up. If necessary, she'd apply a thick coat of concealer under her eyes. "If you can wait an extra ten minutes, I'll come over and we can go to the Coffee Bean together," she told her sister.

"Ten minutes," Angelica threatened. "See you then." She hung up.

Tricia threw back the covers, got up, and took the world's fastest shower. She made it to the Cookery just twelve minutes later.

Angelica and Sarge were waiting in the Cookery. The dog barked a cheerful greeting as Tricia entered. "Are we taking Sarge with us?"

"Oh, no. He's just back in from his morning tinkle break. I'll take him on a proper walk later."

"Let's get this over with," Tricia said, and she went back outside with Angelica hot on her heels.

Despite it being a Saturday, business was booming at the Coffee Bean. The line was five deep with joggers and others who'd stopped for a brew. It was one of the few shops on Main Street that the locals had fully embraced. As always, the aroma of coffee and fresh baked goods was intoxicating. Alexa was taking the orders and Boris was filling them as fast as he could.

"Ange, we might have to wait until the morning coffee rush is over before we can find out if the camera caught the person responsible for lifting the flowers."

"I'll wait here until closing if I have to. I want that guy arrested."

Luckily, no one else came in after them, giving them hope Boris might have time to download the images to a disk.

"What can I get you this morning?" Alexa asked cheerfully.

"The flowers are gone. I hope your camera captured the person who did it?"

Alexa shook her head. "I saw there were none when I came in this morning. I knew you would be here early to see, so I had Boris download the video," she said.

"I have it here," Boris said in his thick Russian accent, and reached under the counter to come up with a jewel box and the disk inside it.

"Thank you so much," Angelica said.

"Would you like something else?" Alexa asked hopefully.

"I'll take a large French roast, and two of those apple-oatmeal muffins to go. Tricia?"

"I'll have the same coffee, but a croissant."

Angelica fidgeted the whole time it took Alexa and Boris to assemble their order. When they presented the cups and bags, Angelica handed Alexa a twenty and called out, "Keep the change," before she practically ran from the store. Tricia had to hustle to keep up.

Angelica had the door to the Cookery unlocked in a flash, and Sarge seemed to think it was some kind of race as he ran to overtake Angelica before she could get to the stairs that led to her loft apartment. He barked with joy and shot up the stairs like a rocket taking off.

Tricia locked the door and followed at a more reasonable pace. By the time she reached the apartment, she found Angelica had already popped the DVD into her player and was waiting for it to start.

Tricia walked past her and into the kitchen, where she took out a couple of plates and set out her croissant, then took the other plate into the living room and retrieved the muffins from the bag Angelica had tossed onto the coffee table. She took a seat on the couch as Angelica paced, holding her coffee in one hand and the remote in another.

Despite Angelica's claim the previous day, the picture quality wasn't what you'd call great. Black and white and kind of murky was the best that could be said of it. Boris must have started recording after business hours. A couple strolled past the Coffee Bean hand in hand, and then there was—nothing but the empty sidewalk for long seconds.

Angelica hit the fast-forward button. People scurried across the screen in a kind of choppy motion, sort of like Charlie Chaplin in his old silent films, and the sky began to darken. The streetlamp came on in a flash, and more people came and went.

"How long do you think this is going to take?" Tricia asked.

"I can speed it up even faster, but I'm afraid we might miss something."

Tricia sipped her coffee and sampled her croissant. Heavenly!

For long periods of time, no one passed in front of the camera, and then they saw themselves putting the flowers back into the closest hanging basket. Angelica hit the pause button.

"Oh, my—I don't look that fat in real life, do I?"

"No," Tricia said emphatically. "You know the camera always adds at least ten pounds." She wasn't sure Angelica believed her and didn't want to elaborate.

Angelica hit the fast-forward button again. Nothing happened.

Nothing happened.

Nothing happened.

And then a figure darted into the frame and was almost instantly gone.

"Rewind, rewind!" Tricia called frantically.

Angelica hit the rewind button and then pressed play. Once again the screen was filled with the image of the empty sidewalk, then someone dressed in dark clothes with a hoodie stepped out of the shadows with a long-handled grabber, the kind used by the infirm who could no longer bend to pick up objects, and plucked the silk flowers from the basket, stuffing them into a dark plastic bag, then quickly moved on.

"So much for the guy being tall. Do you recognize him?" Angelica asked.

"Is it a man?" Tricia asked, not quite sure.

Angelica hit rewind, and they watched the video again. And again. And again.

"I didn't say anything earlier, but the night before Michele was attacked, I felt like someone was watching as I walked back to the Chamber office. When I got inside, I hurried to look out the front window and saw someone dressed like the person in the video and carrying a big black plastic bag."

"But you didn't recognize him?" Angelica pressed.

Tricia shook her head.

Angelica frowned, staring at the still image on the TV screen. "I was so sure we were going to recognize who it was so we could have him arrested."

"You can show the video to Chief Baker, but I don't know what he's going to be able to do."

Angelica shook her head. "I'm sure I've seen that person before."

"Ange, it could be *anyone!*" Tricia said, but Angelica was still shaking her head.

"I'm going to keep watching this until I figure out who it is."

"Well, I think I know who it isn't," Tricia said, and took another sip of coffee.

"What do you mean?"

"It's not the guy who attacked Michele. It seemed like that person was a lot bigger in stature. I know I only saw a glimpse of him, but the person in the video seems a lot shorter and thinner."

"Why would anyone think the two were the same?"

Tricia shrugged. "Maybe because we seem to have a crime wave going on. I know I'd much rather have one villain than two menacing the village."

"I'd rather have *no* villains menacing the village."

Tricia drained her cup and stood. "I've got to get moving. I still have to do my morning walk."

"Boring!" Angelica said. "Thanks to Sarge needing to go out every few hours, I get my exercise running up and down three flights of stairs all day. I've lost ten pounds since I got the little guy."

Sarge barked. He knew a compliment when he heard it.

"Are you coming for supper tonight?" Angelica asked.

"Sure. And I'll probably see you at Booked for Lunch, too."

"Keep thinking about our flower filcher, will you please?"

"I will," Tricia promised, gave her sister a brief hug, and headed for the door. Sarge accompanied her and barked when she didn't grab his leash. "Sorry, little buddy, but you can't come with me."

Sarge barked again, then cocked his head and looked at her with sad eyes. He whimpered, just to make her feel even more guilty.

"Oh, all right," Tricia grumbled. "Ange!" she called. "I'm taking Sarge."

"Thanks!" Angelica called back.

Tricia reached for the leash and Sarge barked excitedly, running around in circles. "Calm down! You'd think you'd never been on a walk with me before." She clipped the leash to Sarge's collar, grabbed a plastic bag from the stash Angelica kept by the door, and picked him up, tucking him under her arm like a football. "Come on."

Once outside the Cookery, Tricia set Sarge down, and he immediately set off, trotting off toward the park. When he came to the
corner, he sat down, waiting for permission to cross.

"We're not going north," Tricia told him and gave the leash a slight
tug. "We're going west. This is *my* walk, not yours."

Sarge looked up at her and blinked, but seemed game to try a new
routine.

Vehicular traffic on Stoneham's side streets was practically non-
existent on that Saturday morning. They crossed Main Street and
started down Locust Street at a brisk pace.

Instead of thinking about the petal pincher as Angelica had suggested, Tricia tried to remember what she could about the figure she'd
seen fleeing the municipal parking lot after Michele's attack. The man—
she felt sure it was a man—had been stocky but had had no trouble
hurdling over the low metal barrier that surrounded the lot and then
taking off at a run. Still, he hadn't had to run far before he was swallowed
by darkness. That meant the guy didn't have to be all that athletic. They
hadn't run after him, so he could have pulled off his ski mask and just
walked away without garnering any attention. The police had searched
the area, but as far as Tricia knew, they hadn't found anything of note.

Tricia turned down Pine Avenue. Mariana lived in the white house
with the navy trim. Her landscaping was primarily low bushes flank-
ing the front steps, but four baskets of purple and white petunias hung
from the soffit on lengths of chain. They were pretty, with their blooms
still intact, unlike the hanging baskets on Main Street. It seemed to
prove the theory that the petal pincher had it in for the merchants on
Main Street and not a hatred of flowers in general. Still, of the two
menaces, Tricia would rather the village had to deal with petty vandalism than murder and attempted murder.

Tricia made it to the end of the block and turned right. She'd had her route figured out only days after the fire and had worn a pedometer for a few weeks until she'd figured out the mileage she wanted to walk per day. Sarge trotted along beside her as happy as only a dog could be. They turned onto Oak Street, where her friend Deborah Black had lived, and where Frannie Armstrong still lived.

They carried on to the corner and turned left up Locust once again. Tricia's stomach tightened as she approached the next cross street, where Bob Kelly lived. She decided to skip walking down that road and walked up to the next block. She didn't have the patience to deal with him that morning.

Bob, Bob, Bob.

Tricia had never liked the man, despite his slight resemblance to Christopher. He was shorter, heavier set, but had the same green eyes that she always found so attractive in men. Still, there was something about him that had set off—well, *alarm bells* was really too strong a description, but she'd disliked him at first sight. The term *lounge lizard* came to mind whenever she thought about him or had to deal with him. That Angelica had found him fascinating, and then had become his lover, had irritated Tricia to no end. But as Tricia now knew, Angelica had a tendency to look for the good in people, even if she made the rest of the world think her just a selfish, vain woman. The fact that her fourth marriage had ended just before she'd met Bob had made her a prime target for a rebound romance.

Bob had done some very dishonorable things during the past that Tricia had not told Angelica about, far more than just the pumpkin-smashing incident. After they'd broken up, he'd rigged a Chamber contest with the prize of a night at a romantic bed-and-breakfast, bestowing it upon Angelica in hopes of a reconciliation. That she chose

Tricia to accompany her had made him angry, and he'd begged her not to tell Angelica. There were other such incidences. In fact, when she thought about it, Bob wasn't at all honorable, and thankfully Angelica had finally acknowledged it—but only after he'd cheated on her.

How low was the man willing to stoop?

Tricia found herself walking slower.

Murder?

"Don't be ridiculous," she said aloud, and looked down at Sarge, who looked back up at her. "I was talking to myself," she said, embarrassed. But again her stomach seemed to quiver.

It was then Tricia remembered the Chamber of Commerce membership list that Betsy Dittmeyer had put together. It wasn't really a list, more a dossier of the Chamber's members, and the information she'd gathered on each member didn't chronicle their nobler aspects. The document was filled with vile assumptions and vicious gossip. Tricia had always meant to delete the file but somehow had never gotten around to doing so.

She abruptly turned, walking into the leash and nearly tripping over the dog. "Come on, Sarge. We're cutting our walk short." And she started down Locust Street once again at almost a jog, with the poor pup struggling to keep up with her.

Tricia only slowed when she entered the driveway of the Chamber's office. She opened the door and unhooked Sarge from his leash. "Be a good boy and go to bed," she told him, thankful Miss Marple was nowhere in sight. She shut the door to the stairs behind her and took them two at a time. At the landing, she turned right toward her sitting room. Miss Marple was asleep on the chair. Tricia headed straight for the small table that served as a desk and booted up her laptop, thankful she'd been good about storing her files on an off-site server.

It took only a minute or two before she pulled up the document and scanned down to the listing for the Stoneham Historical Society. Sure enough, Pete Renquist was listed as their representative.

> A former junkie, who did time in the Essex County, New Jersey, lockup for possession with intent to sell narcotics. Was released when the charges fell through on a technicality and kicked the habit. He was a deadbeat dad, whose ex-wife had to sue for back child support, and his wages at the Stoneham Historical Society were garnished until he paid off the backlog.

Where had Betsy gotten all that information from? Had she had access to Social Security numbers, hacked bank accounts, and other databases?

And then it suddenly occurred to Tricia who else who knew about the file: Angelica, Chief Baker, and perhaps a few of his officers, and, of course, Bob Kelly.

Tricia's stomach tightened.

What possible reason would Bob have had to kill Pete Renquist and brutally assault Janet Koch? The attacks on them must have had something to do with the Historical Society—and possibly the ghost walks. Had Bob ever even mentioned the Historical Society to Angelica?

Angelica might not want to talk about Bob. She had been his lover for several years, but since their breakup, she'd made it clear they were no longer even friends. She had never spoken a word against the man, and it angered her when Tricia did. But surely she'd break that silence if Bob proved to be a killer.

Bob a killer? Tricia still found it hard to wrap her mind around that thought. Still, his life of crime had started early. As a teen, he'd skipped town to avoid the community service he'd been sentenced to perform after being convicted of a youthful indiscretion. And then, of course, there was the legal problem he'd been trying so hard to get out of. His fingerprints had been found at Stan Berry's home after the place had been ransacked following his death. Bob owned the property, and she supposed his attorney might try to say he had a right to be in the home . . . but not when the victim's son had shown an interest in renegotiating the lease. Bob had wanted him out so he could rent the place for more money to someone else. It was going to cost him a lot of money to get out of that one without serving some kind of time in addition to the reinstatement of the sentence of community service he'd skipped out on so many years before.

But Bob a killer?

No, Tricia couldn't believe it.

Could someone else have had access to Betsy Dittmeyer's files? Again, she'd have to ask Angelica.

Tricia bit her lip. What other possible suspects could there be? Earl Winkler? On the last morning of his life, Pete and Earl had exchanged angry words about the proposed ghost walks. Had they argued on other occasions? Earl was a grumpy old man, but that didn't mean he was a killer.

Janet Koch might be the key to knowing who had killed Renquist; was that why Pete's killer had tried to eliminate her, too?

The Historical Society seemed to be the common denominator. No doubt Chief Baker had already spoken with all of its staff. Tricia had told him she'd stay out of it, and she'd meant it. But she also seemed to have a knack for getting people to talk—and often about things they later regretted. And yet, she didn't have a rapport with the rest of the Historical Society's workforce. She'd always dealt with Pete and Janet, and she doubted Angelica knew any of its members on a personal basis, either.

Tricia thought about the cocktail party she'd attended on the Society's grounds when the Italianate garden had been rededicated the previous summer. The Brookview Inn had catered the affair. Would Antonio or one of his staff have dealt with just Pete and Janet, or would someone else on its staff have been assigned to deal with the inn and its personnel? Tricia knew a few of the people who worked at the inn, but they blamed her—not Stan Berry's killer—for the unfortunate events that had occurred after the murderer had been exposed. They wouldn't willingly talk to her, and Antonio wasn't one to gossip, and even now that they were almost related, she was sure he wouldn't do anything to anger Angelica when it came to possibly jeopardizing Tricia's safety. Count him out as an accessory.

Mariana hadn't worked for the Chamber all that long, but Frannie Armstrong had worked for the organization for over ten years before coming to work for Angelica at the Cookery. She was no fan of Bob, who'd treated her poorly, but she'd known him longer than anyone else Tricia could think of. Frannie had an encyclopedic memory, and she loved to gossip—on any subject. Of course, their friendship had cooled somewhat after Tricia had pointed out that Frannie might make a plausible suspect for Betsy Dittmeyer's death. Still, Tricia was determined to talk to her before she shared her suspicions with Angelica or Chief Baker.

Tricia closed the file and shut down her computer. She looked across the room. Miss Marple hadn't stirred. She got up, tiptoed across the room, and went down the stairs. She found Sarge in his basket. "Walkies," she called. The dog hadn't been asleep, and he shot out of his bed like a cannonball.

Hooking the leash to his collar, they started for the door. Tricia only hoped Frannie would be able to tell her what she needed to know.

TWENTY

Tricia and Sarge retraced their steps to Oak Street. This time when they approached Frannie's house, she was outside kneeling in front of the small garden, weeding. "Hi, Frannie," Tricia called cheerfully, so as not to startle her.

Frannie looked over her shoulder. "Well, this is a nice surprise." Sarge barked and pulled at his leash. He and Frannie were great friends, too. "If I'd known you were coming, I'd have made sure I had a dog biscuit for you."

"Both of us?" Tricia asked, and laughed.

"Sorry, I don't eat yogurt or tuna, and that's about *all* you eat," Frannie said pointedly.

Tricia ignored the jibe. "It's been such a long time since we talked," Tricia said.

Frannie looked up, eyeing her suspiciously. "It has."

"How have you been?"

"Fine." Silence fell between them. Then Frannie asked, "Didn't I see you and Sarge walking down my street only half an hour ago?"

"You did," Tricia admitted. "We're just retracing our steps, trying to get in another mile or two. Isn't that right Sarge?"

Sarge barked in agreement. Tricia hadn't known a dog could lie.

"I'm not used to having weekends off, although I'm sure enjoying my stint working at the Chamber. Do you ever miss it?"

"The Chamber? No. Why would I?" Frannie asked, sounding annoyed.

Tricia shrugged. "I don't know. I should think it's a lot more exciting now than when you were there. Probably more interesting, too."

"That's a given. From what Angelica tells me, there's lots of fun stuff going on all the time." She seemed to think it over for a moment. "Yeah, it sounds a whole lot better than when I worked there. Angelica is full of so many ideas, and the membership has sure changed, with lots of new people, new businesses. But I'm happy where I am now," she asserted, and looked at her watch. "I need to finish my weeding before I have to show up at the Cookery an hour from now."

"I don't mean to keep you, but I know what you mean. I hope to be back to Haven't Got a Clue soon, but in the meantime, it hasn't been unpleasant working for the Chamber. I've learned a lot of new things—and a lot about Stoneham."

"Any news from the insurance company?" Frannie asked.

Ah, the perfect opening. "No. But Bob Kelly has been pressuring me to buy the building."

"So I heard," Frannie said. No doubt Angelica had mentioned it.

"He doesn't seem to want to take no for an answer," Tricia said.

"He can be a very stubborn man," Frannie agreed.

"In what way?" Tricia asked, innocently.

"When he wants something, he gets it," she said firmly.

"Unless he lowers the price, I'm not buying."

"Then he'll do what it takes to *make* you buy it."

"You're scaring me a little," Tricia said with a mirthless laugh.

"You ought to be scared. I was lucky he didn't retaliate against me more than he did after I took the job at the Cookery."

"He retaliated against you? How?"

"First, he tried to sabotage my friendship with Angelica. He threatened that he would have me fired within a month of my working there, but then he'd never met anyone who could really stand up to him like she could—can," Frannie corrected herself.

"What else did he do?"

"I could never prove it, of course," she began, "but my credit rating took a huge hit just after I left the Chamber. Bob knows a lot more about computers than he ever lets on, and thanks to his real estate holdings, he has all kinds of ins with various financial institutions."

"You can't mean the Bank of Stoneham," Tricia said, alarmed. She liked its manager, Billie Burke, and couldn't imagine her tampering with files or doing anything illegal.

Frannie shook her head. "Bob deals with a lot of out-of-state banks. A couple of them listed liens against my house. That took a lot of juggling to straighten out. Thank goodness for Angelica. She has more friends in high places than Bob, and pulled some strings to help me set things right."

"Did she believe Bob had anything to do with it?" Tricia asked.

"No. Usually she's such a good judge of character. I don't know what in God's name she ever saw in that sorry excuse for a man."

Neither do I, Tricia refrained from saying aloud.

"He's not still bothering you, is he?" Tricia asked.

"Right now he's got more on his mind than just annoying little people like me—and that's just the way he sees me. Little. Insignificant. Unimportant. I'll tell you the truth, I'm glad he's forgotten about me. That man frightens me."

Tricia had always thought Frannie was fearless; to find out she wasn't startled her. But what had she really told Tricia but conjecture and innuendo—a gossip's best friends. Still, Tricia believed every word Frannie had uttered.

She looked down at the marigolds and red zinnias that populated Frannie's little garden. "They're so pretty, unlike the hanging baskets along Main Street."

Frannie nodded knowledgably. "Angelica has kept me informed. It's a shame. They cost such a lot of money and brought such beauty to our little village."

"Once again, we're probably out of the running for prettiest village in New Hampshire." Tricia shook her head sadly. "I might have seen who is responsible, but it was late and dark, and the person wore a hoodie and was carrying a large trash bag. I'll just bet it was full of the silk flowers we put in those baskets."

"Angelica doesn't like me to gossip," Frannie said, "but I'll bet if you checked a certain Dumpster here in the village, you just might find those missing silk flowers."

"You know who's responsible?"

"As you know, I hear things," Frannie said cryptically.

Tricia met Frannie's penetrating gaze. "I'm listening."

"Sometimes I take a walk in the early morning before it gets too hot. The other day I saw a man walking up Main Street with a big black trash bag in one hand and a—"

"Long-handled gripper in the other?" Tricia guessed.

"Yes."

"I think I saw him, too. But I didn't know who it was. I don't suppose you saw what he did with the flowers he was plucking."

"When he saw me, he stopped at the nearest trash barrel and shoved the bag in."

"Do you remember exactly where?"

Frannie thought for a moment. "Must have been right in front of the *Stoneham Weekly News*."

"Would you be willing to tell Chief Baker what you saw?"

"Absolutely."

"Thank you so much. I'll have him give you a call."

"It took me a day or two to figure out who it was," Frannie said with certainty.

"And?" Tricia asked.

Tricia and Sarge hurried back to the Cookery, but when they reached Angelica's apartment, Tricia found a note taped to the door. *Off to Booked for Lunch to get the salads going. I'll be working with Pixie today. See you at the usual time. Tootles!*

So much for having a Dumpster-diving buddy.

Tricia returned Sarge to the loft apartment, unhooked his leash, gave him a couple of biscuits, and left the building. Once outside, she noticed a truck parked in front of Haven't Got a Clue. Jim Stark stood before the derelict store, staring at it.

Tricia put on a happy face. "Hi, Jim."

Stark turned and nodded in her direction but said nothing. He turned back to the soot-stained façade. Tricia moved to stand beside him.

"The outside fixes are mostly cosmetic," Stark said. "We'll scrub the stucco, repair it, and replace the glass in the window."

"It's the damage inside that's heartbreaking," Tricia said.

Stark nodded.

They stared at the large piece of plywood that covered what had been Tricia's large display window. Could Stark have killed Pete Renquist in a jealous rage? Should she bring up the subject?

She didn't have to.

"I need to apologize for the way I spoke to you when we last talked," he began.

Tricia said nothing, content to let him lead the conversation.

"The truth is, Renquist and my wife were friends—perhaps too close friends for comfort. I guess I was jealous."

"Pete was known to have a glib tongue," Tricia said.

"Toni tells me nothing ever went on between them. I trust my wife. I didn't know Renquist enough to trust him."

"Were you angry at him?"

Stark turned to face her. "You mean enough to kill him?"

"Someone killed him," Tricia said, keeping her voice neutral.

Stark nodded. "I've heard rumors, but nothing concrete."

"I know for a fact that Pete was murdered."

"Yeah, well, I have an iron-clad alibi, if you're thinking of pinning the blame on me."

"Why would you think I'd do that?"

He held a hand up to take in the soot-stained sign over the plywood. "Because you're Stoneham's Queen of Mystery."

Well, that title was certainly better than that of village jinx.

"Every one of my crew—not to mention my client—can vouch that I was on a job site last Monday. Thanks to the port-a-john, I didn't have to leave the site for even a bathroom break from nearly dawn until almost dusk."

"Then you're in the clear."

"With you." He kept staring at the plywood. "Not Toni."

"Why would she think you had a motive?"

"I told you. I was jealous of their friendship."

"I'm pretty sure that's all it was. From what I heard, Pete wasn't able to . . ." Tricia wasn't sure how to delicately express what she needed to say. "He . . ." Oh, hell. "He couldn't get it up."

Stark turned to eye her.

"To compensate," she continued, "he made out like he was a dedicated skirt chaser. From what I understand, it was a condition he'd suffered for quite some time."

"Why are you telling me this?"

"Because I believe men and women can be friends without sexual intimacy."

"Oh, yeah?" he asked, his expression skeptical.

"Take me, for instance. I'm striving to be friends with three men right now."

"But you did once have a deeper relationship with each of them, right?"

Did Stark know all about Tricia's love life since moving to Stoneham? Small town talk . . .

Tricia shrugged. "Okay, bad example. But isn't it just possible that Toni and Pete had a purely platonic relationship?"

"That's what she said."

"Has she ever given you reason not to trust her?"

He didn't look at her but shook his head.

"Do you two talk much?"

He shrugged.

"Are you interested in antiques?" she tried.

"No." He seemed to think about it for a moment. "Well, it depends on your definition. Architectural salvage? Now that's another subject."

"Could that be common ground for you and Toni?"

Stark shrugged. "That would be pushing it."

"How do you know? Seems to me that in your line of work you probably come across a lot of architectural elements that could be salvaged."

"Yeah? So what?"

"Toni's got a fledgling antiques business with empty booths. Couldn't there be an opportunity to share an interest there?"

Stark said nothing, but he did look thoughtful.

They stared at the ugly façade of what had once been the prettiest storefront on Main Street.

"So," Tricia said at last, "that kitchen reno you're doing is going to take two weeks."

"Thereabouts."

Tricia nodded. "Where will you start here?"

"By having a Dumpster delivered. The charred and moldy books will be the first to go."

"Oh, dear," Tricia said, her heart breaking.

"Then we'll pull everything back to the studs."

Tricia raised a hand to stop him. "On second thought, maybe I don't want to know."

"It's probably better you don't. Once we get the new insulation installed and the drywall up, then you should start coming around. Otherwise, it'll just upset you."

She knew she was made of tougher stuff, but she just nodded.

Stark misunderstood her silence. "I didn't do you wrong the first time we did this. You'll be just as pleased with Haven't Got a Clue reborn."

Tricia managed a smile. "Thank you."

Stark nodded. "Well, I'm off to give someone else an estimate. This time, it's an addition to a house on Pine Avenue."

"I'm glad you stopped by. I'm looking forward to working with you again."

"So am I," Stark said. He offered his hand and Tricia shook it. She'd always liked the contractor, and she now believed that he had nothing to do with Pete Renquist's death.

Although the list of suspects was one man fewer, Tricia still wasn't sure who had killed Pete. She'd have to stay on guard . . . as would all of Stoneham's citizens.

Tricia resumed her course for the Chamber office and, once inside, was surprised to hear a radio playing in the office. She was sure all had been quiet when she'd left. She tiptoed toward the office and found Mariana at her desk.

"What are you doing here on a weekend?" she asked, unable to hide her surprise.

Mariana started. "Heavens, you scared me half to death."

"I wasn't expecting to find you here."

"I could use a little overtime, and Angelica said it would be all right for me to finish up work on the mailers. It was kind of a last-minute thing," she said, sounding apologetic.

"Oh. Okay. I guess I'm a little jumpy today. I'm just going up to change and then I've got to go back out again."

"That's okay. Just do what you usually do on weekends."

Tricia nodded and headed upstairs where she changed into a long-sleeved shirt. Afterward, she went out to the garage to scrounge up the pair of gardening gloves she kept for when she trimmed the roses out back. She thought about calling Grant Baker to report what Frannie had told her, but decided against it. He'd only tell her she was being foolish, not to mention trespassing.

Of course, she hadn't been all that surprised when Frannie had confided her suspect for the petal pinching, and Tricia wasn't sure what she was going to say when she confronted the person. First, though, she needed proof.

She stuffed a large clean trash bag into the pocket of her slacks and started off again.

It wasn't far from the Chamber office to the business in question, and since it wasn't yet ten o'clock, Stoneham's main street was still pretty much deserted. Most of the businesses didn't open until at least ten, and where she was headed wouldn't open at all that day, since its personnel worked a five-day week.

As she approached the neat white building, Tricia decided there was no need for stealth and turned in its driveway, heading for the back of the building. As expected, a midsized rusty Dumpster sat behind the place. She approached it and wondered if she should be wearing a mask when she rummaged through its contents, not because she feared the smell, but she wasn't sure what kind of chemical and poison containers might have been tossed there.

She opened the Dumpster's hatch and peered inside. As she feared, there were a number of large black plastic bags. This particular waste company was the same one that the Chamber used and made their pickups along Main Street on Monday, which was why she'd decided to check out the container before it was emptied in two days.

Tricia grabbed the first bag and squeezed its contents. No soft fabric, no plastic-covered metal stems. She had no desire to open any other bags unless absolutely necessary. On the fifth bag, she hit pay dirt. Smiling, she pulled at the plastic until it broke open, and out spilled a variety of colorful silk blooms. But before she could enjoy her triumph, a car roared into the parking lot. A Stoneham police cruiser.

Suddenly the back door of the building burst open and a man came running out. "Arrest her, arrest her! She's trespassing and stealing my trash."

"Whose trash?" Tricia demanded.

The officer got out of the patrol car. It was Hanson, the same officer who had been on duty the night Michele had been attacked. "What's going on here?" he asked.

"Arrest him!" Tricia called.

"Arrest her!" Earl Winkler demanded.

Hanson held out a placating hand. "Not until somebody tells me what's going on."

"I told the dispatcher—this woman is trespassing and stealing my trash."

"And this man," Tricia said, whirling and pointing at Earl, "vandalized all the hanging baskets on Main Street and in the park—not once, but twice. First by snipping off all the live blooms, and then removing all the silk flowers that were put in the baskets in an effort to make them pretty once again." She held up the bag of flowers as proof.

Hanson turned to Earl. "What do you have to say?"

"Why would I want to vandalize the flowers along Main Street?"

"Because he hates the merchants for bringing change to Stoneham," Tricia answered for him.

Hanson said nothing, but he pinned Earl to the asphalt with his penetrating gaze.

"Someone must have planted that bag in my Dumpster," Earl said defensively.

"Oh, yeah?" Tricia challenged. "We could also dust the contents for fingerprints."

It was Earl's turn to be silent.

"And I wonder, if I dug a little deeper, if I'd find the bag filled with the remnants of the flowers that were snipped," Tricia continued.

An imposing Hanson stood with his hands on his hips, towering over Earl.

Earl's head dipped, as though he'd suddenly found his shoes to be very interesting. "I have nothing to say."

Hanson turned to Tricia. "What do you want me to do?"

"If nothing else, I want you to write a report saying what was found in Winkler Exterminating's Dumpster so that it can be presented to the Board of Selectmen at their next meeting."

"Now, wait a minute," Earl protested.

"The village board paid for half the cost of the flowers. I'm sure they won't be happy to learn one of their own destroyed them."

"They're not destroyed," Earl protested. "The flowers will grow back."

"Not anytime soon," Tricia countered.

"How much are the hanging baskets worth?" Hanson asked.

"Thousands of dollars, and this late in the season, they can't be readily replaced," Tricia said. Was it her imagination, or was Hanson on her side? He stood looking at them both for long seconds.

"Technically, you're both at fault. If Mr. Winkler wants to press charges, that's his prerogative. The same could be said for you, Ms. Miles, and I can arrest you both. It'll cost you attorney's fees and will leave a smudge on your reputations. I don't think you want that, Mr. Winkler. Not with your history."

Winkler looked up sharply but said nothing.

"My suggestion is that you two work this out together."

"I won't press charges, but I can't say what my sister will do. Of course, she's in business with Nigela Ricita Associates, and I do believe they are one of your biggest clients, Selectman Winkler. She won't be happy to hear that you're involved."

The threat to Winkler's wallet was devastating. His expression fell and he looked close to tears.

"And as the silk flowers were paid for by Nigela Ricita Associates, I am bound to return them *and* tell them exactly where they were found."

"You'll put me out of business," Earl protested.

"You should have thought about that before you vandalized the flowers in the first place."

"Then I may as well press charges against you."

"Nigela Ricita Associates has very deep pockets," Tricia countered.

That shut Earl up. Suddenly he looked weary.

Tricia considered what Angelica would do. She'd threatened to put the vandal in jail, but Tricia suspected she'd just been blowing off steam. After all, the plants weren't dead. Earl had been right. In time, they would bloom again. Instead of snipping the blooms, he could have killed them with an herbicide.

"I do have a suggestion," Tricia said.

Earl looked up. "What's that?"

"Apologize."

"Are you crazy?" Earl said, his eyes flashing.

"No, I'm not. Apologize and offer to help put back the silk flowers until the plants can grow new blossoms."

"That would take hours."

"It must have taken you hours to cut the blossoms, and then yank out all the silk flowers, too."

"It sounds like the perfect solution," Hanson said. "What do you say, Mr. Winkler?"

Earl seemed to realize that he'd been beaten. "Oh, all right. I'll do it. Monday morning, I'll go over to the Chamber of Commerce and apologize."

"And if you don't . . ." Tricia said, leaving the threat unsaid.

"I said I would, and I will," Earl grated, pivoted, and stormed to the back door to his business. He slammed the door.

Tricia looked at the policeman. "Thank you for brokering a peaceful solution."

"You're the one who came up with the idea."

"Yes, but you made it possible for me to do so. Why didn't you just arrest us both?"

"It's a lot of paperwork," the young officer said wearily.

"May I ask why you seemed to take my side?"

"Mr. Winkler's reputation precedes him." He didn't elaborate. Had Earl pulled the same stunt on residential clients as he had in the business community to try to drum up trade?

"Will you be mentioning this little exchange with Chief Baker?"

"I'll have to file a report, but it's more to chronicle my time off patrol than anything else."

Tricia nodded. "Thank you again."

Hanson tipped his hat. "Ma'am."

Tricia watched as the officer got back into his patrol car, then she turned and closed the lid to the Dumpster, gathered the torn bags of silk flowers, took the big trash bag from her pocket, and transferred the flowers to it. She intended to take them back to the Chamber; it would be up to Angelica to negotiate a time for Earl to restore the baskets. Then again, how good was he at flower arranging? If nothing else, he could accompany Angelica— —or whomever she assigned to do the task—and schlep the ladder up and down Main Street. Tricia was determined it wouldn't be her that did so.

As she turned, the cruiser took off. She gave Hanson a good-bye wave and started back for the Chamber office. She'd put the bags of silk flowers in the garage. As she walked down the road, the bulky plastic bags smacking into her thighs, she decided she'd better warn Angelica about the forthcoming apology. She didn't have to tell her who was going to make it. Then again, she knew Angelica would nag, nag, nag her until she dished the dirt. Her sister could be very persuasive. Tricia figured she'd decide later. For now, she had a date with the shower. She'd never been much of a fan of Dumpster diving.

TWENTY-ONE

Tricia had just made it back to the Chamber office when Pixie's wreck of a car passed. She watched as the car pulled up to the curb in front of the Dog-Eared Page, then Tricia tossed the bag of silk flowers into the shrubbery and took off at a jog. By the time she made it to Booked for Lunch, Michele was exiting the car. She gave Pixie a wave and turned for the door. Pixie pulled out into the street and headed south, turning at the crossroad, no doubt to come up the alley and park in the municipal lot. Meanwhile, Tricia dropped back to a walk and called Michele's name. She turned.

"Tricia, thank you so much for coming to my rescue last night."

Tricia came to a halt before the barkeep. "I'm thankful we were able to chase that guy off."

"I don't know how I can ever thank you and Angelica."

"In the future, have Shawn walk you to your car."

Michele gave a quiet laugh. "Definitely."

"I've been thinking about all that's happened, and I'm convinced you're right. Whoever killed Pete and hurt Janet deliberately came after you last night. Somehow this person is out to stop the ghost walks from happening."

"It probably won't surprise you to hear I'm withdrawing my acceptance of the docent's post."

"I can't say I blame you. But I wonder if you wouldn't mind letting me have a look at the papers Janet gave you."

"I was going to return them to the Society this afternoon—and let the entire village know I'd done so. I don't want you to be hurt."

"Don't worry, I don't intend to make myself a target. But I want to see if buried somewhere in those papers is a reason someone is willing to risk all to stop the ghost walks."

"I must admit I can't make top nor tail out of some of them. Most of them are photocopies of old records. But there are a few odd things in there, too."

"Such as?"

"Notes about a plot of land that's for sale not far from the cemetery. Pete made a notation that he wanted to check out the property, although I don't know why he would. Perhaps he was thinking of building."

Land for sale? And who was—or until recently had been—the biggest realty company in the area: Kelly Real Estate, owned by Bob Kelly. Tricia wondered, if she showed the papers to Karen Johnson of NRA Realty, would she see something others wouldn't?

"If I promise to return them to the Society today, can I take them now?" Tricia asked.

Michele shrugged. "You're welcome to them."

They entered the pub, and Michele immediately went behind the bar. She retrieved the large kraft envelope and handed it to Tricia.

"It's a bit too early in the day to offer you a drink, but I'd love it if you and Angelica could come by this evening so I can thank you properly."

"That's nice of you. Thank you. I'll make a point of mentioning it to her."

"Good. I'll see you then."

Tricia tucked the envelope under her arm, headed for the door, and closed it behind her. Once out on the sidewalk, she pulled her cell phone from her pocket and called the Chamber office. Mariana answered. "Could you do me a favor and tell me the number for Karen Johnson over at NRA Realty?" She did. "Thanks." Tricia punched in the number, and Karen answered on the second ring.

"Tricia, always great to speak to you. What do you need?"

"A favor. You know all the properties that are for sale in the area. Would you be willing to look over some old papers and give me an opinion?"

"Things are rather slow today. I'd be more than happy to give you a bit of my time."

"Great. Can I come by now?"

"Sure. I'll start a fresh pot of coffee."

"You're a doll, Karen. Thanks."

When they had opened shop some seven months before, NRA Realty had rented a bungalow at the back of the Brookview Inn. Since then, they'd moved to what had just a month or two before been another shabby little house at the far end of Main Street. Like the Chamber's new digs, the downstairs had been converted to offices. NRA Associates had painted and landscaped the outside and had spruced up the inside as well, and Karen had hired a receptionist and an associate Realtor.

As Karen had promised, the coffee was hot, and the office was quiet. "Let's go into the conference room, where we can spread out."

The pretty black woman sat at the head of the table, and Tricia took the seat to her right.

"So, what's in this mysterious envelope you've been clutching ever since you entered the office?" Karen asked, and took a sip of her coffee.

"I don't know if you've heard, but the Historical Society was planning on a series of ghost walks at the Stoneham Rural Cemetery this fall."

"Sounds like a great Halloween adventure."

"It did—until Pete Renquist was murdered and his associate Janet Koch was attacked. Last night someone went after Michele Fowler, who had been asked to be a docent for the walks."

Karen frowned. "And you think the answer to who's behind the attacks will be found in those papers?"

"I don't know, but it seems like someone wants to eliminate anyone involved in the project."

Karen looked even more uncomfortable. She let out a breath. "Let's have a look."

Tricia opened the envelope and set the papers on the table before them. "I haven't even had a chance to look at them. And I don't even know what I'd be looking for."

Karen sorted through the pages. "It would seem like the place to start is this map of the cemetery." She lifted the reading glasses she wore on a chain around her neck and perched them on her nose. The black-and-white map was little more than just lines across the page. "Do you know much about the place?"

Tricia shook her head. "Pete was the expert, but Michele has learned a lot about its history during the past few days."

Among the papers were several copies of deeds and other official-looking documents. Karen looked at a site map for a piece of land and tapped a finger on it. "I know this property. It's right next to the rural cemetery. Seems to me I heard a story about it not long after I came to Stoneham." She frowned, thinking. "There was a tentative agreement between Kelly Realty and Marathon Development. I believe an environmental impact study needed to be made."

She frowned again, then pawed through the copies of the old documents, coming up with an old black-and-white aerial photo of part of the cemetery. There were several of them in the package. She lay them on the table in a line.

"I need to check something," she said, got up from the table, and went into her office. A minute later she came back with a color photo printed on copy paper. She tapped her finger on the paper. "This is a satellite photo taken just three months ago. Notice the difference?"

Tricia looked at the photo, unsure what she was supposed to be looking for. Finally she shook her head.

"The old photo of the north side of the cemetery shows a private, probably family cemetery." She pointed it out, then pointed to the corresponding place on the new photo.

"It's not there anymore," Tricia said, not understanding the significance.

Karen nodded.

"What do you think happened to it?"

She shrugged. "The markers were removed, and probably nobody would know the difference."

"But isn't that illegal?" Tricia asked, appalled.

"I'm pretty sure it is. A cemetery *could* be an impediment to development, although not necessarily."

"What do you mean?"

"I'm from Upstate New York, and I know of two large commercial sites that have small private cemeteries in their midst: a mall in Syracuse and the football stadium in Buffalo. Still, a former owner of the land might have seen the old family cemetery as a detriment to selling it." Karen frowned again. "The thing is, if there's a burial plot on a piece of land, it's required by law to be recorded in the property's deed."

Tricia's mind whirled with possibilities. "Have you ever heard of a deed being modified to remove such a reference?"

"That would be illegal."

"Which doesn't mean it would stop someone from doing it." She thought about it for a moment. "What's the value of the property?"

"In excess of a million dollars." She eyed Tricia. "What are you thinking?"

Did she dare voice aloud her suspicion that Bob Kelly was responsible for Pete's death? He had a lot at stake and yet, at this point in time, not much to lose. He was already looking at a possible jail sentence and was desperate for cash. No way would he want to blow the sale of the property by the cemetery when it could increase his bottom line. She knew Bob had been capable of bending the law, but still—murder?

Had Pete discovered the cemetery was missing? Had he been foolish enough to confront Bob over it? Could they have met at the gazebo? But where would Bob have gotten heroin? Silly question. Just about anywhere these days. But how foolish would he have to be to commit murder in a public place? And yet, there'd apparently been no witnesses. Could Bob have seen Tricia and Sarge walking in the park and hightailed it?

"I know what you're thinking," Karen said softly.

"What do you think we should do?"

"We?" she said, and laughed. "I wouldn't name names, but perhaps if *you* spoke about this to your friend Chief Baker, he might want to look into it."

"Good idea. No way do I want Bob to come after me."

"Do you really think he was responsible for Peter Renquist's murder?" Karen asked.

"As you said, I wouldn't want to name names." Tricia gathered the pages together and replaced them in the envelope. "Thanks so much for seeing me on such short notice, Karen."

"Happy to do so anytime," she said, rising. She walked Tricia to the door. "We'll have to get together socially soon. Are you up for having lunch someday next week?"

"I'd love it."

Karen lowered her voice. "I get an NRA discount at the Brookview Inn. It'll be my treat."

"That sounds wonderful, but only if I can reciprocate another time."

"I try to never turn down a lunch invitation," Karen said, and laughed. "I'll call you midweek."

"Great."

"By the way, I wonder if you could give Angelica a message for me when you see her. I've been trying to track her down all morning but haven't had any luck."

"I'll see her at lunchtime. What do you want me to tell her?"

"This morning I came into the office early. We're talking before six."

"How much before six?"

"It wasn't quite light."

"You are dedicated."

"Just part of the job. Anyway, I saw this funny little man with a—"

"Big black trash bag."

"Yes," Karen said, and laughed. "Don't tell me you've seen him, too."

"Yes."

"He seemed to be stealing the flowers from the hanging baskets."

"He was. Someone else saw him, too, and I've already confronted him about it."

"Oh, good. Antonio told me Angelica was almost apoplectic about the flowers going missing."

That sounded like a good description. "The man has agreed to help put back the silk flowers. Now I just have to hope when I tell Angelica about it, she doesn't go apoplectic once again."

Karen laughed. "Okay, but if she wants to talk, I'll be here 'til at least six."

"A twelve-hour day?" Tricia asked.

"Don't feel sorry for me—I thrive on being busy."

"Thanks for helping me with these papers. You're an angel."

Karen laughed. "Just trying to earn my wings."

"See you soon," Tricia said, and left the office, but instead of turning left, she turned right and hoped she'd find Grant Baker behind his desk at the Stoneham Police Station. She had a lot to tell him.

TWENTY-TWO

No doubt about it, Polly Burgess did not like Tricia and didn't keep it a secret. As far as Tricia could remember, she had done nothing to alienate the older woman, who acted as receptionist and dispatcher for the Stoneham Police Department. Polly was especially protective of Chief Baker's time and seemed to consider all of Tricia's visits to be frivolous, even when she had no clue as to the nature of the call. Was Polly angry because she thought that Tricia had broken Baker's heart? Tricia couldn't think of any other reason for the woman's animosity, however mistaken.

As usual, she told Tricia to sit and wait in the small, seedy waiting room, but Tricia didn't have time for Polly's antics that morning. Instead, Tricia pulled out her cell phone and called Baker's personal number.

"Baker here."

"Tricia here. I'm standing in your waiting room."

"Why didn't you come right in?"

"Your gatekeeper," she said simply.

She heard a click, and a few seconds later the door to the inner sanctum opened. "Come on in," he called.

Tricia didn't say a word as she exited the waiting room, but she could feel Polly's angry glare on her back as she sailed through the doorway.

Baker resumed his seat, and Tricia shut the door before taking one of his guest chairs.

"You've been snooping around again," he said with an edge to his voice.

"I wouldn't call it that. I was talking to Michele Fowler this morning."

"I got a full report about what happened last night. Is she okay?"

"A little shaken up, but she'll bounce back. She believes she was attacked because of the attention the ghost walks will bring to the Stoneham Rural Cemetery."

"She's not the only one," Baker muttered, "but so far we haven't got a tangible connection."

"I may have the answer in this envelope."

He held out his hand and she passed it to him. "Why don't you tell me your theory."

Tricia sighed. At least he hadn't called it a *harebrained* theory. While she spoke, he examined the papers. When she stopped talking, he stared at the papers spread out before him on his desk and frowned.

"So, what do you think?" Tricia asked, fearing he was about to blow off her suggestion to look into the situation.

"Didn't I ask you not to keep poking around in this situation?"

"You did ask me to tell you my theory," she reminded him.

"If what you're proposing is true, you've not only put yourself in danger, but Karen Johnson, too."

"Nobody knows what we talked about."

"But someone might make an educated guess."

"I guess that means you think my theory is credible."

He shrugged. He had no intention of agreeing with her.

"Will you at least check into it?" she pressed.

"On Monday, I'll talk to someone at the county clerk's office to see if there's anything about a cemetery on the deed."

"And if there isn't?"

"We'd have to see if we can find other records that support the existence of the cemetery."

"And they'd be at the Historical Society. With Pete dead and Janet out of commission for the foreseeable future, I'm not sure there's anyone there who could help you with that."

"Let's take this one step at a time."

"It could take days, maybe weeks, before you could come up with additional proof. What if the sale of the land goes through before you can prove anything?"

"The wheels of justice don't always turn quickly," Baker said. His indifference was beginning to bug her. How could he still wonder why they hadn't made it as a couple? "In the meantime, I'm taking custody of these pages."

"You can't have them. I promised I'd return them to the Historical Society today."

"I'll call and explain the situation," Baker said. "In the meantime, I don't want you to talk about this—not even to Angelica."

"Why?"

"Because the fewer people who know about it, the better—for everyone's safety."

"Do you know when Bob is supposed to go up before the judge on his past indiscretions?"

"Not offhand, but I can look into it."

"I hope you will. If he is responsible for murder and attempted murder, we need to get him behind bars as soon as possible."

"Tricia, what you've given me might prove fraud, but that's a long way from pinning a murder charge on the man."

Tricia shook her head in frustration. "I can't help but feel an urgency about this. I'm afraid of the man, and he's been hounding me to buy his building. What do I do in the meantime?"

"You could file for a restraining order."

"Sure, and how many women have died at the hands of the men that have been served those papers? Far, *far* too many." She stood. "Thanks for all your help."

"Sarcasm, Tricia? It doesn't suit you."

"Your lack of enthusiasm to track down a killer doesn't suit your job description, either." She headed for the door but paused, turning back to face Baker once more. "By the way, Boris Koslov set a camera up to try to catch the person stealing the flowers. Unfortunately, you can't tell from the video who it was. He was wearing a hoodie, but I did dig up two eyewitnesses who identified the man. I confronted him," she said defiantly. "Well, I and your Officer Hanson, and he's going to apologize and help restore the silk flowers to the baskets. No other law enforcement intervention is necessary. I thought you should know—not that you care."

Without another word, she turned and left his office without looking back.

Polly's sharp gaze seemed to rake through Tricia as she left the building. Tricia hadn't been exaggerating when she'd told Baker she was afraid of Bob. His aggression had been building to a higher pitch each time he'd confronted her, and it was becoming more difficult to avoid him.

Tricia returned to the Chamber office, then went upstairs to shower and change clothes. Twenty minutes later, she was back at her desk.

"I took a message for you," Mariana said, handing her a Post-it note as she passed. "You're insurance agent called."

"Is it good news?" she asked hopefully.

"He didn't say, just that you should call him."

Tricia sat down and found her hands were trembling as she punched in the number on her desk phone. It rang twice before being picked up.

"John Martin."

"John, it's Tricia Miles. Do you always work on Saturday?"

"Just tidying up a few things."

"Please tell me that *this* time you have good news for me."

"I do, and I didn't want you to have to wait until Monday to hear that you've been approved for the entire amount of your claim. The check will be in the mail Monday morning." She could hear the smile in his voice.

"When can I start repairs on my home—my shop?"

"Anytime you want."

"I want, I want—*believe me*—I want!" she cried, suddenly finding herself choking up.

"I assume you've been talking to a contractor."

"I spoke to him just this morning."

"Good. We can recommend specialized professionals to refurbish your apartment and clean the smoke damage."

"I've had a lot of time to research the subject and have a load of tradespeople all lined up. They've just been waiting for the okay to start work."

"Good. Of course you know you can call me for anything."

"You've been an angel, John. Thank you so much."

"Do I get an invitation to the grand reopening?"

"You'll be at the top of the list."

"Take care," he said, and they said good-bye.

"Sounds like good news," Mariana said.

"The best. I'll soon be going home." She laughed. "Well, as soon as all the damage is repaired and I replace nearly everything I own." Suddenly the task seemed daunting.

Tricia spent the next half hour making lists of things to do. She had a lot of plans to make before she could even begin to get her life back.

Looking over her list brought her great satisfaction, and she suddenly wanted to share her good news. Angelica was working at Booked for Lunch. Although it was half an hour earlier than Tricia usually went out for her midday meal, she decided to buck her rut and go early.

"I'm going to lunch," she said, and stood.

Mariana smiled. "You ought to celebrate at the Brookview Inn's dining room. At least you could get an adult beverage there."

"It'll have to wait until later, I'm afraid. But somewhere out there is a martini with my name on it."

"In the meantime, why not splurge with a cupcake?"

"I just might," Tricia said, and headed for the door. The way she felt, nothing could spoil her good mood. Nothing in the world.

TWENTY-THREE

By the time Tricia arrived at Booked for Lunch, the midday crowd had thinned. Instead of being jammed with tourists, she saw a number of her friends. She waved to Russ and Nikki, who were seated in the far booth. Ginny sat alone in the one closest to the front window, kept company by her e-reader. She looked up briefly, saw Tricia, and waved, then went back to her book. Meanwhile Pixie, dressed in a vintage white waitress uniform with *Woolworth* embroidered in green above the pocket, bobbed around bussing tables.

"I'm going to be late getting to the Chamber," she apologized while loaded down with ketchup-and-mustard-stained plates. "Tommy had to leave early, so I'll be finishing up in the kitchen for him."

"Pixie, it's Saturday—your day off from the Chamber."

Pixie laughed. "Good grief. I completely forgot."

"Besides, if you were late, you've got a very understanding boss. Isn't that right, Angelica?"

Angelica stood behind the counter with a calculator in hand; a pencil stuck out from behind her right ear. "Uh-huh," she muttered, although Tricia doubted her sister had even heard what she'd said.

"Thanks for driving Michele into the village this morning, Pixie."

"Oh, it was my pleasure. It's always nice to talk to somebody different."

"Did you get your tattoo?" Tricia asked.

"Oh, yeah. Right now, it itches like hell. I shouldn't have worn this polyester dress. I feel like there's ants crawling all over my chest."

Oh, so *that's* where she'd gotten it.

"If you want to hang around after everybody leaves, I'll show it to you."

"Great," Tricia said, though she wasn't all that excited to witness the presentation.

"Excuse me; the kitchen calls," Pixie said, and hefted a full tray.

Tricia took her usual seat at the counter and waited for her customary tuna plate to materialize. After about a minute and no attention from Angelica, she got up and poured herself a cup of coffee, nudged past Angelica, and got her own lunch. She'd already sat down and removed the plastic wrap before Angelica seemed to realize she was even there.

"Oh. When did you get here?"

"About five minutes ago. What's got you so preoccupied?"

"I'm trying to decide if I should change my standing bread order. But it doesn't matter right this minute. Can I get you—oh, you already have coffee. Well, I think I'll join you." She grabbed a cup from the shelf and poured herself one.

"I came by early to share my good news." Tricia laughed. "Actually several pieces of good news."

The bell over the door jangled, and Tricia turned to see Christopher enter.

"Good afternoon, ladies," he called as she crossed the floor to join Tricia at the counter.

Tricia sighed. Was he ever going to stop bothering her? "Hello."

"Have you got anything good left to eat?" he asked Angelica.

"The grill is closed, but we've still got the soup-and-sandwich special: potato and leek, and egg salad."

"Sounds great. On rye?" he asked.

"Coming right up," Angelica said, put down her cup, and headed for the kitchen.

So much for Tricia's good news. She took a bite of tuna.

"Fancy meeting you here," Christopher said, and smiled.

"I come here almost every day."

"Yes, but today you're early."

Did he keep an eye out for her twenty-four/seven?

Angelica returned with a cup of soup, a spoon, and a couple of packets of crackers, setting them in front of Christopher. "Your sandwich will be ready in a couple of minutes."

"Thanks."

Angelica turned to Tricia. "Now, what were you saying about good news?"

"I heard from the insurance company. The check is being cut, and I can start repairing my store."

Angelica beamed. "That *is* good news. Congratulations."

"Congratulations, Trish. It'll be good to have you living closer—in case you ever need me," Christopher said.

Tricia said nothing and turned back to her sister. "The other good piece of news is that I found your petal pincher."

Angelica's mouth dropped open in surprise, but she quickly recovered, and again beamed. "Who? Who is it?"

Tricia looked right and left before beckoning Angelica closer. "Earl Winkler," she whispered.

Again Angelica's mouth dropped, but this time she didn't smile. "Why, that dirty rat!"

"Funny it should be the rat catcher," Tricia agreed, and used her fork to rearrange the lettuce on her plate. "I'll tell you the whole story when there isn't a crowd listening in," she said with a quick glance at her ex-husband, "but suffice to say, rather than face the humiliation of public knowledge of his indiscretion, he's willing to apologize and help restore the silk flowers."

"Big of him," Angelica said tartly.

"Since the plants themselves weren't destroyed, that's about the best you're going to get."

Angelica scowled. "I'll accept his apology, but that doesn't mean I have to make it easy on him."

Tricia didn't envy the time Earl would have to spend with Angelica to get the job done.

A bell sounded from the kitchen. "That's your sandwich, Christopher. I'll be right back with it." Angelica headed for the kitchen.

Tricia turned her attention back to her lunch.

The door to the street opened, the little bell jangling as Bob Kelly burst in. His face was flushed, and his eyes were red-rimmed. It looked like he hadn't slept in days. He took in the rest of the customers before he reached for the OPEN sign and turned it to CLOSED, then stamped across the tile floor to stand behind Tricia.

"You had to go nosing around, didn't you?"

Tricia's stomach tightened as she swiveled her stool to face him. "Are you speaking to me?"

"Who else?" Bob demanded.

"I don't know what you're talking about."

"I saw you leave the pub earlier with a big brown envelope. What was inside it?"

Tricia's heart skipped a beat. Two people were now watching her every move. "That's none of your business."

"I saw you go to NRA Realty," Bob continued.

Oh, no.

"You know about the cemetery."

Tricia swallowed but said nothing.

"If anyone else finds out, the sale won't go through."

"What's he talking about?" Christopher asked.

Tricia ignored his question and spoke to Bob. "Did you also watch me go to the police station?"

Bob nodded, his expression grave. He unbuttoned his green sports jacket and pulled out a snub-nosed revolver from the waistband of his pants.

"Bob!" Tricia squealed.

"Hey," Christopher protested.

"Get up!" Bob ordered Tricia, waving the gun.

"Bob, what on earth do you think you're doing?" came Angelica's voice as she pushed through the swinging door from the kitchen, holding the plate with Christopher's sandwich.

"Oh my God," Ginny called, sounding frightened.

"Everybody, on your feet," Bob ordered, again waving the gun around for emphasis.

"What are you going to do? Rob the place?" Christopher asked as he rose from his stool, his hands raised.

"Take whatever you want from the till and go," Angelica said.

Bob shook his head, his smile wolfish. "Oh, no. That would be too easy."

"Well, what do you want?" Angelica demanded.

"You. I want you."

"Don't you mean me?" Tricia said. "After all, it's me you want to buy your building."

Bob shook his head. "It's too late for that now."

"Be reasonable, Bob," Russ said as he stood protectively in front of Nikki. Thanks to her burgeoning belly, it was going to take some time to extricate her from the tight booth, and it didn't look like Russ had any intention of doing that.

"I'll go along with whatever you say, Bob, just leave everyone else alone," Tricia said, hoping to spare her friends, but Bob shook his head.

"Oh, no. I'm not leaving any witnesses."

Tricia's mouth went dry. She took a breath. "You haven't got enough bullets in that gun to take us all out."

"Oh, yeah? How would you know?"

"Because I read mysteries, and I know a gun like that only holds six bullets," Tricia said. And she hoped to heaven he was bluffing about it even being loaded.

"I only see six people," Bob said, his voice level.

Stay in the kitchen, Pixie, Tricia thought.

Bob motioned for Angelica to step forward, but before she could, Christopher lunged in front of her and the gun exploded.

Christopher shoved Bob backward, and Ginny cracked him over

the head with one of the café's heavy china plates, the remnants of her lunch flying into the air. Bob fell and the gun exploded again.

Tricia jumped forward as the two men hit the floor in a tangle of arms and legs.

"Christopher!" she hollered, but instead of going to him, she saw that, although Bob was groggy, he still held the gun in his hand. She kicked it several times until he let go, and it skittered across the tile. Bob groaned, but Christopher hadn't moved.

Suddenly, the room seemed to be teeming with people. Angelica and Russ hauled Christopher's dead weight off Bob. They rolled him over onto his back, and his chest, awash in scarlet, heaved as he tried to catch his breath. Russ turned his attention to Bob as Ginny did a fast waddle around them heading for the lunch counter, while in the background Tricia could hear Nikki shouting into her cell phone.

"Christopher!" Tricia practically screamed as she fell on her knees beside him, grabbing his left hand in her own.

Angelica was on her feet again, helping Russ shove a dazed Bob onto the seat Ginny had vacated only seconds before. "Sit on him. Don't let him up!" Russ ordered, and Angelica practically jumped onto Bob's back. Russ handed her the plate that Ginny had hit Bob with. "Use this again if you have to."

She nodded, looking pale and scared.

Tricia turned her attention back to Christopher. His eyes fluttered open and he grimaced in pain. "Don't move," she told him, feeling more frightened than when she'd faced the fire in her shop and had desperately tried to save Miss Marple.

"Nobody . . . nobody ever warned me how much . . . how much it hurts to get shot."

"Don't talk," Tricia said, and placed the index finger of her free hand across his dry lips.

Russ took the wad of clean dishrags Ginny handed him and pressed them against the seeping wound on Christopher's chest. "Did anyone see what happened to Pixie?"

"She went out the back to get help," Angelica said.

Christopher's hand tightened around Tricia's, and he stared into her eyes. She had always loved his mesmerizing green eyes. "I want you to promise me something," he said, his speech breathy.

"Anything, anything at all," Tricia said.

"That after this is all over you'll marry me again."

"You're not going to die," Tricia said, hoping with all her heart that she was right.

"I know it . . . that's why I want you to promise me. If you do, then I know I'll be okay, because I already told you . . . we are destined to be together for all time."

Tricia shot a look over her shoulder at Angelica, who was nodding vigorously. She looked back down at Christopher, who was deathly pale.

"Y-yes. Of course, anything you say." The wad of dishrags beneath Russ's fingers was sodden.

Christopher closed his eyes and a faint smile crossed his lips. "Good . . . good. You can . . . go back . . . to . . . wearing . . . your . . . engagement . . . ring."

Tricia looked down at their clasped hands. Christopher was wearing his wedding band once again.

"Oh my God," Ginny cried, "my water just broke." She stumbled backward and sat down on one of the stools.

Nikki was still on the phone but no longer shouting. "Yes, he's subdued. Please, please hurry!"

The café door burst open, and two of Stoneham's finest darted inside, their service revolvers drawn. "Nobody move!" Hanson shouted.

"Put those things away," Angelica ordered. "I'm sitting on the jerk you want." She struggled to her feet. "Get him out of here!"

They hauled a dazed Bob out of the booth and hustled him out the door. Chief Baker suddenly appeared.

"Get the paramedics," Tricia implored, and Baker pivoted, talking into the microphone attached to his uniform blouse.

"Tricia, he's not breathing," Russ said gently.

"We've got to do CPR," Tricia cried.

"Tricia, he's gone," Russ said, his voice cracking with emotion.

Tricia started down at Christopher, choking back a sob.

Suddenly Angelica was there at Tricia's side. "You can let go now," she said gently.

Tricia stared at her, not comprehending.

Angelica stared down at Tricia's hands tightly clasping Christopher's. Tricia's gaze followed. Wonderful memories from years gone by suddenly bubbled up. Their first date. The first time they made love. Their wedding day. At that moment, she couldn't even remember why they had ever parted. All she remembered was the love.

Angelica placed a hand on Tricia's. "Let go," she said again.

Silent tears trickled down Tricia's cheeks, but she allowed Angelica to disentangle her fingers from Christopher's and pull her onto her feet.

"Ginny, will you be okay for a few minutes?" Angelica asked, her voice calm.

Ginny nodded, wiping tears that cascaded down her cheeks.

Angelica turned back to Tricia, wrapped an arm around her shoulder, and led her toward the door. Outside, the sidewalk was filled with people. Tricia kept her head down as Angelica pushed their way through the crowd and past the police.

"Not now," Angelica said fiercely when Baker appeared in front of them.

He stepped back.

Tricia heard sirens in the background but didn't look up, just watched her feet as they crossed the street and approached the Cookery. Angelica opened the door.

"Angelica—Tricia!" Frannie cried. "What on earth is going on over at Booked for Lunch?"

"We'll talk later," Angelica said. How could she be so damned calm when the world had just turned upside down?

Angelica led Tricia across the store to the door at the back marked PRIVATE.

She closed it behind them.

TWENTY-FOUR

 After the events of the previous day, St. Joseph hospital was the last place Tricia wanted to be, but despite the tragedy she'd experienced, life went on. One life had ended, and another had begun.

A pasty-faced Ginny sat propped up in her hospital bed, draped in one of those hideous blue hospital gowns, but thanks to her radiant smile, she had never looked more beautiful. Beside her, Antonio beamed like the proud poppa he was.

"So," Tricia asked, still finding it difficult to speak after she'd spent so much of the day before crying, "what are you going to name her?"

"After my mother," Antonio said in his lilting Italian accent.

"Sofia? That's a beautiful name for a beautiful little girl," Tricia said.

"That's not all," Angelica said from the end of the bed.

"Sofia Angelica," Antonio clarified.

"Isn't she the most gorgeous baby you've ever seen in your entire life?" Angelica said, nearly bursting with pride.

She was indeed a beautiful little girl, with a full head of red hair, just like her mother.

"Thank you for all the flowers, Angelica," Ginny said, "but you didn't have to send quite so many." On every flat surface stood a vase or a pot filled with colorful blooms, some of them emblazoned with pink ribbons saying *Baby Girl*.

"Well, I didn't know what your favorites were, so I just told the florist to send one of everything."

"Perhaps we can share some with the other patients," Antonio suggested.

"Of course, of course," Angelica agreed, and laughed. It seemed that nothing could upset her on that beautiful, sunny, late-summer morning. Tricia only hoped she'd tone down her excitement later that afternoon when they went to the Baker Funeral Home to make Christopher's final arrangements. As he had no close family, Tricia had decided she'd like to have him buried nearby, where she could lay flowers on his grave. Perhaps it would make her feel better. Perhaps.

She looked down at her hand and the two-carat solitaire diamond ring that once again had taken up residence on her left ring finger. She hadn't been sure she meant what she'd told Christopher in his last moments. Would she really have married him again? But for now, she would honor his last request and wear the ring he had given her so many years ago at a much happier time in their lives. Their wedding had been lavish—ostentatious, really—and Tricia had already made up her mind that the last ceremony she shared with Christopher would be far more simple and dignified.

She found her eyes welling with tears once again and tried to blink them away.

A clatter at the door caught their attention. "Hi," Nikki called out. She sat in a wheelchair, with Russ manning the grips behind her.

"Don't tell me you're here to deliver, too!" Ginny cried, grinning.

"We were just about to check in, but I have a feeling it's going to be a long day, and I thought we should pop up here to see you first."

"Pardon me if I don't get up," Ginny said, and laughed.

"Can I show her the baby?" Angelica asked. She'd only held little Sofia four times since they'd arrived less than an hour earlier.

"Of course," Ginny said, and carefully handed the baby over. Angelica cradled Sofia as if she were a soap bubble as she stepped over to the door. Nikki looked down at the sleeping princess and smiled.

"Aw, I can't wait to hold my little bundle of joy." Then her face collapsed into a grimace, and she bent over as a contraction seized her.

"Speaking of which," Russ said. "We'd better get going. Congratulations, Antonio." He looked at Ginny. "You did great, Mama."

"Thank you. Good luck, Nikki. You've got a tough day ahead of you, but it'll all be worthwhile," Ginny said as Angelica handed the baby back to her.

Russ gave them a wave as he pushed the wheelchair away from the door.

"Nikki's having a boy," Angelica said. "Wouldn't it be fun if Sofia and he got married one day?"

Tricia winced at the mention of a wedding, and Angelica instantly seemed to realize her faux pas. "Oh, Trish, honey, I'm so sorry," she said.

"It's okay."

"Would you have remarried Christopher?" Ginny asked.

"I don't know," Tricia said truthfully. "I'll never know."

"What will happen to Bob Kelly?" Antonio asked.

"I hope they throw him in jail for the rest of his worthless life," Angelica said bitterly. "And to think I once loved that despicable man."

"He's certainly got a lot to answer for," Tricia said. "Two murder charges, attempted murder, and assault, not to mention the trouble he was in before all this happened."

"And don't forget desecration of a cemetery," Angelica said.

Tricia nodded, appalled that anyone would have the temerity to disturb the dead for their own selfish gain.

"How did Bob ever think he would get away with it?" Ginny asked.

"His enormous ego wouldn't let him believe he could fail," Angelica said simply. "But let's not ruin this happy day with talk of Bob." She looked adoringly down at the baby in Ginny's arms.

Happy day? Tricia wasn't sure she would ever celebrate Sofia's birthday without sad thoughts of Christopher. He had sacrificed his own life to save Angelica's. Had he saved Tricia and died, her life would have forever been shadowed with survivor's guilt. That he'd saved Angelica—the one person who meant the most to Tricia—she would be forever grateful. Even so, it was all such a waste.

But they'd had one piece of happy news an hour before when they'd entered the hospital to visit Ginny and the baby. They'd stopped at the reception desk to get the room number, and Tricia thought to ask about Janet Koch.

"She's doing much better. She's now receiving visitors if you'd like to see her."

"I would."

The receptionist had given Tricia the room number, and she intended to stop in after their visit with the baby was over.

Tricia had one more piece of good news to share. "Looks like I owe you five dollars, Ginny."

Ginny looked up at her, confused.

"You were right. I heard from the insurance company before Sofia was born."

Ginny laughed. "We'll put it toward her college fund." She looked at the baby with adoring eyes. "You *are* going to college, young lady." Sofia yawned, rubbing her little mitten-covered hands over her closed eyes.

"Awwww," the three women chorused.

"We should go and let Ginny and the baby get some rest," Tricia said.

"I don't want to," Angelica declared, "but I will. But only if you promise I can come back later and say good night to my"—she stopped, looked around to make sure no one else was listening, and lowered her voice to a bare whisper—"sweet granddaughter."

"Of course you can," Ginny said.

Angelica lavished kisses on her new family before turning to leave.

"Take some flowers," Antonio suggested, and grabbed a large vase filled with pink daisies and baby's breath.

"Good idea," Angelica said, accepting them. "Off we go. We have a very busy day ahead of us."

Yes, they did.

"If you need anything, feel free to call us, dear Tricia," Antonio said sincerely.

"I will," she said, and braved a smile, knowing she wouldn't.

She stepped out into the hall as Angelica made another round of good-byes.

All around Tricia nurses, aides, and technicians scurried. All around were the sounds of new life—of hope and promise.

Her life was about to start another chapter, too, and it would not include Christopher. She hadn't wanted him to be a strong presence in her future, but she had at least expected him to be part of the landscape. That he wouldn't brought her great sadness.

Angelica appeared, all smiles, and wrapped her free arm around Tricia's. "Ready to go see Janet?"

Tricia nodded. "Although I haven't any idea of what I'm going to tell her."

"I'll tell her, if you like."

"Thank you. I don't think I'm quite yet ready to be able to talk about it, but I do want her to know that she's now safe—all of Stoneham is."

"Yes, we are, but at a terrible cost. For what it's worth, I think Christopher is the bravest man I've ever known. He gave me my life, and I'm going to make sure every day counts for something. To honor him, you should, too."

"I will."

They paused at the elevators. "I'd like to do something else to honor Christopher. What do you think about a scholarship? Or maybe Nigela Ricita Associates could buy a piece of land and make another park for the citizens of Stoneham?"

"Why don't we talk about it some other day?" Tricia suggested.

"Of course. I'm sorry I bought it up now," Angelica apologized.

Tricia managed a smile. "I'm glad you were fond of him. He had his failings, but overall he really was a great guy."

"Of course he was, and you brought out the best in him."

Tricia didn't believe that for a moment, but she didn't see any point in arguing.

They took the elevator to the fourth floor, but as they approached Janet's room, Tricia halted. "I don't think I can do this."

"You don't have to, sweetie. Why don't you go down to the lobby and wait for me. I'll only be a few minutes."

"Tell Janet . . ." But Tricia couldn't think of a thing to say.

"I will," Angelica promised, squeezed her hand and then forged ahead.

Tricia turned, but instead of heading for the elevator, she took the stairs and made her way back to the lobby. Never had she felt so alone. She supposed her parents had at one time liked Christopher—after all, he'd taken her off their hands. That must have made her mother feel infinitely grateful. But even if her parents had never really been there for her, she counted Angelica as her staunchest ally. And now she had a new connection to Antonio, Ginny, and sweet baby Sofia.

As Tricia was about to take a seat, she noticed the automatic doors slide open and Grace and Mr. Everett enter the hospital's lobby.

"Tricia, darling girl," Grace said as she approached with her arms held wide. "I can't tell you how sorry I am to hear about . . ." But she didn't say his name.

"Thank you," Tricia said, and embraced her friend. Grace was older than Tricia's mother. She'd had her share of tragedies, but she had bounced back and found a new zest for life. Tricia hoped she would one day find that same resolve. She looked over Grace's shoulder and saw dear Mr. Everett, her employee and, if truth be told, someone she'd come to think of as her surrogate father. His eyes were shiny with unshed tears. She pulled back away from Grace and practically fell into Mr. Everett's waiting arms. And then the tears came once again.

Eventually, Tricia realized she was sitting on a couch, her head still buried in Mr. Everett's shoulder, sobbing as he patted her back murmuring, "Dear girl, dear girl."

Grace pressed a tissue into Tricia's hand, and she wiped her eyes and eventually managed to get her emotions under control enough to sit up straight. "I'm so embarrassed," she murmured, and didn't dare look at her friends.

"But why?" Grace asked, patting Tricia's hand. "We're family. We love you. You, Angelica, Ginny, Antonio, and now baby Sofia."

"Family?" Tricia asked, her throat so tight she felt like choking.

"Not by blood, but by circumstance," Mr. Everett said.

Tricia stared into the elderly man's wrinkled face as a wellspring of love gushed through her.

"And don't forget Miss Marple, too," he added, and smiled.

Tricia felt new tears spring to her eyes. "Yes, we are family."

"We were thinking," Grace began, "that we'd like to host a picnic for our little family. Maybe a potluck next weekend. And maybe we'll invite a few friends, too. Like Pixie and her new gentleman friend, Frannie Armstrong, and Michele Fowler."

"I think that would be lovely," Tricia said, wondering what she could contribute. Then she remembered the deviled eggs Angelica had made for Pete's wake. They seemed simple enough. Maybe she could bring something like that, and she would enjoy making them to share with her friends—her family.

"There you are," Angelica said, arriving on the scene. Her smile wavered, however, when she took in Tricia's tear-streaked face. "Is everything okay?"

"We were just talking about hosting a picnic next weekend for our little Stoneham family. You, included," Grace said.

"That sounds wonderful. What can I bring?" Angelica said, taking a seat next to Tricia.

Grace grinned. "Your wonderful carrot cake."

Angelica's smile was wide. "You got it."

"I'll mention it to Ginny and Antonio when we go upstairs," Grace said. "We can't wait to see baby Sofia."

"You already know her name?" Angelica asked.

"Ginny called us from the delivery room early this morning. She couldn't wait to share the news."

"Isn't she a dear?" Angelica asked with a sappy look that could only be described as motherly pride—despite the fact that she had no claim on Ginny in that respect.

"She's as special to us as our darling Tricia—and you, too," Mr. Everett said.

"Aw, thank you," Angelica said, her smile wavering as her eyes welled.

"We're family," Tricia offered, unsure what Angelica's reaction would be.

"Well, of course we are," Angelica said, and reached over to squeeze Tricia's hand.

In that moment, Tricia realized she had never felt so loved and accepted. "Yes, we are," she reaffirmed, and smiled.

ANGELICA'S FAMILY RECIPES

Grandma Miles's Snickerdoodle Cookies

1½ cups granulated sugar

1 cup shortening

2 eggs

2¾ cups all-purpose flour

2 teaspoons cream of tartar

1 teaspoon baking soda

½ cup salt

2 tablespoons granulated sugar

2 teaspoons cinnamon

Preheat the oven to 400°F. Cream the sugar and shortening; add the eggs. Beat until light and fluffy. Sift the dry ingredients and cut into the creamed mixture. Do not stir or beat. The dough should be very tender and light. Roll into balls the size of small walnuts. Mix together the 2 tablespoons of sugar and cinnamon. Roll the balls in the sugar-cinnamon mixture and place 2 inches apart on a greased baking sheet. Bake for 8 to 10 minutes. The cookies will puff up, then flatten and cool off to a tender, crisp cookie.

Yield: 5 dozen

ANGELICA'S CARROT CAKE

6 cups grated carrots

1 cup brown sugar

1 cup raisins

4 eggs

1½ cups granulated sugar

1 cup vegetable oil

2 teaspoons vanilla extract

1 cup crushed pineapple, drained

3 cups all-purpose flour

1½ teaspoons baking soda

1 teaspoon salt

4 teaspoons ground cinnamon

1 cup chopped walnuts

Preheat oven to 350°F. Grease and flour two 10-inch cake pans.

In a medium bowl, combine the grated carrots and brown sugar, then stir in the raisins.

In a large bowl, beat the eggs until light. Gradually beat in the sugar, oil, and vanilla. Stir in the pineapple. Combine the flour, baking soda, salt, and cinnamon, and stir into the wet mixture until absorbed. Finally stir in the carrot mixture and the walnuts. Pour evenly into the prepared pans.

Bake for 45 to 50 minutes in the preheated oven until the cake tests done with a toothpick. Cool for 10 minutes before removing from the pan. When completely cooled, frost with maple buttercream frosting.

Maple Buttercream Frosting

1 cup butter, softened
2¾ cups confectioners' sugar
2 tablespoons brown sugar
2 tablespoons maple syrup
¼ cup chopped walnuts

Place the softened butter in a large bowl. Beat with an electric mixer for 30 to 40 seconds until whipped. Scrape the sides of the bowl. Sift the confectioners' sugar into the bowl. Beat with an electric mixer for 30 to 40 seconds. Scrape down the sides of the bowl and add the brown sugar and maple syrup. Beat for 2 to 3 minutes or until the mixture is fluffy, scraping the sides of bowl as needed. Stir in the walnuts until just mixed and spread on the cooled cake.

SHRIMP PASTA SALAD

8 ounces elbow macaroni
¾ to 1 pound cooked small shrimp
8 ounces frozen peas, thawed
3 to 4 celery stalks, finely chopped
½ cup onion, finely chopped

DRESSING

1 cup mayonnaise
³⁄₄ cup French salad dressing
1 tablespoon sugar
1 tablespoon white wine vinegar
1½ to 2½ teaspoons paprika
½ teaspoon salt
1 teaspoon garlic powder
1 teaspoon ground black pepper

Cook the macaroni according to package directions; drain and rinse in cold water. In a large bowl, combine the macaroni, shrimp, peas, celery, and onion. In another bowl, whisk the dressing ingredients. Pour over the salad and toss to coat. Cover and refrigerate until chilled.

Yield: 8 servings

BOOKED FOR LUNCH'S
BLACK BEAN SOUP

1 pound dried black beans
4 cups low-sodium chicken broth
2 cups water
3 cloves garlic, minced
1 medium onion, diced
2 medium-sized green peppers, seeded and diced
1 teaspoon kosher salt (to taste)
1½ teaspoon chili powder
1½ teaspoon cumin
chopped cilantro (optional)
diced avocado (optional)
sour cream (optional)

Place the beans in a bowl or pot, cover with cold water, and allow to soak overnight, or add the beans to a medium-sized pot and cover with hot water. Bring to a boil, and let boil for 2 minutes. Turn off the heat, cover the pot, and allow the beans to sit for 1 hour. Drain the beans and rinse them with cold water.

In a medium pot, add the beans, chicken broth, water, garlic, onions, and peppers. Bring to a boil, then reduce the heat to low, cover, and simmer for 90 minutes. At that time, add the salt, chili powder, and cumin, and stir. Cover and continue simmering for another 30 minutes to 1 hour, until the soup is the thickness you desire. (It can be thin to very thick, depending on your preference.) Garnish with cilantro, avocado, and/or sour cream.

Yield: 6 servings

CURRIED DEVILED EGGS

12 hard-boiled eggs, peeled
²/₃ cup mayonnaise
1½ teaspoons curry powder
½ teaspoon yellow mustard
¼ teaspoon black pepper, coarsely ground
¹/₈ teaspoon salt
Paprika (optional)
2 tablespoons chopped chives (optional)

Slice the boiled eggs in half lengthwise. Remove the yolks and place them in a small bowl. Mash the yolks with a fork. Stir in the mayonnaise, curry powder, mustard, pepper, and salt until smooth and creamy. Spoon or pipe the mixture into the egg white halves. Sprinkle with paprika and garnish with the chives, if desired. Refrigerate 1 hour or until ready to serve.

Yield: 12 servings